A Cat in the Stacks Mystery

MURDER
PAST DUE

Miranda James

D0029284

BERKLEY PRIME CRIME, NEW YORK

THE BERKLEY PUBLISHING GROUP
Published by the Penguin Group
Penguin Group (USA) LLC
375 Hudson Street, New York, New York 10014

USA • Canada • UK • Ireland • Australia • New Zealand • India • South Africa • China

penguin.com

A Penguin Random House Company

MURDER PAST DUE

A Berkley Prime Crime Book / published by arrangement with the author

For information, address: The Berkley Publishing Group,
a division of Penguin Group (USA) LLC,
375 Hudson Street, New York, New York 10014.

ISBN: 978-0-425-23603-1

PUBLISHING HISTORY
Berkley Prime Crime mass-market edition / August 2010

PRINTED IN THE UNITED STATES OF AMERICA

20 19 18 17 16 15 14 13 12 11

Cover illustration by Dan Craig.
Cover design by Lesley Worrell.
Interior text design by Tiffany Estreicher.

While I scanned the tiny handwriting of the registrar of the 1840s, I heard snatches of conversation. I paid them scant attention, focusing on my task. But when I heard the words *murder* and *Priest*, I started listening.

I found the incident oddly unsettling, though I couldn't say why. I supposed the conversation was about Godfrey Priest, since he was *the* hot topic in Athena at the moment. And hearing the word *murder* in conjunction with his name wasn't that odd. The man did write murder mysteries. Then I heard the sound of a throat clearing on the other side of my desk. My eyes widened in surprise as I recognized the man. It was Godfrey Priest. What the heck was he doing here?

"Good morning, Godfrey," I said, extending a hand in greeting. Diesel padded right behind me. "It's been a long time."

"What is that? A cat?" Godfrey asked, watching as Diesel made a slow circle around him. Evidently unimpressed, Diesel walked back to the window and jumped up to his bed. Yawning, he turned his back on both of us and settled down for a nap.

"He's a Maine coon," I said. "They're larger than most cats."

"That's the first time I've ever been snubbed by a cat." Godfrey laughed, but his expression revealed annoyance. "They always love me because they can tell I'm a cat person."

I tried not to laugh. "Diesel doesn't take to everybody."

Berkley Prime Crime titles by Miranda James

MURDER PAST DUE
CLASSIFIED AS MURDER
FILE M FOR MURDER
OUT OF CIRCULATION
THE SILENCE OF THE LIBRARY

ACKNOWLEDGMENTS

My first thanks go to Michelle Vega and Natalee Rosenstein, for keeping me in the family. Their support means more than they will ever know. Nancy Yost, my agent, handles the really fun part of the business, so I don't have to.

The Tuesday night crew gave me valuable input on the early stages of the manuscript. Thanks to Amy, Bob, Joe, Kay, Laura, Leann, and Millie for their insights and advice. A special thanks goes to Enzo, Pumpkin, Curry, and their two-legged staff, Susie, Isabella, and Charlie, for allowing us to invade their home each week to critique in such a warm and inviting venue.

I owe a very special thanks to Terry Farmer, Ph.D., proud mom of three Maine coons, Figo, Anya, and Katie, for serving as my technical advisor in all matters having to do with Maine coon cats. Any mistakes in my portrayal of Diesel and his behavior are mine and not hers. (I do have two cats of my own—but neither of them is a Maine coon.) Finally, my love and gratitude to two very dear friends who never fail to encourage me, Patricia Orr and Julie Herman.

ONE

A hurricane slammed through my kitchen this morning, and his name was Justin.

I sighed, surveying the aftermath of my boarder's breakfast. What had gotten into the boy?

An open milk carton sat on the table, accompanied by a bowl, a spoon, and a box of cereal. Justin hadn't closed the box, and he'd left a sprinkle of cereal on the table. Splatters of milk surrounded the bowl and an abandoned plate with a half-eaten piece of toast.

I glanced toward the counter at an open loaf of bread and an uncovered butter dish, sitting in a beam of sunlight. Two pieces of bread occupied slots in the toaster, but from what I could see, Justin had forgotten to press the lever down. I strode over and picked up my newspaper from beside the sink. Justin had somehow managed to dribble water over the paper. I was glad I'd read it earlier, because now it was stuck together.

I stared out the kitchen window into the backyard for a few seconds, calming myself. I turned back. Okay, maybe it wasn't a hurricane. Just a minor tropical disturbance. I was not one of those neat freaks who hyperventilated at the first sign of a mess.

Like most men, I can be messy—but I'm happier when things are clean and well kept. I really shouldn't let myself feel so annoyed over something so trivial.

Maybe Justin was in a hurry to make his first class, but the Athena College campus was only three blocks away. He could sprint there in five minutes tops.

He was acting out of character, and that's what was really bothering me. The eighteen-year-old had been boarding with me for a couple of months and usually was careful to pick up after himself. The past few days, however, he had become increasingly careless about leaving his things lying around the house and not cleaning up in the kitchen after his meals.

Perhaps I should have expected something like this when I relaxed my rule about accepting only older students, preferably those in graduate school, as boarders. They were generally much too focused on their work to cause any disturbances, and I valued the quiet, orderly life I had created for myself these past three years.

But I had accepted Justin as a favor to an old friend. His mother, Julia Wardlaw, and I had known each other since high school and all the way through college. Justin, an only child, wasn't ready for the rough and tumble of dorm life, she said. She wanted him to have a quieter, more homelike atmosphere for his first year in college.

After the grilling Julia had put me through, I felt almost honored that she was entrusting her precious chick to my care.

A large paw pushed against my leg. Diesel, my two-year-old Maine coon cat, chirped in sympathy when I looked down at him. He withdrew his paw and stared up at me.

"I know, Diesel." I shook my head. "Justin has a problem, or he wouldn't be acting this way."

Diesel responded with another chirp—many Maine coons don't meow like other cats—and I reached down to rub his head. He still had his lighter summer coat, soft as down. His neck ruff and tail were less bushy than they would be during the colder months ahead. The tufts on the tips of his ears stood out as he stared up at me, a patient expression on his face. He was a gray tabby with dark markings, and at the age of two hadn't reached full maturity yet, weighing in at twenty-five to thirty pounds. With their broad chests and muscular bodies, Maine coons are the defensive tackles of the cat world.

"We'll have to have a talk with our boarder," I said. Diesel liked Justin and often visited him in his third-floor bedroom. "Just think what Azalea would do if she came in some morning and found a mess like this. She'd skin both Justin *and* me." Diesel returned my rueful glance with a solemn gaze.

Azalea Berry, the housekeeper I inherited along with the house when my beloved Aunt Dottie died, had strict notions about keeping a clean home. She also had strong opinions about large cats as house pets, but she and Diesel somehow managed to reach detente when I brought him home with me a couple of years ago. Even when he was a kitten, Diesel had been smart enough to pick up on Azalea's basic antipathy to cats.

Azalea had more tolerance for college-age boys, but that didn't mean she would allow Justin to get away with leaving the kitchen a mess, even a minor one. Maybe I could help him with whatever his problem was before he did it again and Azalea got after him.

I couldn't blame Azalea for her devotion to the house. Aunt Dottie had lavished her money—and her decorating abilities—on what she considered the center of any home. The kitchen occupied the southeast corner of the house, and the morning sun poured in through the large windows on both outside walls. Light suffused the room, helped by the pale yellow paint on the walls and the white ceramic tile on the floor. The cabinets shone a delicate blue and blended well with the darker hue of the table and chairs.

I could almost smell the scent of the ginger cookies Aunt Dottie used to make when I was a boy. There were only happy memories in this room, but for a moment I ached with the loss of my dear aunt and of my beloved wife, Jackie. They both died within a few weeks of each other three years ago. I pictured them at the table together, laughing and chatting.

Coming out of my reverie, I glanced at Diesel again, and I could swear he had a sympathetic look on his face. "Enough of that," I told him. He twitched his tail, turned, and padded off in the direction of the utility room and his litter box.

I cleared up Justin's mess, and as I was putting the cereal box away in the cupboard, Justin popped into the kitchen.

"Mr. Charlie," Justin said, stopping in the doorway. "I was planning to clean up." One hand clutched a worn backpack, and the other smoothed dark hair out of his eyes. The boy needed a haircut, or else he needed a ponytail.

Diesel reappeared and rubbed against his friend's jean-clad leg. Justin squatted for a moment, scratching the cat's head but watching me through his bangs.

"I thought you already left for your class," I said. "If this was one of Azalea's days, she might have a few things to say about finding the kitchen the way you left it."

I kept my tone mild, but Justin flushed anyway. Down went his head, and his hair swung forward, shielding his face. He mumbled something as he stood. Diesel sat beside him, staring up at his face.

"What did you say?"

Justin shrugged. "Sorry," he said, more clearly this time, avoiding my gaze for the moment. "I really meant to clean up, but I just lost track of time." He shot me a quick glance, then stared down at his feet again.

"No real harm done, Justin. But it seems to me you've been a little careless the last few days. That's not like you."

He shrugged. "Well, I'm gonna be late. Bye, Diesel." He turned and disappeared down the hall. In a moment I heard the front door open. I was relieved not to hear it slam shut.

We were definitely due for a chat, Justin and I. Something was bothering him, and he was bordering on rudeness. In the two months that he'd lived here, he hadn't been the most outgoing young man, but he had been civil until recently.

As the father of two former teenagers, I knew that a

change in behavior could signal any one of several problems. I hoped this wasn't a substance abuse problem. His
father, a conservative Evangelical preacher, would probably yank him out of college and take him home if that was
the case. Julia wouldn't be too happy either, and might
even blame me for letting him get in trouble.

The last thing I wanted was to get involved in the life
of one of my boarders. If Justin's problem turned out to be
serious, he would have to go home to his parents. I wasn't
ready to cope with anything big.

Diesel padded beside me to the wall rack by the back
door, and I lifted his harness and leash off the hook. He
purred as I got him street-ready, emitting the rumbling
sound that inspired his name. He loved going to work
with me.

"Let me get my coat and my satchel," I said. I checked
my tie for coffee and food stains and examined my pants
for cat hair. Why did dark colors attract pet hair like mag-
nets? I did a quick removal job with a lint brush, and then
Diesel and I were ready to go.

In the past two years, since I'd first found a shivering
kitten in the parking lot of the public library, most people
in my hometown of Athena, Mississippi, had grown used
to seeing me walking my cat on a leash. As Diesel grew
bigger, some of them wondered if he wasn't part bobcat,
but that's only because no one in town—including me—
had ever seen a Maine coon. What they'd think when he
was fully grown in another year, I had no idea.

Strangers sometimes stopped us on the street to ask if
he was a weird-looking dog—and I'd swear Diesel looked
offended when they did. He was a sociable critter, but he
didn't tolerate fools lightly—a trait *I* found endearing.

I detected a hint of wood smoke in the crisp autumn air. It seemed early to be lighting a fire in the fireplace, but evidently one of my neighbors disagreed. The odor reminded me of times by the fire in my parents' house on cold winter days.

The homes on my street were over a century old, many occupied by the same families for generations. The graceful architecture, the classic landscaping, and the feeling of a real neighborhood gave me a sense of security after I lost my wife.

Putting thoughts of Jackie aside, I started walking, Diesel preceding me by a few paces. The campus of Athena College—our destination this morning—lay three blocks to the east. A walk that should have taken five minutes usually took fifteen or twenty, because Diesel and I stopped several times so his many admirers could say hello. He took it all in stride, chirping and purring, putting smiles on faces, including my own. One or two even remembered to say, "Morning, Charlie," so I wasn't completely ignored.

Jordan Thompson, owner of the Athenaeum, our local independent bookstore, was out for her morning run. She waved as she zoomed past. I had to admire her dedication to exercise, and wished I could emulate it.

Diesel and I arrived at the college library just as Rick Tackett, the operations manager for the two library buildings, was unlocking the front door. Eight o'clock on the dot, and not a second sooner. We stood on the veranda of the antebellum Greek Revival mansion that housed the library's administrative offices, archives, and rare book collections. The main building, known as Hawksworth Library, stood next door.

Rick nodded in response to my "Good morning" and stepped aside to let me and Diesel enter. About a decade my senior, Rick was pleasant though difficult to engage in conversation. Since he spent much of his time in the main building next door, I saw him only infrequently.

Diesel led the way up the central stairs to the second floor. On the landing, he turned left and paused in front of a door with RARE BOOK ROOM emblazoned in gold leaf on the glass.

When I unlocked the door and pushed it open, I dropped Diesel's leash, then I went around the room turning on lights. By the time I finished, Diesel was settled on his favorite perch—a bed placed on the wide windowsill behind my desk. I unhooked his leash, coiled it, and stuck it beside his bed.

Diesel purred while I readied myself for the workday. My jacket and satchel stowed, I sat at my desk, turned on my computer, and began to organize my day mentally.

I worked two days a week here as a cataloger and archivist, although I enjoyed what I did so much that I never really thought of it as labor. During my career as a librarian in Houston, I had spent much of my time as an administrator. Being able to catalog again was almost heaven after dealing for so long with budgets and personnel. I was content to be here with Diesel and the rare books.

I had barely begun to read my e-mail when I heard a tap at the door.

"Morning, Charlie." Melba Gilley advanced into the room. She was as sleek as she had been in high school. Spectacular figure back then, and she still did. I liked Melba a lot, and she liked me, but so far we had both been content with simply reestablishing our friendship. I wasn't ready to date yet, and now that I was approaching fifty, I wasn't sure when or if I would be. I didn't want the emotional complications a new relationship would bring.

"Morning, Melba," I said. "How are you?"

Melba plopped into the chair by my desk, picked a nonexistent piece of fluff from her immaculate aubergine pantsuit, and said, "Excited. Aren't you?" She looked past me at the window. "Morning, Diesel, honey."

Diesel warbled a response but didn't leave his bed.

"About what?" I frowned. What had I forgotten?

"The big reception tonight. What else would I be excited about?" Melba smiled. "It's not every day Athena welcomes home a golden boy."

"Oh, that," I said. "Big deal."

Melba shook her head at me. "Charlie Harris, you can't tell me you're not curious to see what Godfrey Priest is like after all these years. I know y'all didn't get along in high school, but surely you want to see a famous author in the flesh." She laughed.

I shook my head at her. "He was a jerkwad thirty-two years ago, and he's probably an even bigger jerkwad now, just a rich one."

"He's had four wives," Melba said. "Or so I hear tell. But I guess he can afford the alimony, as much as he makes off his books."

"He hasn't made much off me," I said. "At least not since his first few books came out."

"So you *have* read his books." Melba almost crowed in triumph.

"I'll admit it," I said. "I was curious, like everybody else in Athena. And I even liked the first few. They were entertaining. But then he started writing those violent

thrillers, and the plots got more and more unbelievable."
My mouth twisted in distaste. "Not to mention the violence against women. Surely you don't still read him?"

Melba shook her head. "No, I quit a few books back.
Same reasons as you."

"Then why are you so excited?"

"He's a bestseller, a celebrity," Melba said. "How often
does a celebrity come to Athena? We could use some
excitement."

I rolled my eyes. "Surely you're not forgetting the
time Roberta Hill spray-painted her husband pink when
she caught him dead drunk and naked in Liz Graham's
trailer? I hear tell that was exciting, especially when he
woke up and chased her with an ax down Main Street."

Melba hooted with laughter. "Oh honey, I wish you'd
been here. I've never seen anything so funny in my life.
Delbert all pink, and his personal bits flopping all over
the place. I was coming out of the bank when he and his
wife went flying by. He's lucky Roberta didn't do something worse, like take that ax to his weenie."

I laughed too, trying not to think about an axed
weenie. From behind me I heard Diesel purring, like he
was laughing along with us.

Melba's cell phone rang. Grimacing, she pulled it from
the holster at her waist. She handled it like a gunslinger
with years of practice, twirling it in her hand before holding it still to read the display. "His Majesty wants me."
She answered the call to assure our boss she'd be with
him right away. Then she ended the conversation and replaced her phone after another twirl.

"Duty calls," she said as she stood. "I swear, that man

couldn't find his tiny rear end if I wasn't there to show him where it was." She snickered.

"That's why you're such a valuable administrative assistant," I said. "You know where everything is."

Melba grinned. "See you later, hon."

I chuckled. Peter Vanderkeller, the director of the library, resembled nothing more than a garden rake. His size thirteen feet seemed out of proportion to his emaciated six-foot-four frame. Melba swears she's never seen him eat anything, and most of the time I believe her. I'd never seen him put anything in his mouth other than a pen or a pencil. He invariably chewed on one during meetings.

The silence after Melba's departure felt good. Quiet is the last word anyone would use to describe her.

I turned back to my e-mail, wincing my way through Peter's weekly letter to the troops, as we library employees not-so-fondly called it. Last year at Halloween several of us dressed up in uniform for a staff meeting. Peter didn't get the joke. He never did. I felt sorry for him sometimes.

The subject of this week's homily was recycling. Peter exhorted everyone to stop bringing bottled water to work and to use instead the filtered tap water in the staff lounge. I glanced at my satchel. It usually contained at least two bottles of water. I resolved to use those bottles for refills from the tap once they were empty. Perhaps that would satisfy the boss.

The last e-mail I read reminded me of the gala reception tonight in honor of our celebrity at the president's house. I'd been telling myself I wouldn't go, but I knew curiosity would get the better of me. As much as I detested Godfrey Priest, I wanted to get a look at him after all this time.

Back in high school, I'd let Godfrey intimidate me. He was taller and better looking and was always flaunting his success with girls. I resented him in high school and in college—we were both alumni of Athena College—but that was long ago. Surely I'd left all that behind me?

Perhaps I hadn't, but if living well truly was the best revenge, I wanted to show the jerkwad I was doing fine.

Shaking my head over my foolishness, I turned away from the computer to examine some papers on my desk. Where had I put that letter? I lifted one or two of the piles until I had located what I wanted.

Besides cataloging, I also handled certain kinds of reference questions, those that related to some historical aspect of the college or the library's archives and rare books. Yesterday I had received a request from an elderly woman in Vicksburg who was trying to track down a stray twig on her family tree. Said twig was supposed to have attended Athena College back in the 1840s, not long after the school was founded.

Glancing through the letter, I found the name I needed. Laying the letter aside, I left my desk and approached a shelf of reference materials to the left of the door. What I sought was an old book of attendance records that should answer the question. One of these days I hoped to get a grant to have the records computerized, but until that happened, the old-fashioned way would have to do.

I pulled the book off the shelf and gently turned the pages until I found the years I wanted. Sounds from other parts of the library drifted up. The acoustics often behaved oddly, the grand stairway and the high-ceilinged foyer serving to bounce voices around.

While I scanned the precisely formed but tiny handwriting of the registrar of the 1840s, searching for one Bushrod Kennington, I heard snatches of conversation. I paid them scant attention, focusing on my task. But when I heard the words *murder* and *Priest*, I started listening.

TWO

I kept listening but could discern no other words. The voices faded.

I found the incident oddly unsettling, though I couldn't say why. I supposed the conversation was about Godfrey Priest, since he was *the* hot topic in Athena at the moment. And hearing the word *murder* in conjunction with his name wasn't that odd. The man did write murder mysteries.

I stopped listening and resumed my search until I located old Bushrod.

Back at my desk I made a few notes, planning to respond to the letter after lunch. This morning I intended to spend my time cataloging. I retrieved the truck of books I'd been working on and pulled the next book to catalog. After logging in to the cataloging module of our integrated library system (or ILS, in library parlance), I began to examine the book.

Part of a collection of nineteenth-century medical books, this particular volume was an 1807 treatise on midwifery by Thomas Denman. The binding was in excellent condition, but I opened the book with great care, as always. By now I was accustomed to handling books two centuries old and even older, but I still felt a sense of wonder when I touched them. So sturdy, able to survive two hundred years with proper care, but at the same time so fragile, so easily destroyed. A faint mustiness tickled my nose, and my fingers caressed the cool softness of the pages.

The particular fun of cataloging something this old was noting anything about the copy in hand—inscriptions, stamps, notations—that would set it apart from another copy. In the book I held, the front free endpaper bore, in faded ink, a previous owner's name and date: "Dr. Francis Henshall, March 18, 1809." As I delved further into the book, I found notations in ink in the same handwriting. Dr. Henshall had added comments to the text, based on his own patients.

I turned to the computer and called up the record I had previously downloaded into our system from a bibliographic utility. All the basics were there—title, publisher, date, and so on—and I added the notes to identify the copy in hand.

Engrossed in my work, I started when I heard the sound of a throat clearing on the other side of my desk.

I suppressed my irritation at the interruption as I turned to face the newcomer. Then my eyes widened in surprise as I recognized the man.

Hastily saving my work, I mumbled, "Just a moment."

"Take your time, Charlie," Godfrey Priest said, his voice booming in the quiet of the rare book room.

Beside me, Diesel stretched and yawned. He enjoyed visitors, and he hopped down from his perch to welcome Godfrey.

What the heck was he doing here? We hadn't been that close in high school or college, so why seek me out?

"Good morning, Godfrey," I said, standing. I came around the desk and extended a hand in greeting. Diesel padded right behind me. "It's been a long time."

"It sure has," Godfrey said, his tones still hearty. He clasped my hand in his bigger one and gave it a firm squeeze and a shake. "You're looking good."

"You, too," I said, trying not to wince. I flexed my fingers slightly when Godfrey released my hand.

He was even taller than I remembered. I glanced down at his feet and I could see why. He was wearing an expensive pair of cowboy boots with heels that made him about two inches taller than his normal six-four.

"What is that? A cat?" Godfrey asked, watching as Diesel made a slow circle around him. Evidently unimpressed, Diesel walked back to the window and jumped up to his bed. Yawning, he turned his back on both of us and settled down for a nap. I'd give him a treat later.

"He's a Maine coon," I said. "They're larger than most cats."

"That's the first time I've ever been snubbed by a cat." Godfrey laughed, but his expression revealed annoyance. "They always love me because they can tell I'm a cat person."

I tried not to laugh. "Diesel doesn't take to everybody. Don't pay any attention."

I continued to take in my visitor. Though we were the same age, he looked ten years older. His skin resembled leather, and years of exposure to the sun had added lines to the skin around his eyes. His hair, now a bleached straw mop, had suffered, too. His clothes screamed designer labels, and the Rolex watch he consulted ostentatiously, along with a chunky gold bracelet, made the point that he had plenty of money.

"What can I do for you, Godfrey?" I went back to my desk to sit down. With a wave I indicated he should sit, too. "Did you drop by to talk about the good old days?"

"I have it on good authority that you are the archivist here," he said, patently ignoring my little dig. He settled his long frame into the chair and crossed his arms.

"I am," I said. *Pompous as ever.* I waited.

Godfrey glanced past me toward the sleeping Diesel. "They let you bring that cat to work?" His fingers tensed on his arms, and his eyes searched the room. He seemed nervous, but I had no idea why.

"Obviously."

Godfrey's cheeks reddened as he faced me. I remembered that he had never cared for sarcasm, particularly when it had been directed at him.

"When did you return to Athena?" Godfrey asked. "I don't get here often myself. My schedule is so demanding—book tours, interviews, talking to guys in Hollywood." Again his gaze roved around the room. Was he ever going to get to the point of this visit? How much self-aggrandizement would I have to endure?

"I moved back three years ago," I replied, trying not to sound impatient. Did he think I'd be impressed by his busy life? "Not long after my wife died, my aunt left me her house here."

"Your Aunt Dottie?" Godfrey asked, frowning. "So your aunt died, too?"

"Shortly after my wife."

"Sorry to hear that," Godfrey said. "That's too bad, their dying so close together."

"It was rough." Then a memory surfaced. "You lived with Aunt Dottie for a couple of semesters, didn't you?"

Godfrey nodded. "That would have been my senior year. My parents sold up and moved to Alabama, to Fairhope, and I didn't want to live in the dorm anymore. I was lucky Miss Dottie had a room available. She was a wonderful lady." His face softened with a reminiscent smile.

"She certainly was." This was a side of Godfrey I didn't remember seeing. He had obviously been fond of my aunt. "You're doing well these days. Bestseller list with every new book. That's pretty exciting."

"Thanks. My last seven books have debuted at number one," Godfrey said, the smile giving way to a smug look. "And that's kind of why I'm here."

"I heard you're getting an award for being a distinguished alumnus," I said.

Godfrey shook his head. "That's not what I meant, although that's the ostensible reason I'm back in town. No, I meant the reason I was here talking to you."

Finally. "And that would be . . . ?" I asked, my voice trailing off.

"The archive," Godfrey replied. "I am giving my papers to the university archive. I plan to make the announcement tonight at the dinner." He stared at me. "How do we do this?"

The university administration would be delighted by such a gift, and I thought it was an excellent idea. On one condition. "I know the university would love to have your papers," I said. "But giving them is one thing. Are you willing to donate money to help with the preparation, cataloging, and maintenance?"

"Sure," Godfrey said. "What do you have to do, other than put them on the shelves?" He waved a hand in the direction of the bookshelves. "And how much money? I'm sure I can afford it."

"The papers have to be organized and cataloged," I said, ignoring that last sentence. "That could take some time, depending on the extent of the collection. I'm the archivist, but I work only part-time. It could take years to get your papers done, considering all the other books and collections waiting to be processed here."

"If I give enough money, could you hire someone to catalog my papers and get them done sooner?" He frowned. "I don't want them sitting in boxes, gathering dust."

"Yes," I replied. "We have a tiny budget, and we rely on donations."

"How much?"

"How many papers are we talking about?" I pointed to a nearby box, roughly the size of a box of computer paper. "How many boxes of stuff?"

Godfrey stared at the box. After a moment, he answered. "There are manuscripts of all my novels, and I've published twenty-three. Then there's correspondence,

plus copies of my books, in English and other languages."
He paused. "Say fifty-four boxes."

That was oddly precise, I thought. Had he already
boxed everything? He would never imagine the university would turn down his gift.

"And you would continue to add to it," I said, doing
some mental calculations.

"Sure," Godfrey said. "I'll be writing for a long time
to come, knock on wood." He rapped my desk with his
knuckles.

I found a pad and pencil and made some rough calculations. I named a figure, and Godfrey didn't blink.

"Sounds good," he replied. "I'll double it, just to be
safe. That should take care of things for a few years,
right?"

"Yes," I said. Hearing the voice of my boss in my head,
I added something, though I didn't like doing it. "And of
course you might want to put a bequest in your will, too.
It never hurts."

Godfrey laughed. "You have to say that, don't you?"

"Yes," I said, trying to suppress a sour expression.

"Don't worry, I'm used to it. People are holding their
hands out for money all the time." He grinned. "I'll call
my lawyer this afternoon and take care of it."

"You'll need to talk to some of the administrative people tonight after you make your announcement," I said.

He nodded.

I thought our business was done, but Godfrey didn't
move from the chair.

I waited a moment.

"You're living in Miss Dottie's house, huh?" Godfrey
said.

"Yes."

"Are you taking in student boarders like she did?" He stared past me at the window where Diesel still slept.

"Yes," I said. "It's what she wanted, and it's not so bad having someone in the house, now that my own two children are grown and out of the nest."

"You have two kids?" Godfrey glanced at me, an odd look on his face.

"A son and a daughter," I replied. "Sean is twenty-seven, and Laura is twenty-three."

"That's nice," Godfrey said, his voice soft. "Having kids, I mean."

Maybe I had accomplished something Godfrey hadn't. As far as I knew, he didn't have any children. I was lucky, even if I wasn't a rich writer.

Godfrey shifted in his chair. "What are the boarders like, the ones living there now?"

"Both nice young men," I said, puzzled by the conversation. Why was he asking about my current boarders?

"One of them is named Justin, right?" Godfrey examined his hands with care.

"Yes, there is a Justin boarding with me. The other one, Matt, is actually spending a semester in Madrid, doing research for his dissertation." I was getting more and more uneasy. "Look, Godfrey, what's going on here? Why these questions? Do you know Justin?"

"No, I don't," Godfrey replied. "But I'd like to." He paused for a deep breath. Then he faced me. "He's my son, Charlie, but he doesn't know it."

THREE

"You're Justin's father?" I stared at Godfrey, feeling as if this was a bizarre joke. Back in high school he had a reputation for outlandish pranks.

Godfrey nodded, and I was sure he was serious.

But why the heck was he telling me this? Simply because Justin boarded with me?

"This is incredible." A fatuous reaction, but I had to say something.

"Yeah, it is," Godfrey said. Looking down at his hands, he continued. "I had no idea until about six months ago that I had a son. I can't believe Julia never told me." His voice had an odd note in it.

"Julia Wardlaw?" I sounded like a not-very-bright parrot, I decided.

Godfrey glanced up at me. "Yes, surely you remember

her from high school. Julia Peterson. God, she was beautiful." He smiled.

Julia *had* been a knockout thirty years ago. I saw her on a weekly basis now, when she came on Fridays to pick up Justin and take him home for the weekend. Sadly, the years had not been kind. "Have you seen her lately?" I said.

"No, but I've talked to her," Godfrey said. "She wrote to me through my website. Told me about Justin, and I about fell through the floor."

"I can imagine." Knowing this helped me put a few things together. When Julia brought Justin to my house, helping him move in his things, she told me more about her family. Obviously as reluctant to tell me as I was to hear it, she seemed to feel it her duty anyway. Justin and his father, Ezra, argued over Justin's choice of schools. Ezra Wardlaw wanted Justin to attend a small Bible college and follow him into the ministry. Justin rebelled, supported by Julia. He was their only child, and the betrayal—that was the very word Julia had used, quoting her husband—had hit Ezra hard.

"This is really none of my business," I said, "but are you sure Justin is your son?"

"Absolutely." Godfrey looked at me like I was an idiot. "You don't think I'd take someone's word for it? But I knew it was a possibility. In my position, I have to be sure, so I insisted on a DNA test."

"Naturally," I said, my tone wry. "It's still none of my business, but what do you plan to do?"

"I want to meet Justin," Godfrey said. "Talk to him, explain the situation. Now that I know, I want to be part of his life."

Perhaps Justin already knew about his famous biological father, I thought. Julia could have told him recently, knowing that Godfrey was coming to Athena.
It had been announced in the local paper a couple of
weeks ago.

If Justin knew, that might explain his behavior the past
few days. News that his father wasn't Ezra Wardlaw, but
Godfrey Priest, would have come as a huge shock. Poor
kid, I thought.

"What is it?" Godfrey stared at me.

"Thinking about Justin, that's all." I was not going to
share my thoughts on this with Godfrey. Besides, I was
only speculating.

"You like him? Think he's a good kid?" Godfrey
sounded so eager, I felt sorry for him. But I was more
concerned with Justin's reactions to all this. Would he be
able to cope with another father in his life?

"Yes, I do. He's a nice, intelligent young man." Behind
me, Diesel added his opinion, emitting a few trills and
chirps. He knew whom we were discussing. "He's a son
you can be proud to acknowledge."

"Thank you, Charlie," Godfrey said. "You have no
idea what that means to me." He sounded pathetically
grateful, and I sympathized.

"When will you talk to him?"

"I'm supposed to meet Julia for lunch," Godfrey said.
He checked his watch. "If she can get away from Misery,
that is. I still can't believe she married that guy."

"Misery" was an old nickname for Ezra Wardlaw. He
was several years older than Godfrey, Julia, and I, and by
the time we were in high school, Ezra already had a reputation as a fire-and-brimstone Evangelical preacher.

"I was in Texas by the time they got married," I said. "The last time we had heard from her, she was dating Rick Tackett and it sounded pretty serious." I had forgotten about that until now. Funny how things popped back into the memory sometimes.

"Rick Tackett?" Godfrey's tone was sharp. "How do you know that?"

"We came to spend Christmas with Aunt Dottie around then, and we ran into Julia and Rick somewhere. At the grocery store, I think." I paused. "You know him?"

"Yeah, I know him," Godfrey said, but it didn't sound like he cared much for him.

"Anyway, that's why I was so surprised when I heard she married Ezra."

Godfrey stared down at his hands. "Guess that's my fault. I spent a few months here, about nineteen years ago, doing research for one of my early books. We spent some time together. I'd divorced my first wife, and Julia seemed to be on her own."

"Seemed to be?"

"She was attending Ezra's church, and they had been dating. But while I was here she didn't see much of him." He squirmed in the chair, his eyes still cast downward. "I had no idea I'd gotten her pregnant. I finished my research and went back to California."

I'd bet there was more to the story than Godfrey told me. I got the feeling he lied about not knowing about Julia's pregnancy.

"You left, and she married Ezra Wardlaw." I watched him, wondering if he would look at me. "And she never got in touch with you to let you know she about Justin?"

Godfrey shifted in his chair again. "No, she didn't."

This behavior convinced me he was lying, but I wouldn't call him on it. What would be the point?

"Why are you telling me all this?" I said.

Examining his hands again, Godfrey said, "You're the only old friend I have in Athena—besides Julia, of course—and my son is living in your house. I thought you should know, since I'll be in town for a while, hoping I can get to know my son."

His only "old friend"? I almost laughed at that. Considering our history in high school and college, Godfrey had to be pretty desperate to call me his friend. After the way he treated me, I shouldn't even be talking to him.

Even though he was still a jerk, I couldn't, in good conscience, turn my back on him. As a father, I could sympathize with his situation.

"I'll do what I can," I told him.

His face brightened.

"But you need to keep in mind that Justin is in his first semester of college. He's facing a lot of stress as it is, and you need to be careful about adding more."

"I understand," Godfrey said. "I just want to be a part of his life, if he'll let me." He leaned back in his chair. "But I'd really like to take him to California with me for a while. We could get to know each other, he could have a little fun—which we both know he hasn't had with Misery in the picture. Maybe take off for Europe, if he'd like that."

Protesting would do no good, I realized. Julia would be horrified if she heard this, because I knew she wouldn't want Justin that far away from her. But they would have to work this out themselves. It was none of my business.

Diesel jumped down from the window and walked

over to Godfrey's chair. He sat up on his hind legs and stretched out one of his front legs, resting his paw on Godfrey's knee. Godfrey stared down at Diesel in surprise.

"He does that sometimes," I said. "He seems to sense people's feelings, and he tries to comfort them."

"Thank you, buddy," Godfrey said, his voice soft as he touched Diesel's paw lightly with his hand.

Diesel muttered, withdrew his paw, and went back to his window.

Godfrey shook his head. "I've got to put him in a book. That was freaky."

"Diesel is a special cat." I smiled and reached for a piece of scrap paper. Picking up a pen, I jotted down my telephone number. "Call me and let me know when you'll be coming by the house, okay?"

Godfrey accepted the paper. "Thanks, Charlie. I've got another appointment before I meet Julia for lunch." He stood.

I stood too and accepted the hand he proffered. "Good luck. I hope things work out for you with Justin."

Godfrey thanked me again, and I watched as he strode out of the room.

"What a mess," I said.

I didn't realize I had spoken the words until I felt Diesel's paw on my shoulder. When I turned to face him, Diesel gazed at me, his head cocked a bit to the right. It was uncanny, the things this cat seemed to understand. "Yes, it's a messy situation. Poor Justin." I shook my head. "Poor Godfrey, poor Julia, and even poor Ezra."

Diesel trilled a couple of times.

"Somehow I think we'll be in the middle of it, too. With Justin in our house, there's no way to avoid it."

Diesel chirped.

"We'll support Justin any way we can." I spoke with more assurance than I felt. "If he wants our help, that is." I couldn't believe I was saying such things. What had happened to my resolve to steer away from emotional complications?

I stared at my cat as if he could answer that for me. Diesel blinked slowly before settling back down to nap.

For a few minutes, I thought about what had just occurred in my office. Godfrey started out as I remembered him—cocksure, swaggering, self-involved. His manner changed, though, his self-assurance seemingly gone when he told me about Justin. Perhaps having a son humbled him.

But there was more to it. The way he squirmed when talking about Julia. He lied to me about that. He had been lying to himself for years. He knew all along Julia was pregnant, but for whatever reason he hadn't been willing to acknowledge it. Until now. Why? I wondered. Maybe hitting fifty had done it.

I turned to my computer. All this speculation gave me a headache. I needed to focus on work and forget about distractions.

I managed to keep myself busy until lunchtime, continuing with my cataloging. Around eleven-thirty I put down my pencil, set my computer to standby, and stood.

"Come on, boy." I rubbed Diesel's head. "Let's go home for lunch."

A few minutes later, Diesel and I were heading for home. The temperature had risen a few degrees, but the weather remained pleasantly cool. Being back in northern Mississippi, where there were actually four seasons a year, made a welcome change from Houston with its two seasons. Summer and not-summer, as I liked to call them.

As I inserted my key in the front door, I heard voices inside. Loud voices, full of anger.

I opened the door, Diesel on my heels.

Ezra Wardlaw stood in the living room, shaking a finger at Justin. The boy sat, head bowed, on the sofa. They were so involved in their argument, they paid no attention to Diesel and me.

". . . get your things right now. You're coming home." Ezra's face was so red I thought he might stroke out.

"I'm not leaving." Justin looked up at his father and yelled back at him. "And you're not my father!"

"Don't you dare speak to me like that." Ezra's arm drew back.

I winced as Ezra's hand connected with Justin's face. Justin's head rocked back, and Ezra stepped closer.

I stepped forward, determined to prevent any more violence in my house.

"Stop that." I dropped Diesel's leash, and I heard, rather than saw, Diesel run out of the room. He hated loud voices. "Don't strike that boy again."

Ezra whirled to face me. "This is none of your business. Keep out of it."

Justin rubbed his face gingerly. He looked straight at me. He mouthed the word *please*.

"It *is* my business. You're in *my* house." I kept my voice and tone firm. "You will not strike anyone in this house, or I'll call the police. Understood?" I took a step closer to him. I was taller, by about three inches, and I outweighed him by a few pounds, too. If I had to, I'd knock some sense into him.

Ezra glared at me, but his hands stayed by his sides as he turned back to his son. "Get your things. Now."

"I'm eighteen. I don't have to go anywhere with you." Justin stared up at Ezra, resolve in his eyes.

Ezra's chest heaved. He seemed to be struggling for breath.

"You should leave now." I waited, ready to intervene if necessary.

Backing away from his son, but never losing eye contact, Ezra said, "This isn't over. That bastard will rot in hell before he takes you away from me."

FOUR

After that statement, Ezra stomped out of the room. Moments later, the door slammed so hard the windows in the living room rattled.

"I hate him." Justin's voice bore such loathing. What had Ezra done to this boy to make Justin despise him so?

"Come with me, son. We need to put some ice on your cheek. It's swelling already."

Justin blinked at me. I think he'd forgotten I was in the room. "Yes, sir." He stood but didn't move forward.

I took him gently by the arm and led him into the kitchen. After his last outburst, he appeared listless, watching me with dulled eyes.

He leaned against the sink while I got ice cubes from the dispenser and wrapped them in a dish towel.

"Here," I said. "Hold this to your cheek. It will feel better."

His cheek was still an angry red. He was going to have a terrific bruise there.

Justin accepted the towel and put it against his face. He winced, but he held the towel in place.

As I watched, concerned, wondering what else I could do for him, he started crying. Quietly, at first. Then harder and louder, the sobs beginning to wrack his body.

Poor kid. This was more than he should have to bear. I put an arm around his shoulder, and he hugged himself to me with his free arm.

I spoke to him, keeping my voice low and soothing, and the sobs diminished.

Feeling a cat rubbing against my leg, I looked down. Diesel had come out of hiding, and now he watched me, wanting to help.

"Justin, look. Diesel's here. He wants to talk to you."

Sniffling, Justin pulled away from me, gazing down at the anxious feline face. He sat down on the floor, towel still against his cheek. Diesel rubbed his head on Justin's chin.

The cat climbed into the boy's lap, his rumbling purr loud in the room. Head bent, Justin let Diesel lick his un-covered cheek.

Smiling, I left the kitchen, knowing that Justin was in good paws. Diesel could bring him comfort, and Justin needed it.

I used the downstairs bathroom, taking my time wash-ing my hands. I stared at my reflection. For all my talk of minding my own business, I had walked right into a messy situation. How would Julia react when she found out what Ezra had done? She had a fiery temper as a young woman. She might light into Ezra the way he had lit into Justin. What a mess.

Finished washing my hands, I judged it okay to go back to the kitchen.

Justin now sat in a chair, Diesel in his lap. Boy and cat glanced at me. Justin seemed calmer, and Diesel no longer looked anxious. A bruise was forming on the boy's cheek.

"How about some lunch, guys?" I went to the refrigerator. "Diesel has his crunchies if he wants them, but I need something else."

I stared into the fridge, waiting for Justin to respond. He was probably embarrassed, poor kid. He might be eighteen in years, but he was still a boy in so many ways.

"There's still plenty of that ham Azalea baked. I think I'll make some sandwiches." I turned to face the table. "How about you, Justin? I make a pretty good ham sandwich."

Justin's head dipped down for a moment. He rubbed Diesel's head. "That sounds good. But I can make my own."

"Tell you what," I said. "I'll slice the ham, and you can get everything else together. Okay?"

"Yes, sir," Justin said. Diesel jumped down from his lap and padded off in search of his own lunch.

Justin came to the sink and washed his hands, still avoiding looking directly at me.

I set the plated ham on the counter, found a knife, and started carving thick slices. Azalea cooked a mighty fine ham, and my mouth was already watering.

Justin retrieved mustard and mayo from the fridge, along with a jar of Azalea's homemade pickles. He set it all on the table, along with the bread and a big bag of potato chips. Next he found plates and knives, along with napkins, and arranged them.

"Would you get me a can of Diet Coke?" I asked.

Justin went back to the refrigerator, pulling out my Diet Coke and a can of regular for him.

He sat down at the table, waiting for me to finish. I had sliced enough ham for four or five sandwiches, I figured. That should do.

I brought the ham to the table and sat down, cater-corner from Justin. He held out the loaf of bread to me, and I took four slices. "I don't know about you, but I'm betting I can eat at least two sandwiches."

"I'm kinda hungry too." He seemed surprised that he had an appetite. He waited while I helped myself to the mayo and mustard before making his first sandwich.

I poured some chips onto my plate, watching as Justin carefully spread a thick layer of mayo on two slices of wheat bread.

He still wouldn't look at me.

"I want you to know, son," I said, "that you can talk to me, if you want to. I'll help you any way I can, and Diesel will, too."

Justin smiled at that and looked me in the face finally. "Thank you, Mr. Charlie. I appreciate that." He took a bite of his sandwich and winced. When he finished chewing—slowly—he spoke again.

"I'm glad you came home when you did." He paused for a moment. His gaze shifted away. "He would've beat the crap out of me if you hadn't."

My stomach clenched in anger. "Has he beaten you before?"

Justin nodded. "Yes, sir. He doesn't like it when I defy him."

He said it so matter-of-factly that my heart ached for him. "You don't have to put up with that anymore. Don't let him in the house when I'm not here."

"No, sir, I won't." Justin ate some more of his sandwich. He touched his bruised cheek a couple of times. I was sure it was pretty sore.

Trying to appear calm, I was stewing inside. I'm not normally a violent man—far from it—but violence against children makes me furious. My father had been, like Ezra Wardlaw, a devout Evangelical. Stern, demanding, but he never once raised his hand against me. I tried his patience often enough, but his firm and loving discipline taught me what I needed to know. I felt the back of my mother's hairbrush on my bottom a few times, but she never struck hard enough even to bruise me.

Justin cleared his throat. "Um, guess I should explain why I said he isn't my father." He pushed some potato chips around on his plate. "Not my biological father anyway. But Mom is really my mother." He watched my face carefully for a reaction.

Feigning surprise at this point would be ridiculous. Justin deserved the truth.

"I know," I said. "Your biological father came to see me this morning."

"You know him? I suppose you would, you and him both being from Athena." Justin tried to appear nonchalant, but his curiosity was obvious.

"We grew up together. Same class in school and at the college, too."

"That's cool." Justin ate in silence for a couple of minutes.

I could have volunteered information, but I thought it was better to let Justin ask me what he wanted to know. I'd have to be diplomatic, though. I didn't want to tell the boy his biological dad was a jerk, in my opinion.

Finished with my first sandwich, I started on the second one after a sip of my drink. By this time Diesel had come back. He crawled into the chair opposite mine and sat, looking back and forth between Justin and me.

"It's so funny how he does that." Justin laughed. "Do you ever let him eat at the table?"

"No, because he doesn't get people food very often." I arched an eyebrow at my boarder. "Remember?"

Justin nodded, a guilty expression flashing across his face. "Yes, sir, I promise I won't do it again unless you say I can."

"Thank you."

Diesel trilled a few times.

"Yes, we're talking about you," I said. "And don't think you can con any ham or potato chips out of me or Justin."

If cats could frown, I'd swear Diesel frowned at me then.

Justin snickered. After drinking some of his Coke, he set the can down and looked at me. "What's he like? Godfrey Priest, I mean. I've, like, seen him on TV, and I even read some of his books. But I don't know much about him."

Definitely the time for tact. "We always knew Godfrey would do something big." I sat back in my chair and regarded Justin. "Even as a boy, he made plans. Talked about traveling all over the world. At first he was going to be a reporter, and by the time he was a teenager, he decided he was going to be a famous writer."

"That's pretty amazing," Justin said. His eyes glowed with the beginnings of hero worship. Godfrey might have a lot to live up to with Justin.

"When Godfrey set his mind to do something, he did it." *No matter what it cost anyone else*, I added silently. "He always had the drive and the ambition. I don't think anyone who knew him doubted he'd succeed."

"Were you friends?"

"Not really. I was pretty competitive too, and we were always vying for the same honors in school." With a rueful laugh I admitted, "Godfrey usually won. The only thing I ever beat him in was math."

"Yeah, I know what that's like." Justin shook his head. "This girl in my class was always beating me for things. I hated coming in second."

"I did, too," I said. Odd how the memories of those many defeats still rankled on occasion. "But I had plenty of other accomplishments to be proud of. You will, too."

Justin nodded his thanks. I could see he was burning to ask another question but was probably afraid to.

I wanted to set his mind at ease. "He's looking forward to meeting you. I know he wanted to talk to your mother first, but I'm sure he'll come to see you as soon as he can."

"Yeah, I guess," Justin said. "But he's this rich, famous writer, and I'm a hick from a little town in Mississippi."

I suppressed a smile. "He's from this same little town.

He knows he has a son now, and that's the only thing that matters. You could be purple with seven eyes, and he wouldn't care."

Justin laughed at that, and Diesel joined in, chirping. The sound of a ringing phone interrupted their merriment.

"Excuse me," Justin said. He stood and pulled a cell phone from the pocket of his jeans. "It's my mom," he said after glancing at the display. "Be right back."

Justin walked out of the kitchen as he answered the call. "Hi, Mom."

That was the last Diesel and I heard. Diesel stared hopefully at the potato chips left on Justin's plate.

"No, siree," I said. I picked up the plate and took it over to the sink. "That's not Diesel food."

I walked back to the table where Diesel sat. As I scratched his head, his rumbling purr started.

"Mr. Charlie."

Justin stood in the kitchen doorway, a stricken look on his face.

"What's wrong?"

"My father—Ezra, I mean—is in the hospital. He got in a fight, and now he's in bad shape." He paused, his body trembling. "Can you take me to the hospital?"

FIVE

I hate hospitals. I have spent far too much time in them, first with my parents and then with my wife. As I parked my car in a visitors' lot at Athena Regional Medical Center, I remembered the last time I was here—when Aunt Dottie succumbed to pancreatic cancer. I was at her side, trying to see not her ravaged face and body, but the happy, healthy woman I adored.

Beside me, Justin unbuckled his seat belt, the sound breaking into my reverie. "I don't like hospitals," he said. "But I guess I have to go in." He made no move to open his door, but he touched his bruised cheek a couple of times.

"I don't like them either," I said. "But your mother wants you to be here. She needs your support." I opened my door. "Come on, let's go in."

Justin sighed heavily, but he did as I instructed.

He followed me, lagging a little behind, to the emergency room entrance. I couldn't blame him for not wanting to go inside, not after what Ezra had done to him earlier.

I had no idea how serious Ezra's condition might be. "Bad shape" could mean any number of things. Julia hadn't given her son any details, but I doubted Ezra was in critical condition.

And if Ezra had been fighting, who was his opponent? The logical answer was Godfrey Priest. Was he injured as well?

Inside the ER, we paused at the desk to inquire about Ezra, but before I finished speaking, Julia appeared beside us.

She was better dressed than I remembered seeing her for a long time. Her usual shapeless cotton or polyester frock was gone, replaced by a serviceable black dress. Probably the one she wore to funerals, I decided. It gave her a certain dignity, offering a sharp contrast to her gray hair, pulled into a severe bun at the nape of her neck.

"Thank you for bringing him, Charlie," Julia said. She touched Justin's arm. Then she gasped as she saw the bruise on his cheek. She touched it gingerly, and Justin shied away. "Sweetie, what happened?"

"He hit me." Justin glared at his mother.

Julia whirled to face me. "What on earth do you mean, striking him like that?" By the fire in her eyes I could see she was about ready to strike out at me.

"Not me," I said, holding up a hand. "Calm down, Julia."

"Then who?" Julia asked, turning back to Justin.

"Ezra." He said the word with such loathing, even

Julia flinched. "A little while ago. He came to try to make me go back home with him. But I told him I wouldn't go, Mama. I said he wasn't my father, and he couldn't make me. That's when he hit me."

Julia threw her arms around him and hugged him close. "My poor little lamb. I don't know what's gotten into the man, I swear to the Lord. He was very upset this morning, honey. It's my fault. I should have handled him better."

Justin pulled away from his mother. "I don't want to see him ever again."

"Honey, that's foolish," Julia said. "He *is* your father, in all the ways that count. Even if he struck you like that. You have to give him the chance to apologize to you. By now he must be very upset with himself for doing it."

Justin had a mulish expression on his face. "I don't have anything to say to him."

"Just do what I tell you." Julia's sharp tone surprised both Justin and me.

"Yes, ma'am."

"Come with me." Julia turned and walked away. Justin, after a quick glance at me, trailed after her. I wasn't sure forcing Justin to talk to Ezra right now was a good idea, but Julia would no doubt have brushed aside any objections I could raise.

I moved to the small waiting room and sat down. Resigning myself to an indeterminate period of twiddling my thumbs, I wished I had brought a book with me. Or Diesel.

Diesel was confused when I told him he had to stay home. He went almost everywhere with me, except to church, and he knew today wasn't Sunday. He sat in the kitchen, watching as Justin and I went out the back door to the garage. I knew he'd still be sitting there when I came home again.

I glanced around me. There were only a couple of other people in the waiting room, an anxious-looking elderly woman and a man who had to be her son. He had the same nose, the same angles to his face. He kept patting his mother's hand, speaking in low tones, but she didn't seem to be hearing him. Who were they here for? I wondered. Her husband, his father? I hoped whoever it was would be all right.

Julia appeared in front of me, blocking out the harsh fluorescent lighting for a moment. I looked up into her face, not surprised to see the weariness and anger there.

"How is Ezra?" I asked as I stood. I motioned Julia to the seat next to me, and she sank into it like a woman twice her age.

"Are you okay?" The stiffness of her movements worried me.

Julia grimaced. "Just getting old, Charlie. And tired."

"You're the same age I am. You're not old." I tried to keep my tone light, but Julia heard the concern in my voice.

"It's not the years, it's the mileage. Isn't that what they say?" The specter of a smile passed across Julia's face. "I'm okay. Tired is all. The past couple of months have been pretty rough."

"Ever since Justin left home."

Julia nodded. "Ezra has been beside himself for months. He loves that boy with all his heart, and Justin defying him the way he has, well, it's about broken his heart." She paused. "But I'm about ready to wring his neck over what he did. He should never have struck Justin like that. He almost cried, though, when he saw the bruise he made."

I forbore commenting on Ezra's behavior at the moment. "Justin has the right to live his own life." I probably should have kept my mouth shut, let Julia talk.

"I know that as well as you do. I had to make a choice when Justin told me he didn't want to be a preacher, and I made it." Julia's angry tone didn't offend me. I was treading on ground where I had no business stepping.

"Do you regret it?" I was prying, but instinct told me Julia needed to talk about all this.

"No, I don't." Julia closed her eyes and leaned back in the hard plastic chair. "You're a parent. Would *you*?"

"No." I waited a moment, but she didn't reply. "How did Ezra wind up in the hospital? Justin mentioned a fight."

Julia turned her head and looked me in the eye. "Godfrey told me he came to see you this morning. Told you everything."

"Yes, he did. I'm sure you'd rather he kept this private."

"He's bound and determined to make this some kind of public spectacle. But if he thinks he's going to take Justin away from me, just because of all his money and his fame, he's going to get a rude awakening." Julia sat up. The loathing in her tone didn't surprise me. Godfrey had that effect on people, at least in my experience.

"If I can do anything to help, you know I will." I wasn't thrilled about being dragged into this mess, but for Justin's sake, I wanted to do what I could.

"Thank you. You always were a good man, even when

you were a boy. Did the right thing, and stood by your friends." Julia smiled, some of the tension and anger draining out of her. She sounded fatigued as she continued. "It's such a nightmare. I was sitting in a restaurant having lunch with Godfrey so we could talk about Justin. And then Ezra walked in. He and Godfrey started arguing. I tried to get between them, but I couldn't."

"I doubt you could have done anything to stop Ezra," I said, recalling the scene at my house. "When a man's that angry . . ."

"Ezra has a terrible temper. He has prayed for so long, asking the Lord to help him overcome it. But he never can."

Did he take that terrible temper out on his wife as well as his son? After what I witnessed earlier, I was afraid he did. Could that explain the stiffness in Julia's movements?

Julia perhaps sensed my concern. She looked at me again. "Ezra has never struck me, if that's what you're thinking."

"I'm relieved to hear it. But he struck Justin this morning. Very hard."

Julia's hands clenched, and her breathing grew labored. From the glint in her eye, I figured it was just as well Ezra was already in the hospital or Julia might have put him there herself.

"How badly is Ezra hurt?"

"Not as bad as he's going to be if he strikes Justin again." Julia made an effort to regain control of herself. For a moment I thought she might go flying into Ezra's room. "Sorry, Charlie, this is all so sordid."

"You don't need to worry about that with me. We've

known each other too long." I took her right hand and patted it. "Now, tell me what happened to Ezra."

"It was ridiculous, a man his size laying into Godfrey like that. Godfrey hit him twice, once in the nose and once in the eye, and it was all over. I don't think Godfrey did anything except bruise his knuckles a little."

"Did he break Ezra's nose? Or injure the eye badly?" I could picture the scene all too easily. I fought Godfrey a couple of times myself in the folly of adolescence. Godfrey won both times, but thankfully my face didn't suffer lasting harm.

"Ezra's nose is pretty swollen. So is his eye. I don't think there'll be permanent damage, except to his pride. There were several of our church members in the restaurant. Ezra shamed himself in front of them." The grim satisfaction in Julia's voice didn't bode well for Ezra. Any sympathy I could have felt for him evaporated the moment he struck Justin. "What can I do for you?" I said.

"I'll be fine," Julia replied. "I'm sorry that you got dragged into this, but I know you'll help Justin if you can. Just be there if he needs someone to talk to, if you don't mind."

"Of course I don't." I paused for a moment. There was a question I felt I had to ask, but Julia might not want to answer it. "What made you decide to get in touch with Godfrey after all this time and tell him about Justin?"

Julia threw me an odd look, but any answer she might have given me was forestalled by Justin's abrupt entrance into the waiting room.

His stormy face said it all. The time spent with his father had not gone well.

Julia stood and held out her arms. Justin walked into

them, and they embraced. I turned away to give them some privacy. The elderly woman and her son were gone now. I got up and moved to the other end of the room. Julia and Justin conversed in low voices.

After a few minutes, while I stared out a window into the parking lot, Julia called my name. I strolled back to her and Justin.

"Thank you for coming," Julia said, one arm still around her son. "I think Justin's ready to go. I really appreciate your bringing him here."

Mother and son both appeared worn to the bone now. The best thing I could do was to get Justin home and let him have some privacy or maybe some time with Diesel. My cat had a tonic effect on people, and Justin needed that now.

"Glad to do it," I said. I took her free hand and held it between both of mine for a moment. Julia smiled, and I released her hand. "If there's anything else I can do, let me know."

Julia nodded. "Put some ice on that bruise if it hurts very much." Justin gave her a quick kiss on the cheek, and I walked out of the waiting room with him a couple of steps behind.

In the car, Justin didn't say anything. After he buckled his seat belt, he leaned back and closed his eyes. I kept silent. If he wanted to talk, I'd listen.

Justin stirred, opened his eyes, and looked out the window. "He apologized for hitting me." He touched his cheek briefly and then let his hand slide back down to the seat.

I left the car in park. "I'm glad to hear that," I said.

"He said he'd never hit me again. He was crying." Justin turned to look at me. "You think he means that?"

"I sure hope so." Faced with alienating his son completely, perhaps Ezra was trying to change his behavior.

"He kept telling me he was my father, that he had taken care of me for eighteen years. Like he wanted me to be grateful, I guess."

"In his way I think he's trying to tell you that he loves you and considers you his son," I said, choosing my words with care. "I don't think he's really looking for gratitude. He doesn't want to lose you, but he might not be able to find the right words to tell you that."

Justin frowned. "He won't listen when I try to tell him things. He just preaches at me and tells me what I ought to do, instead of trying to understand me. I'm not him."

"No, you aren't. But sometimes fathers have a hard time letting their sons be their own men. I think some fathers feel their sons have to be just like them in order to justify their own choices in life. Does that make sense?"

Justin's eyes had grown big. "I never thought about it like that. That's why he wants me to be a preacher too, huh?" He turned to gaze out the window again, his head against the glass.

I had given him enough to think about. I backed the car out of the parking space and headed for home. Justin stayed silent the whole way.

When I turned onto my street, I glanced ahead and swore under my breath. A strange car, a late model Jaguar, sat on the street in front of my house. It could only be Godfrey.

SIX
||||||||||||

I was tempted to drive right by. Justin needed some time to himself, I thought. But this meeting with Godfrey was inevitable. Maybe it was better to get it over with.

As I passed the car I looked inside. Sure enough, Godfrey waved as I turned into the driveway. I clicked the garage door opener. Justin stirred as I drove inside.

I turned off the car and clicked the opener again. The door came down behind us.

In the dim light provided by two windows high in the wall in front of us, I examined Justin's face. He still bore signs of strain from his time with Ezra.

"That's him in the car out there, isn't it?" Justin unbuckled his seat belt.

"If you're not ready to talk to him, you don't have to."

Justin blinked a couple of times. "No, I want to talk to him." He paused. "But what do I call him?"

"Only what you feel comfortable with. He'll understand if you call him Mr. Priest. You both need to know each other better before you decide anything else." I smiled at him.

Justin nodded. He opened his door and got out.

I followed him into the house, and sure enough, Diesel was waiting near the kitchen door. Justin knelt on the floor beside the cat and rubbed Diesel's head.

"You talk to Diesel for a few minutes," I said. "I'll let Godfrey in. I want to have a word with him first if you don't mind."

"Yes, sir," Justin said. Diesel climbed into his lap and was butting the boy's chin with his head.

For a moment Justin looked much younger than eighteen, and I worried about the burdens piling up on those boyish shoulders.

Godfrey was waiting on the doorstep. I motioned him inside.

"Hi, Charlie. Where have y'all been?" As he stepped past me into the hallway, he showed no signs of his fight with Ezra.

"At the hospital," I said, closing the door behind him. "Julia called and asked Justin to come."

"The hospital?" Godfrey shook his head. "Man, I didn't hit Ezra that hard, did I?"

"They wanted to make sure his nose isn't broken," I said. I led the way into the living room and motioned for Godfrey to sit down in one of the two overstuffed armchairs. I sat in the other, and we regarded each other for a moment.

"Ezra will probably be fine," I said. "Though I don't think Julia's very happy with him at the moment. Or with you."

"Julia." Godfrey leaned back in his chair. "I wouldn't have recognized her, she's changed so much since the last time I saw her." He was frowning.

"We're all fifty years old," I said, my tone deliberately harsh. "You don't look like you did thirty years ago either, you know."

Godfrey scowled at me. "You think I don't know that? I wasn't criticizing Julia, anyway. It was just a bit of a shock."

"Forget about Julia and Ezra for the moment. Let's talk about Justin."

"Where is he? I really want to see him." He turned in his chair, half rising, and looked toward the door.

"He's in the kitchen with Diesel. He'll be here in a minute. I wanted to talk to you first, though." I held up a hand, and Godfrey sat back.

"So talk." Godfrey folded his arms across his chest. "What are you going to lecture me about now?"

"I'm not going to lecture you," I said, wanting to add an epithet or two but restraining myself. "Julia has entrusted Justin to my care, and I simply wanted to tell you to move slowly with him. He's had a rough day so far, and he doesn't need you charging into his life like a bull in a china shop. You need to focus on what Justin needs, and not so much on what you want."

"Yes, Mr. Harris. Thank you for telling me what to do." Godfrey's tone mocked me, but I ignored that.

"I have no reason to expect that you've changed much

in thirty years, Mr. Priest," I said just as mockingly. "You never did think much about anyone but yourself. But you have a son now, and that has to change."

Godfrey stared at me. "Lord, I had no idea you despised me so much. What did I ever do to you?"

I almost laughed in his face. The man had a colossal ego. "We don't have enough time to go into that. Just stop and think for a moment about what you did to Julia nineteen years ago. Walking away and leaving her pregnant, knowing she would probably marry Ezra. You have a lot to answer for."

Godfrey's face whitened, and I knew I was right. He had lied about not knowing Julia was pregnant when he left her. To his credit, he didn't try to deny it now.

"I'll go get Justin," I said, rising from my chair. "And you take it easy with him."

Godfrey didn't answer. I left him gazing at the wall.

In the kitchen, Justin and Diesel were still on the floor. Justin's face was buried in Diesel's neck, and Diesel was muttering away. "Are you okay?" I stopped a few paces away from the pair.

Justin looked up at me, his face slightly tearstained. "Yes, sir."

"Why don't you wash your face and hands?" I said. "Do you still want to see Mr. Priest?"

Nodding as he got his feet, Justin went to the sink and splashed his face with water. After patting himself dry with a towel, he washed his hands.

"I'm ready," he said as he turned to me.

I put a hand on his shoulder and kept it there as he

preceded me out of the kitchen and to the living room. His steps were slow but steady.

We paused in the doorway of the living room. Godfrey stood, facing us as we came into the room.

Justin stopped several feet away from his biological father, and Godfrey drank in the sight of his son like a man who hasn't had water for weeks.

"Justin, this is Godfrey Priest. Godfrey, this is Justin Wardlaw."

"It's nice to meet you, sir," Justin said. He took a step forward, his hand out, but Godfrey didn't move. Justin faltered.

Godfrey started to speak. He stopped to clear his throat. "It's nice to meet you, too." He finally held out his hand, and Justin stepped forward to take it.

Godfrey shook his son's hand, his eyes still fixed on the boy's face. Now that I saw the two of them together, I spotted certain features they shared. Justin had Julia's coloring and her eyes, but his nose and cheekbones were just like Godfrey's.

Godfrey drew Justin toward the couch, and they both sat down, neither one of them speaking, each simply staring at the other.

"What happened to your face?" Godfrey asked.

I turned and stole away, leaving father and son alone together. I would let Justin explain the bruise.

Back in the kitchen, I picked up the phone and punched in Melba Gilley's number. I had called her earlier, before I took Justin to the hospital, to tell her I might not be back this afternoon. As Diesel rubbed against my legs, I glanced at the clock. It was now almost two-thirty.

"Hey, Melba, it's Charlie." I listened for a moment as I leaned back against the kitchen counter. "I'm not sure. I might be back a little later. Oh, so you've already heard about that?"

I shouldn't have been surprised that news of Ezra's set-to with Godfrey had already hit the Athena grapevine. And trust Melba to be one of the early grapes on the vine.

"Yes, I do know what it's all about. I'm surprised your informant didn't tell you that, too."

Melba squawked a bit in my ear.

"You'll find out soon enough." I hated the fact that this scandal would be all over town, and all over the college, before long. Justin and Julia deserved some privacy, but thanks to Ezra and Godfrey, they had lost all chance of that.

"I'll tell you more about it when I see you," I said. She might as well have the real story from me instead of who-knew-what wild rumors were flying around.

Diesel had his paw on my thigh now. He chirped at me.

"Gotta go now. I'll talk to you later." I listened a moment longer and then hung up the phone.

"What is it, boy?" Diesel was talking away.

Then I heard the front door close.

Diesel followed me from the kitchen into the hallway. The living room was empty.

"Justin? Where are you?"

There was no answer. I went to the window and looked out in time to see Justin getting in the car with Godfrey.

"Well, they're gone," I said to Diesel. "That's what you were trying to tell me, weren't you?"

Diesel looked up at me as if to say, *Of course.*

"I really wish they hadn't," I said, heading back to the kitchen. "But nothing I can do about it now. Guess we'll go back to work, okay, boy?"

About fifteen minutes later, back in my office, Diesel and I were settled in for the remainder of the afternoon. I planned to work till around six, then we would head home. I needed to change for the big dinner tonight, an occasion I did not anticipate with much joy.

I had hardly sat down in my chair before Melba popped in, eager to get the scoop from me. I gave her a bare outline of the facts, and her jaw dropped a couple of times.

"Poor Julia," she said when I finished. "That Godfrey is a rat bastard, if I do say so myself. Running off and leaving her pregnant like that."

I hadn't needed to spell it out for Melba. Anyone who knew Godfrey in our high school days wouldn't be a bit surprised.

Melba left after a few more comments on Godfrey and his behavior, and I was able to work for a while with no interruptions.

Around four o'clock I realized I was thirsty. I rummaged in my bag, but I had forgotten to bring any bottled water with me. Taking a large plastic mug with me, I headed downstairs to the staff lounge for the filtered water cooler there. Diesel yawned at me, declining to come with me.

The walk down and up the stairs would do me good. I spent so much time hunched over the computer that my back generally ached by the time I got home at night. I hardly ever remembered to get up and stretch the way I should.

I rounded the bottom of the staircase and walked down the short hallway to the back of the house. The room that had once been the study-cum-office of the master of the house had been converted into a congenial space where library employees could eat lunch, have some coffee, and relax.

I hadn't expected to find anyone in the lounge at this time of the afternoon, but Willie Clark sat at one of the tables, frowning down at the legal pad in front of him. He put down his pen as he heard me enter and scowled at me.

Since this was Willie's general greeting to everyone, I took no offense. He, too, had been one of my classmates in high school. He had never been friendly, but that probably wasn't his fault. He was the kid who was always the butt of the joke, the one the football team—Godfrey was captain our senior year—never failed to harass. Even those who, like me, tried to be nice to him didn't get very far. He hadn't changed much as an adult, sad to say.

"How are you, Willie?" I regarded him with a smile as I filled my mug from the cooler.

"Fine," he snapped back at me. For someone who served as the head of the library's reference department, Willie was lacking in people skills. "Trying to work, if people will let me."

As long as I had known him, Willie had been scribbling words on pieces of paper. I presumed he wanted to be a writer, but I never heard that he managed to publish anything.

"Sorry, didn't mean to bother you," I said. I turned to leave, but Willie spoke again, and I turned back.

"Godfrey Priest came to see you," Willie said. "Heard he got into a fight, too." He smirked.

"Yes, he did," I said. "I guess the whole town has heard about it now."

"Too bad Ezra didn't put Godfrey in the hospital," Willie said, his face dark with hatred. "Or in the grave, where he belongs."

SEVEN

Willie was so often the target of Godfrey's bizarre practical jokes in high school, it didn't surprise me that he harbored intense feelings against his old nemesis.

But wishing Godfrey dead?

"That's a bit strong," I said, trying to keep a mild tone.

Willie sucked at his prominent front teeth—an irritating habit—as he glared at me. I remembered that Godfrey started calling Willie "Bugs" because of those teeth. The nickname stuck, unfortunately for Willie.

"Godfrey's a colossal jackass, and you know it." Willie slapped a hand down on his legal pad. "He made you look like a fool more than once."

"Yes, he did," I said. "I don't like him either, but that doesn't mean I wish he was dead."

"More fool you, then." The contempt in Willie's voice

surprised me. "You don't know everything he's done. No one does. But I do." He stood, pushing his chair back with a violent gesture, grabbed his pad and pen, and stalked out of the room.

The nickname "Bugs" was cruelly apt, because physically Willie was a rabbit-like specimen. Godfrey and I both towered over him, and I knew Willie resented us for that. Godfrey hadn't been content with physical domination, however. He enjoyed tormenting Willie because Willie always reacted. That simply egged Godfrey on.

I wasn't the only one who tried to make Godfrey leave Willie alone, but Godfrey wouldn't—or couldn't—stop.

Having Godfrey in Athena was bringing back too many unpleasant memories from the past, and I had an uneasy feeling more unpleasantness lay ahead, as long as Godfrey stayed around. I wondered briefly what Willie had been talking about when he said "everything he's done." Probably his own list of grievances against Godfrey, and I had no doubt they were legion.

I left the staff lounge and was about to mount the stairs when a voice hailed me. I turned to see Peter Vanderkeller, the library's director, standing in the doorway to his office suite.

"Afternoon, Peter," I said. "Did you want to see me?"

"Yes, please," he said before he turned and disappeared.

I suppressed a sigh of irritation and followed him. Conversations with Peter on occasion lasted an hour or more. Melba rolled her eyes at me as I passed her desk— her signal when our boss was in one of his odd moods.

"Please shut the door behind you," Peter said when I entered his office.

I did as he asked and then advanced toward his desk. Peter stood behind it, hands on hips, so thin he made me think of the old TV character Gumby. If Peter were green, he'd give a fair imitation. I dismissed the foolish notion as Peter gestured to one of the comfortable chairs in front of his desk.

This was my favorite room in the house. Originally, Peter's office and Melba's had been one larger room, the front parlor. The high ceilings with their ornate moldings bore witness to the era in which the house was built. A magnificent mahogany dining table served as Peter's desk, though he used a contemporary office chair with it. I envied Peter that table. The machines of modern technology—computer, printer, and telephone—looked sadly out of place. If I closed my eyes for a moment, I could easily conjure up the figure of a woman in a hoop skirt, her beau paying court.

"What can I do for you?" I sipped at my water while I waited for a response.

Peter removed his horn-rimmed glasses and twirled them idly by one earpiece. He blinked at me. "It has come to my attention that our eminent alumnus and hometown boy wishes to endow our institution's archive with his papers, accompanied by a considerable sum of money. It has also come to my attention that he has discussed this matter with you."

"Yes, on both counts," I said. Listening to Peter made me want to be as terse in response as a character in a Dashiell Hammett novel. "I should have told you about it right after Godfrey spoke to me. But I guess I just got busy and didn't think about it."

"That is quite okay." Peter waved my apology away.

"No doubt the man believes he has bestowed an honor of great magnitude on his alma mater." His mouth twisted in a grimace. "If it were in my power to do so, I would tell Mr. Priest we don't wish to house the work of a man who has prostituted himself to the bestseller lists."

I had no idea Peter held such a low opinion of Godfrey and his work. I had never considered Peter a literary snob, either. He read fiction widely and counted several Mississippi mystery writers, like Carolyn Haines and Charlaine Harris, among his favorites. They had both spoken at Athena College, and Peter had been beside himself with excitement during their visits.

Why did he have such disgust for Godfrey Priest, then?

"I don't think the president would be very happy if you did such a thing," I said.

"No, he wouldn't," Peter replied. "More's the pity. Athena College has always prided itself on its rich literary heritage." He smiled sadly. "And now, having to add the work of a hack to our archives is a sad comedown and a none-too-subtle comment on the priorities of our current administration."

"It's not so bad. We also have the complete works of that nutty doctor from the nineteen fifties who fancied himself the next Walt Whitman." One hundred and twenty-three privately bound, handwritten volumes of poetry so execrable it made rap songs sound like Shakespearean sonnets—but the man had left the college three quarters of a million dollars along with his so-called art.

Peter ignored that. "I should thank you, I suppose, for confirming the awful truth for me. And so I do. I know that I can leave the matter in your more-than-capable hands, Charles."

"You certainly may, Peter," I said. Peter never unbent so far as to call me Charlie. I stood. "If that's all, then?"

Peter nodded. "I suppose I shall see you tonight at this absurd fête the president has planned?"

"Yes, I'll be there."

Nodding again, he turned his attention to the papers on his desk.

I retreated to the door and let myself out, careful to close it softly behind me.

When I turned, I saw Diesel on top of Melba's desk. Woman and cat were enjoying a conversation.

"Diesel got lonely, I guess." Melba glanced at me over the cat's head.

"Diesel, get down off the desk," I said. "You know you're not supposed to be up there."

The cat muttered as he jumped to the floor. Padding to the doorway, he sat down and started to groom himself.

"He was looking for you," Melba said.

"I know. He doesn't like being left alone for long."

"Did Peter talk to you about Godfrey Priest?" Melba leaned back in her chair.

"Yes," I said. "I suppose I should have come and talked to him earlier, right after Godfrey dropped by this morning." Now I felt a bit guilty. Peter should have heard the news from me.

"You know how he hates to think he's always the last to find out something." Melba glanced toward Peter's door. "Like when he found out his wife was having an affair with Godfrey."

"What?" I stepped closer to the desk. "When was this?"

"About ten years ago," Melba said. "Not long before Peter came to Athena, in fact."

"He was at some small college in California before, wasn't he?"

Melba nodded. "Near Los Angeles. And guess who Mrs. Vanderkeller became friends with?"

"Godfrey. How did they meet?"

"Apparently she had these big plans to be a fancy Hollywood screenwriter." Melba's nose wrinkled in disgust. "The way I heard it, she was always dragging Peter to any party she could get herself invited to. She was supposed to be real attractive, and she met Godfrey at one of the parties."

"She left Peter for Godfrey?" This was beginning to sound like the story line of a soap opera.

"She did. She divorced Peter and married Godfrey. His second wife, I think." Melba thought a moment. "Yes, his second. His first wife was some C-list actress who actually made porn films, from what I heard." The scandalized look on her face was priceless.

"How did Peter end up here, of all places? Didn't he know this was Godfrey's hometown?"

"No, poor man, just his luck." Melba glanced toward Peter's door again. "I guess he wanted to get as far away from California as he could, but he had no idea until after he got here that Godfrey was from Athena."

The man was jinxed. I felt sorry for Peter. No wonder he had such a venomous attitude toward Godfrey.

"Is there anyone Godfrey *hasn't* pissed off?" I gave Melba a rueful smile.

"I'm beginning to think not." A buzzer sounded. Melba looked cross. "I'd better find out what he wants. I'll see you tonight."

"We'll be there," I said, heading for the door. "Come on, Diesel. Let's finish upstairs and go home."

Diesel bounded up ahead of me. He knew the word *home*.

I finished cataloging a couple more items, and when I remembered to look at my watch, I was surprised to see that it read 5:37. "Definitely time to go," I said.

Diesel was ready, practically pulling me down the stairs once I locked the door to the archive behind us.

Back home again, I freed Diesel from his harness, and off he went to find crunchies and water. I headed to my bedroom on the second floor for a quick shower. I paused on the landing to listen for sounds of habitation on the third floor, where Justin's room was.

"Justin? Are you there?"

I waited a moment and called again. There was no answer, only silence. I supposed he could still be with Godfrey, but Godfrey was due at his reception at seven. I went up the stairs to Justin's door and tapped lightly. I called his name, but there was no response.

I listened for a moment longer and then tried his door. It was unlocked. Normally I wouldn't have done it, because my boarders deserved their privacy. I couldn't shake the feeling that Justin could be in trouble.

The room was empty, the bed unmade.

I shut the door and walked slowly back down the stairs to my room, telling myself not to worry. There was surely some innocuous reason for Justin's absence.

Coming out of the bathroom twenty minutes later, still

toweling my hair, I spotted Diesel in the middle of my bed. His head was cocked to the side, as if he were asking me a question.

"Yes, I'm going out, and yes, you're going with me." I frowned. I talked to Diesel a lot, I realized. Some people might find that odd, but it didn't really matter. So I talked to my cat.

I was about to tie my tie when the phone rang. It might be Sean, my son. He sometimes called around this hour.

"Hello."

Melba's excited voice boomed out at me. "You won't believe this. The party's canceled."

EIGHT

"Canceled?" I was stunned. "But why?"

"I heard Godfrey called the president's office about half an hour ago and told them he was too ill to come. Peter just called me, and I called you right away."

"Thanks for letting me know. But Godfrey seemed perfectly fine earlier."

"It sure is strange," Melba said, and I agreed.

"Look, Melba, I've got to go. Diesel's demanding his dinner." I knew that was the easiest way to get her off the phone. "See you tomorrow. Bye."

I hung up and looked down at Diesel, lying half-asleep on my bed. He turned his head to look up at me, then blinked and yawned.

What had happened to Godfrey?

He reveled in attention, so there had to be a serious reason he'd canceled on a party in his honor.

Did it involve Justin in some way?

On that thought, I left my bedroom and proceeded back upstairs to the boy's room. I might as well check in case he had come home while I was in the shower. Diesel passed me and scooted up the stairs well ahead of me. He was sitting in front of Justin's door when I reached the third floor.

I knocked, but there was no answer. I opened the door, and there was still no sign of Justin.

"Come on, boy," I said to Diesel as I shut the door. "He's not here."

Diesel bounded down the stairs before me. I headed for the kitchen, thinking vaguely about having something to eat. But by the time I reached the kitchen, my uneasiness over Justin's absence had become more urgent.

I couldn't help feeling that something was wrong. Why had Godfrey skipped out on his own party? Where was Justin?

Even if it turned out to be a waste of time and there was some simple explanation for all this, I decided not to sit home and wait.

So much for my not getting emotionally involved in this mess. But my paternal instincts were kicking in, I guess.

Diesel followed me to the back door, but I told him he couldn't come with me this time. He assumed a long-suffering expression, as if I were always abandoning him.

"I won't be gone too long," I said, adding, "I hope," under my breath.

Farrington House, Athena's ritziest hotel, was my destination. Godfrey had to be staying there, probably in their best suite. The hotel occupied half a block on the town square, about ten minutes' drive from my house. It was dark outside now, and I switched on my headlights as I backed the car out of the garage.

I hoped Justin was safe with Godfrey, probably in the hotel still talking and getting to know his biological father.

There were no empty parking spaces in front of the hotel. I had to settle for one across the street, facing the square. As I turned off my lights, preparing to get out of the car, I observed someone sitting in the shadows of an old gazebo about ten yards in front of me.

He moved, and I recognized him as Justin. He watched me, obviously nervous, as I approached. The night was cool, and Justin was in short sleeves. He shivered a bit, his face turned away from me as I sat down next to him. The stone bench chilled me even through the wool of my pants.

"What are you doing sitting out here?" I asked in a mild tone. "Aren't you getting cold?"

"A little, I guess." Justin's teeth chattered. "I, um, I can't go back in there."

"The hotel? Why not?"

"I just can't."

The desperation in Justin's voice alarmed me. I put a hand on his shoulder to try to calm him a bit.

"What's wrong? You can tell me." I spoke in my most benign, fatherly manner.

"No, it's horrible." The boy shuddered, whether from the cold or something else, I wasn't sure.

"Is something wrong with Godfrey?" I tried to keep my voice even.

Justin nodded. He still wouldn't look at me.

"Does he need a doctor?" I stood. "We'd better go and check on him then."

"It won't do any good," Justin said, his voice barely above a whisper.

"Why not?"

"It just won't."

I was getting a really bad feeling about this. "Did you call nine-one-one?"

Justin shook his head. He still seemed too dazed to do anything.

I pulled out my phone and punched in the emergency number. I reported a possibly injured man.

"What's the room number?" I asked Justin.

He shrugged. "The Lee Room, I think."

I gave the operator the information and hung up before she tried to keep me on the line.

"Come on." I grasped the boy gently by the arm and pulled him up. "Maybe there's something we can do." I was afraid Godfrey was beyond help at this point, but I had to try.

I expected resistance, but for whatever reason Justin came docilely enough. Though I peppered him with questions on the way, he wasn't saying anything more.

In the bright light of the lobby, I could see that Justin was pale and in obvious distress. I felt an even stronger sense of urgency. Had Godfrey had a heart attack?

"He gave me a key," Justin said when I veered toward the front desk.

"Fine." I headed for the elevator, my hand still firmly on Justin's arm. Inside, Justin punched the button for the fourth floor.

There were five large suites on this, the top floor. All

were named for Confederate generals. Justin headed for the grandest of the five, the Robert E. Lee (of course), and paused in front of the door.

I took the card from Justin and inserted it in the lock. I opened the door and stepped aside. If anything, Justin's face was paler now than it had been before. He leaned against the wall.

I caught a whiff of mingled scents through the open door, and my sense of unease grew. After I took two steps inside, I knew by some instinct that this was a crime scene. I had to move with care and not disturb anything. But I still had to check on Godfrey.

Overhead lights illuminated the room, the reception area of the suite. The smells were stronger now, and I approached one of the two couches with dread, certain of what I would find.

Three steps more and I could look down over the back of the sofa.

Godfrey sprawled prostrate on the floor. The back of his head was a bloody mess.

The coppery tang of blood had mingled with the unpleasant scent of Godfrey's bowels, loosened in death.

I heard a faint roaring in my head. I couldn't tear my gaze away from Godfrey's corpse. He had to be dead with a wound like that.

But in the faint hope that he was still alive, I steeled myself to walk around the couch and approach Godfrey's body. I bent down and grasped his left wrist, lifting the arm just enough to get my fingers in the right spot. I detected no pulse, though I held the wrist for what seemed an eternity.

As I put the arm gently back against the carpet, I

caught a glimpse of something sticking out from under Godfrey's waist. My brain didn't register it for a moment. I was going to throw up if I didn't put some distance between me and that horror on the floor.

Out in the corridor again, I drew a deep breath of clear air. I closed my eyes for a moment, but all I could see was Godfrey, his head bashed in.

And Justin's cell phone by the body.

It had to be his. The phone in that room was purple, and Justin had a purple phone.

Justin had his arms wrapped around his body, and he was shivering. He looked at me, fear in his eyes.

What had happened in that room between father and son? Had they argued? Over what? They hadn't met before today.

But as I looked at Justin, I couldn't believe he was responsible. He wasn't a killer, not this miserable, frightened boy.

Even though I had already called 911, I took out my cell phone and punched in the number of the sheriff's department. When the dispatcher came on the line, I gave him my name and a quick report. "I'll be in the lobby, waiting for you."

Justin was crying now, quietly. I was torn. I wanted to comfort him, but I was also tempted to get back into Godfrey's room and retrieve the cell phone. I couldn't believe I was even considering doing something like that, but the last thing Justin needed right now was to be the chief suspect in Godfrey's murder.

The sheriff's department was only three blocks away. They'd be here in five minutes or less. The EMTs should be here any second too, though there wasn't anything they could do for poor Godfrey.

As I wavered, the decision was made for me. The elevator opened, and an elderly couple stepped out.

"Come on, son, let's go downstairs." I put an arm around Justin's shoulders.

The couple cast inquiring looks our way as we passed them, but I ignored them. I had to get Justin downstairs and find us both something hot and sweet to drink—my aunt's favorite cure for any kind of shock.

The elevator seemed to take forever, and the bland music playing in it stretched my already frayed nerves even further. Finally the door opened into the lobby, and I led Justin to the restaurant.

The hostess took one look at my face and the crying teenager with me and asked, "What do you need?"

"Hot coffee, two cups, with a lot of sugar."

I sat Justin down at the closest table, and the hostess returned right away with the coffee. "Here, son, drink this. You need it."

Justin stared at me for a moment, but with trembling hands he picked up the cup and began to drink. The hostess hovered, a worried look on her face.

"Is he going to be okay?" she said.

I nodded. "Just a bit of a shock." I took a drink of my own coffee, feeling the welcome warmth spread through me.

"Okay," she said. "If you need anything else, let me know."

I thanked her, watching Justin as the color slowly came back into his face. I pulled a handkerchief from my pocket and handed it to him. He scrubbed at his face with it, drying away the tears, and then he blew his nose.

"Thank you," he said. He wiped his nose again. "I guess I kind of freaked out when I found him."

"I understand," I said. "I don't blame you. I'm kind of freaked out myself." I took another sip of my coffee. "How long were you sitting out there on the square?"

"I don't know," Justin said. "I'm not really sure." He sipped at his coffee. "Who would kill him? It's crazy."

"I know," I said. "It doesn't make any sense right now, probably never will." I debated whether to tell him about the cell phone. Would it be better for him to know now?

If I told him, though, his reaction later might seem more suspicious. Probably best not to say anything so whatever he told the sheriff's department would be unrehearsed.

Lord, what a mess.

"Do you think my dad, I mean Ezra, killed him? He was so angry earlier." The expression on Justin's face was heartbreaking.

Lord, I prayed, *please don't let it be Ezra. Or Julia. I don't think Justin could take it.*

What could I say to the boy now that could possibly comfort him? I had no assurances for him. This would force him to grow up brutally fast.

"I just don't know," I finally said.

Before I could say anything else I spotted an arrival in the lobby. "You don't move from this spot, and ask for more coffee if you need it," I said. "The EMTs and the sheriff's deputies are here, and I need to talk to them."

"Yes, sir," Justin said. "I won't go anywhere."

I had an inspiration. I gave Justin my cell phone. "Call

your mother. Ask her to come here as quickly as she can. I don't know how long I'll be, and I don't want you to be by yourself."

Justin nodded. He picked up my phone, examined it for a moment, and then punched in a number.

I left him at the table and braced myself for the coming interview. I had been so concerned for Justin that I hadn't taken time to alert the hotel staff. The manager on duty, I could see now, was reacting badly to the news of a dead body in her hotel. She handed one of the EMTs a key, and they headed for the elevators with a couple of deputies.

As I neared the front desk, a tall, thin black woman in uniform turned to face me. Her expression was enigmatic, to say the least. She had her hair scraped back into a bun, and she regarded me with cold brown eyes.

"Mr. Harris," she said, her voice neutral. "You reported this incident."

"Yes, Deputy Berry, I did." I stopped a couple of feet away from her.

Kanesha Berry and I had a difficult relationship that stemmed from the fact her mother was my housekeeper. Kanesha had tried, once Aunt Dottie passed away, to get her mother to retire. Azalea paid no attention to her daughter. She wasn't ready to stop working, and she told me the day I moved into the house that she was going to look after me and she wasn't about to listen to any arguments.

Since it would take a braver man than I—or a more foolhardy one—to argue with Azalea, I simply smiled and said, "Thank you."

Kanesha couldn't argue with her mother, so she chose

to blame me. Every time I encountered her, I felt like I'd
run up against a buzz saw.

After glaring at me for a moment, Kanesha summoned
another officer. "Deputy Bates," she said, her voice taut,
"Mr. Harris here called it in. Go with him and take a
preliminary statement."

"Yes, ma'am." Bates gazed into the distance, not at
Kanesha, when he spoke. His tone verged on insubordi-
nate.

Kanesha's eyes narrowed for a moment. She did not
reply. She turned and walked in the direction of the
elevator.

"Come with me, sir," Bates said. "We'll be using the
manager's office." I had seen Bates around town, but I
didn't know him. He appeared to be about Kanesha's age,
mid-thirties.

Praying that Julia could get here quickly, I followed
Bates around the desk. The manager came with us into
her office and flapped about for a moment, still obviously
unsettled. Bates calmed her down and asked her to step
outside.

When we were alone, Bates sat behind the desk and
motioned for me to sit across from him.

I sank into the chair, my stomach churning. Images
of Godfrey, dead on the floor, flashed through my mind.
Lord, I needed something to settle me down. A nice shot
of brandy would do the trick, but I doubted Bates would
let me ask for one.

Bates asked me my name, address, and so on. Then he
got down to the meat of the interview.

After a couple of false starts, I was able to give an or-

ganized account of finding the body. I carefully omitted
for the moment that I hadn't been alone.

"How'd you get in the room?" Bates asked when I
finished.

"I had a key."

"And how'd you come by that?" Bates eyed me with
suspicion.

"Godfrey's son gave it to me. Godfrey had given it to
him earlier." That much was true.

Bates jotted something into his notebook, then he
asked me to go through it all again, starting with why I
came to check on Godfrey in the first place.

I explained again about the party having been canceled
and my worries that Godfrey was ill, because he would
have never, as far as I knew, skipped an opportunity for
a lot of attention.

"I tried calling, but there was no answer."

"And you didn't ask somebody here to check on him?"
Bates watched me, his face blank.

"No, I didn't think of that," I said. "My house isn't that
far away, so I just hopped in the car and came here."

Bates nodded, and I continued telling my story for the
second time.

During all this, I continued to worry about Justin.
Surely Julia had arrived by now. She'd be upset at the
news too, but the most important thing right now was
looking after her son.

Bates sat examining his notes, and I ventured a
question.

"Is Deputy Berry in charge of this investigation?"

Bates nodded, his expression unreadable. "Acting

Chief Deputy Berry," he said. "Chief Deputy Dan Stout is out on medical leave right now."

"I see." And I did. This case could be a big break for Kanesha if she managed to solve it quickly. She was the only African-American woman deputy in the department, and I knew her well enough to understand how ambitious she was.

Justin and I both were probably in for a rough time. Kanesha wouldn't put on kid gloves for us, even though I'd bet her mother would have a few things to say if she pushed us too hard.

The door opened, and Bates rose to his feet. I turned in my chair.

Kanesha stood a couple of paces inside the room. She held up a plastic bag with a cell phone inside. A purple cell phone.

"Mr. Harris, did you lose this?"

NINE

My eyes fixated on the cell phone in the plastic bag. "No, that's not mine." The land mines lay ahead, and I had to avoid them.

"Do you know whose it is?" Kanesha lowered the bag but her gaze did not waver from my face.

"I do not." That much was true. I thought it was Justin's, but I didn't know for sure.

"Do you know someone named Justin?"

I did not reply for a moment. Kanesha ought to know very well that I had a boarder named Justin. She lived with her mother, and I couldn't imagine that Azalea hadn't mentioned Justin to her.

"I do," I finally said. "Justin Wardlaw. He boards with me."

"Where is he now?" she asked.

"I don't know." That was the truth. Justin might still

be waiting in the hotel restaurant, but it was likely that Julia had arrived and taken him away. "If you want to come by my house tonight or tomorrow, you'll probably find him there."

Kanesha nodded. She moved closer to the desk and set the bag down. Deputy Bates vacated his chair, and Kanesha took his place. She held out a hand, and Bates gave her his notebook. She read through his notes, and I saw her frown a couple of times.

When she finished, she pushed the notebook aside, and Bates retrieved it. Kanesha settled back in the chair and regarded me, her eyelids slightly hooded.

I tried not to squirm in the chair.

"I believe that's all we need for the moment," Kanesha said.

What the heck? I thought. *She can't be serious.*

"I'll have more questions for you and young Mr. Wardlaw later, but I know where you live." The ghost of a smile played across her lips.

It wasn't a benevolent ghost.

"Fine," I said. "I'll be at home tonight." As I rose, I nodded at both deputies. I knew I'd eventually catch hell from Kanesha for not telling her I wasn't alone when I discovered Godfrey's corpse. But I don't think I would have done anything differently. Justin needed time to recover from the shock of Godfrey's violent death before he had to deal with the law. I had bought him some time, though it could cause me trouble.

I made a beeline for the hotel restaurant, but the table where I left Justin was unoccupied. I hurried to my car. When I reached home a few minutes later, an aging Honda was parked near my mailbox.

In the kitchen, Julia and Justin sat at the table. Diesel was ensconced in Justin's lap, and the boy cuddled the cat to his chest. Teapot, cups, spoons, and cream pitcher were neatly arranged on the table between mother and son.

Julia looked up at me, her face troubled. "Oh Charlie, what an unholy mess this is. I'm so sorry you and Justin had to see something like that."

"I'm okay," I said, giving her shoulder a reassuring squeeze. "Justin, how are you?"

"Okay," he said, his voice muffled. He was rubbing his head against Diesel's neck. Diesel's purr rumbled through the room.

I fetched a cup and saucer from the cupboard, and when I sat down Julia poured me some tea. I added cream and sugar and sipped. The warmth of the tea soothed and comforted, as always.

After a few sips, I set the cup down. Neither Julia nor Justin had spoken, perhaps waiting for me to break the silence. I could feel the tension in the room emanating from both mother and son.

"I spoke with the investigators from the sheriff's department," I said. "The person in charge of the investigation is Kanesha Berry."

"Azalea's daughter?" Julia frowned. "I hadn't heard she was promoted, but that's good for her, I guess."

"It's apparently temporary." I shrugged. "The chief deputy is out on medical leave, and Kanesha is the acting chief deputy."

"Why aren't the police in charge?" Justin asked.

"In a big city, they would be," I said. "But here it's the sheriff's department that investigates homicides. Our police department isn't equipped for a major crime."

"Thank the Lord things like this don't happen very often in Athena." Julia cradled her teacup in both hands and gazed down into it.

"I didn't tell Deputy Berry that Justin was with me at the hotel," I said. There was no gentle way of doing this.

"Thank you." Julia smiled, but the lines across her forehead deepened.

"But they're going to know, of course, that Justin spent time with Godfrey in that room today," I said.

"Yes, he did. But other people could have visited him. Obviously, someone else did." Julia's tone was as sharp as her gaze at me.

"Obviously." I looked at Justin. "When was the last time you used your cell phone?"

Justin didn't meet my gaze. Instead, he leaned back in his chair and stuck his hand in his jeans pocket. He pulled out my cell phone and returned it to me without a word.

"Thank you." I put the phone on the table. "Now how about answering my question?" My tone was as cutting as Julia's had been, moments ago. Justin's lack of response annoyed me.

"Don't speak to him that way." Julia glared at me. "He's done nothing wrong."

"I didn't say he had." I returned Julia's fierce look. "But he needs to answer my question. It's important."

Julia leaned back in her chair, arms crossed over her chest. I thought she was going to speak again, but after an intake of breath, she remained silent.

I repeated my question to Justin.

Diesel rubbed his head against Justin's chin, and the boy finally looked at me. "I dunno, sometime this afternoon, I guess."

"Do you have your cell phone now?"

Julia watched me intently.

"No, sir." Justin pushed his dark bangs back from his face. "I lost it."

"Why is this so important?" Julia leaned her elbows on the table, her hands clasped together. "People lose cell phones all the time."

"Because they found Justin's cell phone with Godfrey's body." I watched them both carefully to gauge their reactions.

Julia blinked rapidly, and Justin remained mute.

"Justin, was Godfrey alive when you left him this afternoon?" I made my tone neutral, unthreatening.

"Yes, sir," the boy said.

"But you went back to his room and found him dead. How long was it between the time you left him and came back?"

Justin thought for a moment. "About an hour, I guess." He glanced at his mother, clearly concerned about something. She avoided his gaze.

"Why did you go back?"

"I wanted to talk to him some more." Justin focused on me again. "He didn't answer when I knocked, so I used the key and went in." His voice caught. "I thought maybe he'd gone somewhere, and I was just going to write him a note. But . . ." His voice trailed off, and I thought he might start to cry.

"When he found Godfrey's body," Julia said, her expression bleak, "he got out his phone to call someone. But he panicked."

"And he dropped the phone and didn't retrieve it." I could picture it very easily.

"Yes, sir," Justin said. He had his voice under control.
"I was really scared. I got out of the hotel, but I didn't
know what to do. So I went across the street and sat there
until you came."

"What are we going to do, Charlie?" Julia sounded
angry. "Kanesha will probably think Justin killed Godfrey. But he didn't. The idea is totally ridiculous. I'm not
going to let anyone treat my son like a vicious killer."

"No, I didn't kill anybody." Justin hugged Diesel to
him. He eyed his mother warily, it seemed to me.

"I believe you," I said, putting as much conviction into
my voice as I could. "I mean, what motive would you
have?"

Justin shifted in his chair, and Diesel protested. He
rubbed the cat's head, but then he lifted Diesel and set
him on the floor. Diesel chirped before stalking off to the
utility room.

"Sorry," Justin looked straight at me. "We did have an
argument, and I guess I kind of yelled at him." He paused
and turned to his mother.

Julia sighed. "Godfrey wanted Justin to go back to
California with him, stay a few months. But he didn't
want to go. Godfrey . . . well, you know what he was like
when he didn't get his way. As if I'd let him take Justin to
California anyway."

"I remember only too well." I remembered Godfrey's
rages when he was thwarted. "He could be extremely
unpleasant."

"He was," Justin said, his eyes sad. "He kinda calmed
down after I yelled back. But I could tell he was still mad.
So I left."

"And when Justin went back, Godfrey was dead." The

horror in Julia's voice brought the nasty scene back to mind.

I squirmed in my chair. It would be a long time before I could get that vision out of my head.

I sipped at my tea, hoping to settle my stomach a bit. "You'll have to tell all this to Deputy Berry."

Justin looked mutinous, and Julia was none too happy, either.

"I know you don't want to," I said. "I'd like to keep Justin out of this too, but I don't think we can."

"If you don't say anything, they're not going to know Justin was there." Julia looked ready to throw the teapot at me. She intended to protect Justin at all costs, it seemed. She wasn't being rational.

"Show some sense." I had just about had it with both of them. I had tried to buy Justin a little time to recover, but there was no way I was going to lie any further about his presence at the hotel. "They have his cell phone, and they'll probably find his fingerprints all over the place. How are you going to explain that away?"

"I suppose you're right," Julia said after a moment's silence. "Honey, we have to be truthful. They need to find out who really did this, and if we lie to them, it only makes things more difficult."

"Is it okay if I go up to my room now?" Justin stood up. "I'm really tired."

"Of course, honey," Julia said. "Get some rest. But you haven't had any dinner. Are you hungry?"

"I've got something to eat in my room," Justin said. "Can I just go, Mama?"

"Yes, you can." Julia stood and held out her arms. Justin approached her for a hug, but he didn't let it last long.

He pulled free from his mother and walked swiftly out of the kitchen. Moments later we heard him clumping up the stairs.

Julia and I sat at the table and watched each other for a moment. She was still unhappy with me, I could tell, but I wasn't particularly happy with her, either. Protecting her son was one thing, but trying to pretend he was never in the hotel was completely absurd.

"How about you?" I said. "Have you had anything to eat? I haven't." As an olive branch, it might do.

"No, I was still at the hospital when Justin called. I got over to the hotel as quickly as I could to get him away from there." Julia relaxed enough to lean back in her chair.

"Is Ezra still in the hospital?" I had forgotten about him until now.

"Yes." Julia glanced away from me.

"Was he that seriously hurt?" I frowned. Something didn't add up here. "Surely Godfrey didn't injure him that badly."

"He didn't," Julia said, her tone flat. "But being in a fight didn't help anything."

"What's wrong with him?"

"He's dying." Julia burst into tears.

TEN

"I'm so sorry," I said, knowing how inadequate that was. "I had no idea."

I got up and found a box of tissues for Julia. She pulled a couple from the box and dabbed at her eyes as I sat down again.

"No one knows except Ezra and me and his doctors." Julia's voice was husky from the tears.

"You haven't told Justin yet?"

"No," Julia said. "But I have to, I know. I was putting it off until after he met Godfrey, but now . . ." Her voice trailed away.

"Is it cancer?" I asked. I had noticed, when Ezra was in my house assaulting Justin, that he looked thinner and older than I remembered.

Julia nodded. "Pancreatic cancer."

"I'm so sorry," I said. "My wife had it too."

"I know," Julia said softly.

"Where has he been going for treatment?"

"Memphis," she said. "They wanted to send him to Houston, to that big cancer hospital, but Ezra doesn't want to go."

That big cancer hospital in Houston, M.D. Anderson, had done its best for Jackie, but the cancer had won.

"The survival rate is so small," I said.

"Yes, it is." Julia rubbed her temples as if her head ached.

"There's not much you can do, then," I said.

"No, there isn't." Julia smiled so sadly that I wished I could do something to comfort her. "And miracles seem to be in short supply at the moment."

Before I could respond, I heard the doorbell.

Startled, Julia glanced at me.

"Probably Kanesha," I said, rising.

Julia paled. "I wish I didn't have to talk to her tonight."

"It's best to get it over with. Maybe I can stay with you while you talk to her." I smiled at her before I left the room.

I peered through the peephole in the front door. Kanesha Berry, along with Deputy Bates, stood on the front porch. I couldn't postpone this, no matter how much I wanted to. I opened the door.

"Hello again, Mr. Harris." Kanesha nodded at me. "I have more questions for you, like why you forgot to mention the fact that you weren't alone at the hotel."

"I'll be happy to explain that. Come in, please," I said, standing aside.

"I also want to speak to Justin Wardlaw. Is he here?" Kanesha remained on the doorstep.

"He is, and so is his mother. I think she would like to speak to you first." I motioned for her to enter, and this time she did.

"How long has Mrs. Wardlaw been here?" Kanesha turned to face me after I closed the door.

I thought for a moment. "Perhaps half an hour."

Kanesha grimaced, and I could tell she was not happy about this. She probably thought Julia and I had been cooking up alibis together.

"This way, please," I said. "Mrs. Wardlaw is in the kitchen, if you don't mind talking to her in there."

"Wherever you like." Kanesha and Bates followed me.

Julia was standing by the table when we entered the kitchen. Diesel had disappeared, probably upstairs with Justin. Julia appeared composed, but I knew how anxious she must be.

"Good evening, Mrs. Wardlaw," Kanesha said, halting on the other side of the table from Julia. "This is Deputy Bates."

"Ma'am," Bates said, removing his hat and sticking it under his arm.

"Good evening." Julia nodded at them each in turn. "Is it okay if Mr. Harris stays with me?"

"He might as well." Kanesha's tone was sharp enough to cut through stone. "I'm sure he's already heard everything you have to say."

Julia frowned at that, and I shrugged. The damage was done. Any investigator with a shred of intelligence wouldn't take anything we said at face value anyway.

"Why don't we sit down?" I indicated empty chairs. "Can I get you something to drink?"

Both deputies declined my offer. Julia and I sat first, then the two deputies took seats. Bates pulled his notebook and a pencil from a pocket and prepared to take notes.

"Charlie told me you're in charge of the investigation," Julia said. Her complete attention seemed to be focused on Kanesha.

"That's correct," Kanesha said. "I'm sure you're aware by now that Godfrey Priest was found dead under suspicious circumstances. We are investigating his death, and I have some questions for you and also for your son." She nodded in my direction. "And for Mr. Harris, too."

"I'll be happy to answer your questions," Julia said.

Kanesha regarded Julia with a bland expression. "Mrs. Wardlaw, what was your relationship to the deceased?"

"I've known him most of my life," Julia said. "We were not particularly close, at least in recent years." Her face colored slightly. "But I suppose you could say we were friends."

"I see," Kanesha said. "And your son? What was his relationship to Mr. Priest?"

Did Kanesha already know? The way gossip traveled in Athena, I figured she must.

But why didn't she ask directly?

"Godfrey was Justin's biological father." Julia's cheeks stayed red. "They met for the first time today."

"Is your husband aware of this?" Kanesha was an excellent poker player, I was willing to bet.

"Yes, he is," Julia said.

"How does he feel about it?"

"He's not happy," Julia said, in a tone that indicated she thought it a stupid question. "He has always considered Justin his own son."

"He knew he's not the boy's biological father?" Kanesha was poking at every possible sore spot—and none too gently.

"Yes, he knew. He has always known." Julia's color heightened.

"Where is Mr. Wardlaw?" Kanesha asked.

"In the hospital," Julia said. "Where he has been since about one o'clock this afternoon. I was with him until about thirty minutes ago."

Julia had stated her own alibi and Ezra's very clearly, but Kanesha did not appear interested.

"There was an altercation between your husband and Mr. Priest today." Kanesha appeared to be well informed about the day's events.

"They had words." Julia frowned and crossed her arms over her chest. "My husband struck Godfrey, and Godfrey hit him back. In the face. My husband was bleeding and in pain, so I took him to the emergency room."

"Did you see Mr. Priest again after that?"

Julia hesitated. "No, I did not."

That was the first question Julia hadn't answered right away. Was she lying?

"You're sure about that?" Kanesha had noticed the hesitation, too. She looked ready to pounce.

"I am." This time Julia didn't falter.

"So you have no further knowledge of Mr. Priest's movements after you saw him at lunchtime?" Kanesha leaned back in her chair, relaxing her rigid posture for the first time since the interview began.

"Only what Justin and Charlie have told me." Julia smiled briefly. "But I'm sure you'd rather hear it from them."

"Yes," Kanesha said, "and I'll also need to talk to your husband. How long will he be in the hospital?"

"It's possible he'll be released tomorrow." Julia relaxed her arms, letting them slide into her lap. "But he's ill. You cannot upset him."

Kanesha pulled a business card from one of her shirt pockets. "Please call me at this number tomorrow, and let me know when I can speak with him."

Julia accepted the card and placed it on the table in front of her. "Certainly."

"Thank you. I may have more questions for you later." Kanesha said. "Now I'd like to speak to your son."

"I'll get him, if you like," I said to Julia.

"Thank you, Charlie," she said. "If you don't mind."

"Back in a minute," I said, rising from my chair.

As I left the kitchen I heard no further conversation. Would Kanesha continue to question Julia while I was out of the room? I was concerned about Julia and that one hesitation in answering. I doubted Kanesha would let that go for long.

Nothing I could do about it now, I thought as I climbed the stairs to the third floor.

I knocked on Justin's door and waited for a response. When none was forthcoming, I opened the door and looked inside. Justin, still dressed and with his shoes on, appeared to be sound asleep on the bed. Diesel, stretched out beside him, raised his head and blinked at me.

I entered the room, moving quietly. I found three candy wrappers on the floor by Justin's bed. Some dinner, the poor kid. He'd had a terrible day, and it wasn't finished yet.

Laying a hand on his shoulder, I shook him gently and called his name.

Justin's eyes popped open, and he stared up at me in confusion. "Mr. Charlie? What . . . ?" The memories of the day evidently came back, and he sat up, rubbing his face.

"Sorry to wake you," I said. "But the deputies are here. You need to come downstairs now."

"Yes, sir," Justin said, his voice dull.

Diesel jumped to the floor and rubbed against my legs as I turned to leave.

"Please wait. I need to ask you something." I turned to face him as Justin stood.

Diesel began chirping at me, and I reached down to rub his head. The cat pushed his head against my hand, and I rubbed a little harder. He really loved head rubs.

"What is it, son?" I asked.

"I don't know what to do." Justin ran a hand through his hair.

"About what?"

Diesel walked over to Justin and rubbed against his legs.

"What if I found something in the hotel room?" Justin asked. "Something that could get somebody in trouble?"

ELEVEN

"In the hotel room, you mean?" I examined Justin's face. He was clearly worried.

Justin nodded.

"You should tell the deputies, like we discussed earlier." My tone was firm. "It's best to be truthful. What you found could help them solve the case."

"I'm afraid to." Justin looked miserable. "And you're the only person I can talk to about it."

"What did you find?" I asked. Who was he afraid of incriminating? I had an uneasy feeling I knew.

Justin stuck a hand into his pocket and withdrew something. He held his palm out to me, and lying across it was a gold pen.

"It's my dad's."

"Your dad's? You mean Ezra's." I was so shocked by what Justin had, I didn't know quite how to respond.

"Yes, sir," Justin said. "I gave it to him for his birthday last year. I had it engraved." He held the pen closer, pointing to the letters on the shaft with his free hand.

I suddenly recalled Justin's question when we were sitting in the hotel restaurant. He'd asked me if I thought Ezra had killed Godfrey.

Now I knew why. The evidence lay in Justin's hand.

But how could Ezra have left the hospital and made it over to the hotel without anyone knowing he was gone? Julia said she had been with him all day, and surely the hospital staff would have noticed if he had been gone for very long.

"What should I do?" Justin asked as we both stared at the pen.

"You have to show it to the deputies," I said.

"I can't," Justin said. "Even after what he did to me."

I stared at the pen in his hand, torn. Justin's fingerprints were all over the pen now, and had probably obliterated any others. Deputy Berry already knew he was in the room.

I made a snap decision—with my heart, not my head. I wasn't keen on suppressing evidence, but until I knew how that pen ended up in Godfrey's room, I was going to continue to protect Justin—and whichever of his parents left that pen behind.

"Put it back in your pocket, and don't say anything about it to them yet. Let's see how things go with their questions."

Obviously relieved, Justin nodded. He shoved the pen back into his pocket. "Guess I'd better go downstairs."

"Yes." I strode to the door and held it open. "Come on, boys."

Diesel scampered out, and Justin and I followed. The cat had already disappeared by the time Justin and I reached the stairs.

Back in the kitchen we found Deputy Bates regarding Diesel with awe. "That's really a cat?"

"Yes," I said. "He's a Maine coon, and they get to be as big as thirty or thirty-five pounds."

"Dang, he's bigger'n my dog." Bates shook his head.

Kanesha frowned at her subordinate while I exchanged an amused glance with Julia. If nothing else, Bates's reaction to Diesel had relieved some of the tension.

"Deputy Berry, this is my son, Justin Wardlaw." Julia stepped forward, stretching an arm around the boy's waist and pulling him close.

Kanesha introduced herself and Bates to Justin, then motioned for him to have a seat. "I'd like to speak to Justin alone," Kanesha said.

"No." Julia shook her head. "No, I need to be with him."

Kanesha frowned. "How old are you, Justin?"

"Eighteen," he said.

Kanesha nodded. "In that case, Mrs. Wardlaw, I have to insist I talk to Justin without you. Justin is an adult."

Julia bridled at that. She looked like a lioness about to attack. "That's ridiculous. If you're not going to let me stay with him, then I don't think he should talk to you."

Kanesha opened her mouth, but I spoke first.

"Julia, Deputy Berry is right. Justin is an adult now, and I think it's best to let her talk to him now. Otherwise, I imagine he might end up doing it down at the sheriff's department. Wouldn't you rather avoid that?"

Kanesha shot me a severe look. She wasn't happy with

my interference, but I thought I'd better do something before Julia got really riled up.

"Very well. You're right. I don't want that." Julia let
go of Justin after a moment. "I'll be close by if you need
me." She smiled at her son.

Justin nodded. He might be eighteen, and therefore an
adult in the eyes of the law, but when I looked at him, I
saw a tired, frightened boy. I hoped Kanesha would handle him gently. He'd had a very difficult day.

I offered Julia my arm and escorted her across the
front hall into the living room. She sank into an armchair
and covered her face with her hands.

At the moment I wasn't sure how to comfort her, other
than by patting her shoulder a few times.

I pulled a chair close to hers and sat down. "Julia, it's
going to be okay." I hoped I sounded convincing.

Julia let her hands fall to her lap. Her face was wet
with tears. "Oh Lord, what are we going to do?"

"They won't arrest Justin," I said, to myself adding, *at
least not tonight, I hope*.

"Please, Lord, no," Julia said, her voice soft. She
leaned back in the chair, looking suddenly older than her
fifty years. "Ezra will be so upset when he finds out about
all this."

"He'll have to know," I said, and Julia nodded. "And
while we're talking about Ezra, I have a question."

Julia regarded me warily.

"You were with him at the hospital all day? Until
you left to get Justin from the hotel?" I watched her
carefully.

Her gaze dropped away for a moment. "Yes, I was."

"Then there was no way Ezra could have left the hospital?"

Startled, Julia sat upright. "Of course not. Whatever made you ask something like that?" She frowned. "Ezra did not kill Godfrey. You can get that notion out of your head right this minute."

Julia was getting angry with me again, but I wasn't going to back down.

"Okay," I said. "I'll get it out of my head for a moment. But let me ask you another question." I hated doing this, but Julia was obviously—at least to me—lying about her time at the hospital.

"Well, go ahead." Julia glared at me.

"If I asked Ezra whether you were with him all day at the hospital, what would he say?"

Julia's eyes narrowed. "What is that supposed to mean? Of course Ezra would say I was with him."

"Then one of you would be lying." I said it as gently as I could. "It's no use. I know one of you was in Godfrey's room today." I paused for a moment to let the words sink in.

Julia paled, and I knew I was right. I felt no satisfaction from it.

"How?"

"Justin found something belonging to Ezra in the room," I said. "When he went back and found Godfrey dead."

"Oh dear." The fight seemed to have gone out of her—for the moment. "Is Justin going to give it, whatever it is, to the deputies?"

"No, I told him not to, for now," I said. "He's very worried about it, but I wanted to find out who left it there. You haven't told him yet that you went there, have you?"

"No, I haven't." Julia shook her head. "I see now I should have told him."

"You have to tell *me* the truth too, if I'm going to be any use to Justin," I said.

"I will." Julia's tone was firm.

"The question is," I said, "well, two questions, actually. First, which one of you went to the hotel? And second, when?"

She leaned back in the chair again. "It was me. Ezra never left the hospital. What did I leave there?"

"Ezra's pen, one Justin gave him."

"Of course. How stupid of me." Julia shook her head. "Godfrey wanted to give me a check, but he didn't have a pen. I had Ezra's things in my purse, so I must have pulled out that pen and then left it behind."

"Godfrey was alive when you left?" I hated to ask it, but I had to.

"Yes." Julia's eyes flashed. "Alive and mad as a hornet."

"Why?"

"Because I read him the riot act," Julia said. "I went there expecting to find Justin with him. And he wasn't. When I asked Godfrey where Justin was, he told me they'd argued and why."

"So you lit into him?" I had to suppress a smile. I recalled that Julia had a rather fiery temper as a girl.

"I did," Julia said with a trace of satisfaction in her voice. "I told him he had to think more about what was good for Justin, and not what he wanted. He got the point."

"I'm sure he did," I said. "How long were you there?"

Julia thought for a moment. "No more than fifteen minutes, maybe only ten. I had to get back to the hospital."

"What time was that?"

"I got back a little after three. They were changing shifts."

"So you left Godfrey alive before three?" I was trying to get the chronology straight in my head.

"Yes."

"You didn't try to find Justin before you went back to the hospital?" I asked.

"No. I was concerned about him," Julia said. "But I had to check on Ezra, and I wanted to stop by the bank to deposit Godfrey's check. Justin would have called if he needed me." She turned away for a moment. "Or so I thought."

"You'll have to tell the deputies about this," I said.

"I know. They'll think Justin or I killed him. Or maybe that we did it together." Julia rubbed a hand across her eyes as she faced me again. "Lord, I wish I could hear what's going on in your kitchen right now."

"I know. I wish I could, too," I said. "But there's nothing we can do at the moment except wait."

Julia nodded.

"It's possible they might think you or Justin killed him," I said. "Depends on what they think your motive is. Revenge, maybe."

"Why would I suddenly decide I wanted revenge now?" Julia snorted. "If I'd wanted to kill Godfrey because he got me pregnant and ran out on me, I would have done it years ago."

"Possibly," I said. "But now your husband is terminally ill, Godfrey appears and wants to take your son back to California, and maybe you're so stressed you lose control and strike him down."

Julia blanched. "I hadn't thought of that. It does sound plausible when you put it that way. The Lord knows my stress level is through the roof."

"No wonder," I said in sympathy. "Anybody's would be, with what you're going through with Ezra."

Julia smiled her thanks. "But I didn't kill Godfrey, and neither did my husband nor my son."

"Then we have to look elsewhere." I paused. "How often did Godfrey come back to Athena over the years?"

Julia thought for a moment. "Every few years, probably. A few times he came on a book tour. Other times for research of some kind."

"Once his parents left Athena, did he have that many ties here, other than college?"

Julia didn't appear to have heard me.

"What is it? Have you remembered something?" I leaned forward in my chair.

"Talking about book tours made me think of it," Julia finally said, focusing on me again. "When I was leaving the hotel earlier today, I saw somebody at the front desk with a box of books." She shrugged. "At least, that's what I thought it must be, because I saw the name of Godfrey's latest book on the side of the box."

"Who was it?" A potential new suspect, I hoped. All the better for Justin and Julia.

"That woman who owns the bookstore on the square, Jordan Thompson," Julia said. "And I know for a fact she hated Godfrey with a passion."

TWELVE

"I didn't think ministers' wives listened to gossip." I said it teasingly, but Julia didn't take it that way.

"I don't run around gossiping with anyone." Julia's tone was frosty enough to make me wish I was wearing a sweater. "But people tell me things, even when I don't ask them to. Besides, Melba Gilley's niece Patty works there. Has since she got out of high school five years ago. She used to babysit Justin, and whenever I run into her, she always wants to talk."

I nodded. I knew Melba's niece, Patty Simpson. Plus, I knew Melba. If Patty was at all like her aunt, she knew what was going on around her within a ten-mile radius.

"Okay, let's say something happened between Godfrey and Jordan Thompson." I regarded Julia warily. "Something that pissed off Jordan so much she wanted Godfrey dead. How the heck are we supposed to find out what that was? Other than calling up Patty Simpson and asking her, since she seems to know everything."

"I'm not suggesting that." Julia scowled. "Although I have no doubt Patty would be happy to tell you that, and a dozen other things besides." She paused. "I know you go into the bookstore. I've seen you there myself, several times."

"Yes, I do. I go in there at least every couple of weeks." I have always loved bookstores, and though I have plenty of access to books through the two libraries where I work and volunteer, I can't resist the lure of the bookstore.

"Then go by there tomorrow and talk to Jordan," Julia said. "She's fond of older men, from what I've seen. You can probably get her to talk to you."

"Julia, I can't believe you're suggesting such a thing." I pretended to be shocked, but I was more amused than anything. I couldn't see myself in the role of *homme fatal*, persuading attractive young women to spill their secrets.

She didn't respond. Instead, she turned in her chair and peered in the direction of the kitchen. "What's taking so long? Shouldn't they be done by now?" She started to rise.

"No, I'll go." I motioned for her to stay where she was, and she sat down again. "Kanesha won't like it, I'm sure, but she's probably already so annoyed at me it won't make much difference."

A few feet from the kitchen I could hear the low murmur of voices. Then one rose above the rest—Justin's.

"Yes, I went back, but he was dead. I keep telling you that. Why do you keep asking me?"

The note of near-hysteria in the boy's voice worried me. When I stepped into the kitchen, I could see Diesel in Justin's lap, peering angrily at Kanesha. He looked like he was ready to launch himself over the table at her.

"Diesel, no."

At the sound of my voice, the cat warbled, and I could tell he was upset. But some of the tension left his body, and he sat back against Justin. The signs of exhaustion in Justin's face emboldened me.

Kanesha stood up and faced me. "I'd appreciate it if you'd remove that cat from the room."

I didn't care for the way she said *that cat*. "It's his house too, and if he wants to be in this room, he can. What are you doing that's upsetting him?"

The surprise in the deputy's face pleased me. Obviously she hadn't expected me to talk back to her. I pressed my advantage without allowing her to answer.

"I think you've had enough time now to ask Justin your questions," I said. "He's had a long and very upsetting day. Unless you're going to charge him with something, I think this interview should be over."

Over Kanesha's shoulder, I caught sight of a smirking Bates. That wasn't good. Kanesha might take it out on Justin because she knew she had to prove herself in front of her good ol' boy of a subordinate.

"I am conducting an investigation into what looks like homicide, Mr. Harris." Kanesha enunciated each word so carefully, I could tell she was furious. "I will conduct the investigation as I see fit, and that means questioning anyone with any connection to the victim." The intensity of her gaze made me want to take a step back. "Do you understand that?"

"I do." A smarter man would have tucked tail and run. She was one pissed-off deputy, but another look at Justin's face was all I needed to make me stand my ground. "My point is, you've questioned Justin and his mother. You've pushed your luck far enough as it is, since Justin hasn't had time to talk to a lawyer. They're both very upset about what happened, and if you have a humane bone in your body, you'll give them time to recover. They haven't even had their dinner yet, and neither have I. You can continue this tomorrow."

Bates stood and moved close to Kanesha. He appeared ready to step between Kanesha and me.

I must have looked more threatening than I realized, because now both deputies were glaring at me. I took a step back, my hands up to show that I meant no harm.

Kanesha jerked her head once, and Bates moved away.

"I have more questions for you, Mr. Harris." Kanesha folded her arms over her chest. "But they can wait until tomorrow. I'm sure I'll have more questions for Justin and Mrs. Wardlaw as well. Have a good evening."

She stalked past me, Bates behind her. He gave me a cocky grin as he went.

Moments later I heard the front door open and close, and Julia appeared in the kitchen right after. She took one look at Justin, then hurried to his side. Diesel jumped down from the boy's lap and came to rub against my legs.

"Honey, how are you? Did they mistreat you?" Julia examined Justin, her fingers trembling as she touched his face.

"No, I'm okay, Mama." Justin leaned against her, his head at her waist. Julia stroked his hair. "It was pretty intense. She kept asking me the same questions over and over."

I went to the refrigerator and retrieved a can of Coke for Justin.

"Thank you, sir," he said as he accepted it. "You should've heard Mr. Charlie, Mama. He came in here and told the deputy that she should stop. And she did. But boy was she mad." He popped the top on the can and took a long swig of Coke.

"Thank you." Julia threw me a glance full of gratitude.

"You're welcome," I said. "Now, anyone hungry? How about I order us a pizza?"

Both Julia and Justin shook their heads. "Not for me, thanks," Justin said.

When a teenager turned down pizza, he was obviously worn out.

"Okay," I said. "Why don't you go on up to bed? And if you get hungry in the night, there's plenty of food in the fridge."

"Yes, sir." Justin stood, his shoulders tensed. "Mama, will you come upstairs with me for a few minutes? I need to talk to you about something." He glanced at me, and I nodded. He relaxed.

I knew he wanted to talk to Julia about the pen he found in Godfrey's room. Julia could explain, and then they could decide what to do about it.

"If you need anything, let me know." I watched as they left the room, Julia's arm around her son.

Diesel started after them, but I called him back. "Not now, boy. Justin and his mother need to be alone. You stay with me."

The cat looked at me for a moment, then sat down and started cleaning his left front paw.

I've never had a pet that seemed to understand what

I said so well. Sometimes it freaked me out a little. I watched Diesel a little longer, until hunger pangs claimed my attention.

I decided against pizza and settled for scrambled eggs with cheddar cheese and a couple of pieces of toast instead. When my meal was ready, I poured a glass of water and carried it with my plate to the table.

Diesel could smell the eggs and cheese, and approached my chair, chirping. He loved scrambled eggs, and I usually gave him a few bites. If I didn't, I got a heavy paw on my leg as a reminder.

I took my time eating, and when I was done I cleaned up the kitchen. Azalea would be back in the morning, and I didn't want her to find a mess. She would have enough to do with dusting, vacuuming, and laundry without having to clean up in here.

Julia still hadn't come back down by the time I finished. I was tired and ready to climb into bed with a book, but I didn't want to go upstairs without seeing Julia to her car. Aunt Dottie would haunt me if I neglected my duties as a host.

I went up for the book I was reading, planning to take it back downstairs while I waited for Julia. Diesel trotted along with me. I retrieved the book from my bedside table, and Diesel followed as I left my room and walked back to the stairs.

From above me I heard Julia telling Justin good night, and moments later she was coming down the stairs. I moved forward to intercept her as she reached the second-floor landing.

"You must be about ready for bed." Julia paused, her hand on the banister. "What a day this has been."

"Yes, it has." Somehow it seemed three days long, but it was only this morning that Godfrey Priest had appeared in the archive. "I wanted to see you out and ask if there's anything else I can do."

Julia placed a hand on my arm as we walked down the stairs together. Diesel had zipped ahead and disappeared before we were halfway down.

"You're a good friend," Julia said. "And I'm so sorry if I was rude to you earlier. I'm just terrified of what's going to come of this." Her grip tightened on my arm. "I have to keep Justin safe."

"How is he?"

"Very tired and confused, poor lamb." Julia sighed. "Like both of us, I expect. We talked, and I explained about the pen."

"Good." I wanted to ask whether they decided to tell Kanesha about it, but Julia looked exhausted.

We reached the bottom of the stairs, and I turned to face her as her hand dropped from my arm. "I'll keep my eye on him, and I'll keep my ears open, too. Someone else had a powerful motive, and I'm sure the truth will come out. It's just going to take some digging."

"You're a good man, Charlie Harris." Julia surprised me with a peck on the cheek, and I could feel my face redden a bit. "I'll get my purse and be right back."

I waited, hoping my face had lost any vestige of red by the time she returned.

When Julia reappeared, purse clutched in her hand, I moved to open the door for her. I started to follow her down the walk, but she insisted that I not.

"It's not that far to the car, and I'll be fine. I'm going by the hospital to check on Ezra, and then I'll head home and collapse." She smiled before she turned and moved down the walk to the street.

"Good night, then," I called after her. I waited until she pulled her car away from the curb before shutting the door.

I turned off the lights downstairs, watching for Diesel, but there was no sign of him. I found him sprawled across my bed when I got back upstairs.

After putting my book back on the nightstand, I undressed and got ready for bed myself. I was tired, but my brain was buzzing with all kinds of thoughts about the events of the day.

I read for a while, trying hard to concentrate on my book, and eventually I put it aside and turned out the light. Diesel snuggled close to my legs.

Praying that I wouldn't have nightmares about dead bodies all night long, I did my best to fall asleep.

THIRTEEN

||||||||||||||||||||||||||||||||||||||||||||

If I dreamed about corpses, I didn't remember it when I woke the next morning. I came out of a sound sleep to feel a paw gently prodding my nose and then a head butting lightly against my chin.

With Diesel around I had no need of an alarm clock. He got me up most mornings by six-thirty, and today was no exception.

After I came out of the bathroom, wearing my robe over my pajamas, I went down to the kitchen, where I knew Diesel would be waiting. I filled his bowl with fresh water and replenished his food. He began eating his breakfast with enthusiasm.

I hadn't remembered to fill the coffeepot last night and set it so that I would have coffee when I got up. And no wonder. I felt dazed as I recalled the events of the day before.

While I waited for the coffee, I went to the front door to retrieve the paper. Standing on the doorstep, breathing in the fresh, cool air, I began to feel more awake. I scanned the front page, but there was no mention of Godfrey's death. Tomorrow's paper would be full of it, I was sure. And there would probably be national news crews all over the place. The mysterious death of a bestselling writer would attract attention across the country.

I was working the crossword and sipping coffee when the back door opened. I looked up to greet Azalea Berry. Today, Wednesday, was one of her three weekdays at my house. She had other clients on Tuesdays and Thursdays.

At nearly six feet tall, Azalea was an imposing figure. She had a regal bearing and she rarely smiled, but she was kind, with a warmth that belied her reserve. She was only about three or four years older than I, but she possessed the poise of a grande dame in her eighties.

"Good morning," I said.

"Good morning, Mr. Charlie," Azalea replied. She closed the door behind her and set her purse and keys on the counter nearby. "It sure is some beautiful morning."

"Yes, it is." I wondered whether she had heard about Godfrey Priest's death. Surely Kanesha had mentioned it to her mother.

"Terrible thing about that poor man." Azalea retrieved her apron from a hook by the back door and put it on.

"It sure was. It seems like a nightmare instead of something real."

"And you finding him that way." Azalea shook her head. "It's a wonder you wasn't up all night."

"It was pretty grisly." I took a sip of my coffee.

"How is Justin this morning?" She shook her head. "That poor child."

"I haven't seen him this morning. He was completely worn out last night."

"Then he's going to need a good breakfast. Build up his strength. You, too." She went to the refrigerator and began pulling out eggs, sausage, and milk. Next she retrieved the flour canister, and I knew she was going to make hotcakes.

My mouth began watering. Azalea made wonderful hotcakes.

Diesel wandered into the kitchen and sat down a few feet away from Azalea.

She regarded him with a gimlet eye, and he stared back unfazed. "I don't need no help from you," Azalea said.

Diesel warbled at her, and Azalea turned her back on him, busying herself with preparing breakfast.

"Diesel, let's go see if Justin is up." I put my coffee cup aside and stood. "Come on, boy."

Diesel was off like a streak. I followed at a much more leisurely pace.

When I reached Justin's room, I found the door open and Justin sitting at his computer with Diesel climbing into his lap. I tapped lightly on the door, and Justin looked up at me.

The worn, frightened look had left his face, and this morning he appeared more his usual self, I was glad to see.

"Good morning." I smiled. "Azalea's downstairs making hotcakes for breakfast."

Justin's face lit up. "I sure am hungry." His head ducked down for a moment. "Uh, about yesterday . . ."

"Yes," I said when he paused.

"Thank you," Justin said, raising his head to look at me. "I'm glad you were there, sir."

"You're welcome." He seemed younger than eighteen right then. He'd had more than one deep shock yesterday, and the Lord only knew how it would all affect him in the long run. "Come on downstairs when you're ready. Breakfast will be on the table soon."

"Yes, sir. I will." Justin rubbed Diesel's head, and the cat chirped happily.

I reached the kitchen in time to answer the phone. The appetizing smells emanating from the stove made my stomach rumble. Justin wasn't the only hungry one.

"Hello."

"Good morning, Mr. Harris. This is Ray Appleby from the *Athena Daily Register*. I'd like to talk to you about the murder of Godfrey Priest."

I glanced at the clock. It was only seven-fifteen.

"You're calling pretty early, Mr. Appleby. I haven't had my breakfast yet." My tone was sharp, but I didn't care.

"I apologize if I woke you," Appleby said. He didn't sound apologetic. "But I really need to talk to you as soon as possible. According to my sources you found the body."

"If you want to call back at a more civilized hour, I *might* be willing to talk to you. Until then, I have nothing more to say." I hung up the phone.

I turned to find Azalea regarding me, her expression inquisitive.

"Somebody from the paper, wanting to talk to me about yesterday." I sat down at the table.

"That's mighty rude, calling somebody this early."

She turned back to the stove. "People just ain't raised right these days."

"It's only going to get worse," I said. I picked up my coffee cup and, seeing that it was empty, got up to refill it.

"I guess he was pretty big news." Azalea expertly flipped a couple of hotcakes as I poured the coffee.

"He was, and there'll probably be news crews from all over the country here." I stirred some sugar substitute into the coffee. "And it looks like your daughter may be center stage, since she's in charge of the investigation."

Azalea made a noise that sounded like *hmmph*.

"It's a big chance for her." I sat down at the table again and drank some coffee.

"That girl wanna be on TV, she should've been an actress." Azalea set a plate with three hotcakes and three sausages on the table in front of me.

"Thank you," I said, reaching for the syrup she had placed on the table, along with a napkin and cutlery.

Justin appeared a few minutes later when Diesel was begging for another bite of hotcake. Justin saw it and grinned.

"Good morning, child." Azalea treated the young man to one of her rare smiles. "You set on down here and eat you some breakfast. You need your strength."

"Yes, ma'am," Justin said, eyeing the plate of hotcakes and sausage avidly. "Thank you, Miss Azalea. I'm starving."

Azalea stood, arms folded, watching Justin eat for a moment. Then she inspected my plate. "How about some more?"

I groaned and pushed my plate away. "No, thank you.

That was delicious, but if I eat any more I'll have to go run around the track for two hours."

The housekeeper cocked an eyebrow at that. She knew I was not a runner. "Just go up and down them stairs a few times. That'll do it."

The doorbell rang, and I started to get up from the table.

"You set still." Azalea motioned me back into my chair. "I'll take care of whatever heathen that is, ringing the bell this time of the morning."

"Thank you," I said. I knew better than to argue with her.

As I watched Justin shovel the food into his mouth with Diesel sitting hopefully by his chair, I heard raised voices come from the hallway. I recognized one of them and sighed.

The voices neared.

"I done told you, girl, you ain't going in that kitchen. You go and set yourself down in the living room. Mr. Charlie'll come in there when he's done finished with his breakfast."

"Mama, this is ridiculous." Kanesha Berry sounded angry.

"Git on in there like I told you. Ain't gonna hurt you to wait five minutes."

"Oh good Lord. If this don't beat all."

Justin stared at me, round-eyed, and I tried hard not to laugh. The stern, commanding deputy of the night before was starting to sound like a petulant teenager.

Azalea entered the kitchen alone, and I hastily drank some coffee to hide my smile. Justin dipped his head down and stuck another forkful of hotcake and sausage in his mouth.

"Miss High and Mighty Deputy is waiting to talk to you, Mr. Charlie, when you be done with your breakfast." Azalea proceeded to the stove as if Justin and I had heard nothing of the argument between her and Kanesha.

"Thank you, Azalea," I said. "I'm not exactly dressed for an interview, but I don't think she'll want to wait while I shower and dress."

Something like *hmmph* sounded from the direction of the stove, and I shrugged at Justin.

"Are you going to your classes this morning?"

Justin regarded his plate for a moment. "I guess so. Do you think I should? Or maybe I should go over to the hospital?"

"Why don't you call your mother and talk to her about it? My guess is she'll say you should go to your classes and keep busy."

"Yes, sir." Justin appeared relieved.

The last thing he needed was to be hanging around the house all day. I was hoping the media didn't know who he was yet, so they'd leave him alone.

"But if people start pestering you with questions," I said as I thought about it, "you come on back here and don't worry about your classes, okay?"

"You mean like newspeople?"

I nodded.

Justin made a face. "I'm not talking to them. I don't want to be in the news."

"Then you don't have to talk to them. Remember that."

"Okay."

I stood. "Now I'd better go talk to Deputy Berry."

As I was leaving the room, I glanced back to see Azalea serving Justin more hotcakes and sausage. Diesel remained with him, ever hopeful.

If only I had a metabolism like that, I thought wistfully.

I tightened the belt of my robe before I entered the living room. I should have washed my hands, I realized too late. Oh well.

"Good morning, Deputy. You wanted to see me?"

Kanesha turned from studying one of the bookcases against the far wall. Lines of tiredness had etched her face overnight. I wondered whether she'd had any sleep at all.

"Good morning, Mr. Harris." Kanesha frowned. Whether she was still riled up from the argument with her mother, I couldn't tell. "Yes, I do."

"Why don't we sit down?" I gestured toward the sofa and chairs.

Kanesha chose one of the chairs, and I sat in the other, bracing myself for an onslaught of questions.

"I came by to tell you not to speak to any newspeople." Kanesha glared at me. "I don't want this investigation compromised by someone letting details get loose."

"I'm in no particular hurry to talk to any reporters," I said, somewhat stung by the sharpness of her tone. "One of them called me already this morning, but I hung up on him."

"And who was that?"

"Ray Appleby, from the local paper."

Kanesha's eyes narrowed. "I've already given him a statement. If he bothers you, let me know. Same thing goes for any other reporters."

"Thank you, I will. I have no desire to see myself or anyone in this house on national television." I crossed my arms and gazed blandly back at her.

"So far none of them know that Justin Wardlaw was with you last night." Kanesha shifted position in the chair. "I'd like to keep it that way as long as possible. They'll find out eventually, though."

"They won't find out from me," I said. "He wants to go to his classes today. Do you think that's a good idea?"

Kanesha considered that for a moment. "I don't see why not. I need to question him again, but I have other things to do this morning." She stood.

"That's all?" I shrugged. "I thought for sure you had more questions for me."

"I do, but they can wait. You'll hear from me."

I stood, ready to show her to the front door.

"I'll see myself out."

I nodded as she walked past me toward the hallway. Moments later I heard the door open and close behind her.

I headed back to the kitchen. Justin was gone, along with Diesel. Azalea was clearing the table, putting things in the dishwasher.

She probably wouldn't ask me what Kanesha had said to me, so I told her.

"Any of them come sniffing around the house, I'll just turn on the water hose."

I laughed. I could see her doing it. "Go right ahead."

As I picked up my coffee cup to get a refill, I saw Azalea regarding me with a frown.

"Is something wrong?" I asked.

"She gone need some help." Azalea, for the first time in my acquaintance, looked worried.

"Kanesha?"

Azalea nodded.

"She seems pretty capable to me," I said. "She seems to know what she's doing."

"She's a smart girl, I know. Always worked real hard. Ambitious, too." Azalea smoothed her apron, and I waited for her to continue.

"But people ain't gonna talk to her. You know what they're like." Azalea looked at me expectantly.

"You mean because she's black." There was no other way to say it, and I knew what Azalea meant. Old attitudes die hard, and many people in Athena weren't used to the idea of a young black woman in a position of such authority. That could cause Kanesha some problems.

"I sure do," Azalea said. Her eyes bored into mine. "That's why you got to help her, only don't let on like you're doing it."

FOURTEEN

Showered, shaved, and dressed, I contemplated the day ahead. Wednesday is my day for errands. I worked at the college library on Mondays, Tuesdays, and Thursdays, and on Fridays I volunteered at the public library.

Justin had gone off to his classes, and Azalea would be here most of the day working and keeping an eye on things. She had already taken another phone call from the local reporter, Ray Appleby, and I doubted he would call back anytime soon.

Before I went upstairs, Azalea extracted a promise from me to help Kanesha as discreetly as possible. I knew there was some truth to what Azalea said, and I couldn't help being curious about who had killed Godfrey and why. Everyone else in town would be talking about it, so there was no reason I couldn't, too. And slip in the occasional question.

Was this how the Hardy Boys got started? I laughed at myself in the mirror. I didn't have a famous detective for a father, but I had read hundreds of mystery novels. I would poke around, but I wasn't planning to investigate houses on cliffs, old mills, or secret caves anytime soon.

Diesel followed me to the room next to my bedroom, another bedroom that Aunt Dottie had converted into a sitting room for herself. With a few small changes I had turned it into an office of sorts, mainly by adding my computer and printer.

The cat jumped up onto the desk by the computer—his usual spot—and watched as I turned the computer on and got comfortable in my chair. I had a little time to kill—an unfortunate phrase, I realized—before shops would open, so I might as well check my e-mail.

The first message I opened was from my daughter Laura, who had moved to Los Angeles two years ago to pursue a career as an actress.

The news about Godfrey had apparently hit the media in California last night, because Laura's message was full of questions. She had no idea, of course, how closely involved I was in the case. I glanced at the time stamp on her message. She had sent it around two A.M. Pacific time.

I replied to her message at some length, explaining what I knew about Godfrey's death and my own involvement. I knew there would be many questions to come, because Laura loved mysteries as much as I did. As a ten-year-old she wrote her own plays based on the Nancy Drew books, and naturally she starred as Nancy. If I wasn't careful, she'd hop on the first plane home, determined to help me.

Then I remembered she was in a successful play at the moment, so I was safe from her enthusiastic assistance. Smiling, I clicked the SEND button.

There was no message from my son, Sean, but that wasn't unusual. Much more taciturn than his younger sister, Sean wrote me an e-mail every week or so and called about as often. He and his mother had been very close, as Laura and I are, and I knew he was still struggling to come to terms with Jackie's death.

Finished with e-mail, I shut down the computer. Diesel yawned at me, and I reached out to scratch his head.

"Are you ready to go, boy? It's almost ten."

The cat hopped to the floor and rubbed against my legs. He knew the word *go*.

Downstairs I heard Azalea running the vacuum in the living room. I fastened Diesel into his harness, and soon we were on our way in the car. I had decided not to walk this morning, despite fine weather, in case I needed to get somewhere quickly.

My first destination this morning was the independent bookstore, the Athenaeum. Some locals and visitors might scratch their heads over the name, but I thought it was clever. Its present location was on the town square, across from Farrington House, but it had started life about twenty years ago in a house on a street near downtown. The present owner, Jordan Thompson, had inherited it from her father, and when I moved back to Athena, I was delighted to find it thriving.

It was a few minutes past ten when I pulled my car into a spot directly in front of the store. The neon OPEN sign was on. Diesel hopped down from the car, eager to go inside. Jordan always made a fuss over him and gave him a kitty treat or two. Or five. Diesel sometimes went into starving-cat mode around her, and I pretended not to notice.

I paused at the front window. There was a large pile of Godfrey's latest book, a hardcover with a garish cover, on display. It would probably sell even more copies now that he was dead.

With that morbid thought, I entered the bookstore, Diesel stepping ahead of me. The bell hung from the door handle jangled and, as usual, Diesel swatted at it until I pulled him away.

"Good morning." I called out the words because I didn't see any staff members in evidence.

The head of one of Jordan's assistants popped up from behind the counter. "Let me know if you need help with anything." The head disappeared.

"Thanks." The head belonged to Jordan's younger brother, Jack, who was about the same age as Justin. He was always in a hurry, it seemed, and I took no offense at his abrupt manner.

The Athenaeum occupied about four thousand square feet, and there were thousands and thousands of books lining the shelves. I could easily spend two hours here— and often had—such was the wealth of the printed word available. I headed for the mystery section, where I usually started. I had been here the previous Saturday, so there might not be anything new in. It never hurt to look, though.

I was checking the *H*s for three of my favorites—Haines, Harris, and Hart—when I heard a voice behind me.

"Good morning, Diesel. What a beautiful boy you are."

Diesel tugged at the leash, and I let him go as I turned to greet Jordan.

"Good morning, Charlie," she said, bending down to give my cat an affectionate greeting.

Her long red hair pulled back in a ponytail, Jordan looked younger than thirty-one. Tall and willowy, she was a striking woman, with flawless skin and flashing green eyes. "Good morning," I said. "How are you?"

"I'm fine," she said, standing up. "Can Diesel have a treat or two?"

"Sure," I said. "You spoil him, you know."

Jordan laughed. "He's a big guy. Needs to keep up his strength."

I passed over the leash, and Diesel padded happily after Jordan.

I hoped that by the time Jordan brought Diesel back I could figure out an approach. I scanned the bookshelves in front of me, as if I could find inspiration there.

I heard the bell on the door, and then a voice called out, "Morning, everybody. I brought doughnuts."

Recognizing the voice of Patty Simpson, I smiled. With Patty here it shouldn't be too hard to steer the conversation around to the death of the town's famous writer.

I left the mystery section for the front counter. Her back to me, Patty was setting down a box of doughnuts along with a purse and a bag of books. Jack Thompson had disappeared from behind the counter.

"I finished the galley of that new thriller you gave me," Patty said without turning her head. "It was pretty awful, so I don't think you should order more than one."

Then she turned and saw me. "Oh, sorry, I thought it

was Jordan. How are you, Mr. Harris? Would you like a doughnut?"

I would very much have liked a doughnut, but after the breakfast I had consumed, I knew I shouldn't. "No, thank you," I said, surprised that the words actually came out of my mouth.

"There's plenty," Patty said.

"No, really, I'm okay. But thanks for the offer."

"I'll be right back." Patty grabbed her purse and scurried off in the direction of the back room.

While I waited, I turned my back on the doughnuts, lest I be tempted further. Instead I focused on a nearby display of diet cookbooks. I ought to buy one, but I knew I'd never cook anything out of it.

When Patty returned, she eyed the box of doughnuts. She helped herself to one, stuffing half of it in her mouth. Judging from the plumpness of her figure, she wasn't interested in diet cookbooks any more than I was.

"Have you heard the big news?" She popped the rest of the doughnut into her mouth while she waited for my reply.

There was no point in playing coy. Sooner or later everyone would know I found the body.

"Yes, I have. Poor Godfrey."

Patty swallowed. Her expression turned sour, and I didn't think it was from the doughnut.

"He was a colossal jerk, that's what he was." Patty reached for a second doughnut before pulling her hand back.

"I went to school with him," I said. "He wasn't always a nice person. Did you know him?"

"Only through the bookstore. And from things my

Aunt Melba has told me about him." She shot me an arch
look. "I know you know my Aunt Melba. Don't you think
she looks good for someone her age?"

I suppressed a laugh. Patty was anything but subtle.
"She sure does."

Patty grinned, and I knew the minute I left she'd be on
the phone with Melba, reporting my comment.

"So Godfrey came to the store to sign books, I guess."
If I didn't steer the subject back to Godfrey, no telling
what Patty, trying to get a response from me, would say
about Melba next.

"Not as often as he should have." Patty frowned.
"You'd think Mr. High-and-Mighty Bestselling Author
would have the decency to help out his hometown bookstore. But not him. He was too good for us."

"You mean he wouldn't sign here?" That was rather
ugly of Godfrey, if it was true.

"Well, he did sign a couple of times," Patty said. "But
the last time he was going to come, he canceled at the last
minute and went over to that big chain bookstore out on
the highway instead. The jerk."

"What are you talking about?" Jordan and Diesel
walked up to us, and I could tell that Jordan wasn't happy
as she gave Diesel's leash back to me. Diesel stared back
and forth between us, sensing the sudden tension in the
room.

"About Godfrey Priest," Patty said, not the least fazed
by Jordan's forbidding expression. "And about the dirty
trick he played on us the last time he was supposed to
sign here."

"We all have better things to do with our time than
talk about that jackass," Jordan said. "You need to finish

checking those backlist orders." She turned and stalked off.

Patty waited until Jordan was safely out of earshot before moving a step closer to me and Diesel. "She used to be in love with him, you know."

"Really?" I felt awkward. This was the kind of thing I had come for, but it suddenly seemed a bit embarrassing.

Patty was not embarrassed. "Oh yeah, she would go off to those mystery conventions, when he was still showing up at them, and I think they had a big ol' fling. But then he must've dumped her."

"That's too bad. He did have a terrible reputation with women, though." I kept an eye on the back room. Jordan might reappear at any moment, and I didn't want her to catch us.

"And that was when he stopped coming to the store." Patty sounded triumphant, as if she'd just solved a puzzle.

That was interesting. Hell hath no fury, etc. Not to mention a bookstore owner whose business could be hurt by the defection of a big-selling writer.

Jordan stuck her head out of the back room. "Patty, have you started on that backlist order yet?"

"Just starting it now." Patty's tone was cheerful in reply. She winked at me. "If you need help with anything, you just let me know." She turned to look around the counter for something. She picked up a printout and brandished it at me. "I have to go through the romance section and decide what we need to reorder. I'm the expert for that section."

As she turned, her foot caught on something, and she stumbled toward me. I put out a hand to steady her, and Diesel scooted out of the way.

"Thank you," she said. "Now what's this doing here?"

She stooped down and picked up a box of books that had been sitting on the floor behind the counter. She set the box, labeled with Godfrey's name and the title of his new book, on the counter next to the doughnuts.

Julia's words from last night flashed into my mind. "Could I have a look at one of those? I haven't read it yet."

Shrugging, Patty pulled one out of the box and handed it to me. "It's pretty awful. I gave up after fifty pages."

I heard her only dimly as I opened the book to the title page. There, below the printed name, was Godfrey's signature.

And yesterday's date.

FIFTEEN

"This is pretty interesting." I held the book out to Patty.

She took it from me and glanced down at the title page.

"Whoa. This is going to be worth something, let me tell you." She snapped the book shut and stuck it back in the box.

"I suppose so." I was annoyed she hadn't given the book back to me, but perhaps she was so surprised she didn't realize her rudeness.

"So that's where she was." Patty muttered the words under her breath, but I was close enough to make them out.

"What *are* you doing?"

Neither of us had heard Jordan approach. Patty stared at her boss like a fox caught in the proverbial henhouse, while I mustered as innocent-looking a smile as I could.

"Just looking at this box of books," I said. "I was thinking about buying one. I haven't read it yet."

Jordan's eyes narrowed with suspicion as she looked from Patty to me. "These aren't for sale."

"Then what are you going to do with them?" I thought that was a reasonable question. She could surely sell them for a lot more than list price—books signed by a famous mystery writer the day he was murdered. Talk about collectible.

"I meant they're all spoken for," Jordan said in a more conciliatory tone. "They're all special orders." She turned and reached for the box.

"You know, I saw Godfrey yesterday morning," I said. "I know he had plans for lunch. Was that when he signed them?"

Jordan stepped back from the box and glared at me.

Patty watched avidly, her eyes going back and forth between her boss and me.

"No, it wasn't," Jordan said, her face flushing. "If you must know, he signed them yesterday afternoon. I went by his hotel room."

"Gosh, then maybe you were the last person to see him alive." Patty could hardly contain her glee. "I bet the police will want to talk to you."

Jordan, in the act of reaching for the box again, stumbled against the counter. When she turned, her face was dead white. For a moment I thought she was going to faint, but she rallied. She pulled a high-seated stool over and sat down on it. "What happened?"

"You haven't heard?" I was surprised. She was probably the one person in Athena who hadn't. "Godfrey was found dead in his hotel room last night. The sheriff's department is treating it as a suspicious death."

"Oh dear Lord." Jordan muttered the words over and over.

"Can I get you some coffee or something?" Patty, suddenly contrite, appeared anxious.

Jordan waved her away. "No, just go do your job for once."

Patty's sulky expression didn't bode well for her dedication to the task, but she went away quietly.

"Are you okay?" I asked, concerned by how shaken Jordan still seemed to be.

Diesel, sensing her distress, stood up on his hind legs and stretched his right paw out, touching her thigh. Jordan gave him a shaky smile and a rub on the head.

"If she ever does penance for anything, it'll be for that double-jointed tongue of hers." Jordan paused and breathed deeply. "Yeah, I'll be okay. It's a shock, hearing news like that. So completely unexpected." She continued rubbing Diesel's head.

"You really had no idea?" Was she a consummate actress, only pretending to be stunned?

Jordan shook her head. "No, why should I? I never make it to the ten o'clock news. I'm always too tired. And nobody called me, either." She snorted. "Though I'm surprised Patty didn't."

"Was Godfrey a particular friend of yours?" I wasn't sure how she would react. This might be my last visit to her bookstore if I wasn't careful, and I certainly wouldn't like that. "Sorry, but you seem pretty shaken up."

"More than a bookstore owner should be for a writer who hadn't deigned to enter her premises in five years?" Jordan laughed, a bitter sound. Diesel sat back on his haunches and stared up at her.

"I suppose so, yes. If you put it that way." Perhaps I should have excused myself and gotten the heck out of there, but curiosity kept me.

"I'll tell you one thing: I'm not sorry the bastard's dead." Jordan stood up, and Diesel scooted back beside me. "He embarrassed the hell out of me by not showing up here—twice—for advertized events. Not to mention the money I lost on returning hundreds of copies of his books—books I could easily have sold. But he didn't have to balls to show his face in here."

"That's too bad. No wonder you were pissed at him." I didn't know what else to say. The passion in her voice startled me. Right now, she sounded angry enough to have killed him.

But anger this intense because of business?

Or was there something more personal behind it, as Patty claimed?

I couldn't ask her that outright, or I really would be banned from the bookstore. At the moment I couldn't think of a subtle way of getting at the information either.

"Now, is there something I can help you with?" Jordan became very businesslike.

"I would still like a copy of Godfrey's latest book." I nodded at the box of signed copies. "If those aren't available, an unsigned copy will do."

Jordan stared at the box for a moment before reaching into it and pulling out a book. "It's okay. You can buy one."

"Thank you." I went around to the front of the counter, Diesel at my heels. As Jordan rang up my purchase and bagged it, I pulled out my debit card.

The transaction finished, Jordan returned my card and handed me the bag. "Thank you very much." She didn't smile the way she usually did, but she also didn't look like she never wanted to see me in her store again. That was a relief.

"Come on, Diesel. Got to finish our errands." I flashed Jordan a smile as the cat and I headed for the door, but the bookstore owner had already turned away.

Outside the store, I paused. Diesel sat down and looked up at me. I gazed back at him, lost in thought.

Why had Jordan changed her mind and let me buy one of the signed copies?

Should I take it as some sort of bribe? Because the book would probably soon be worth a lot more than the $26.95 plus tax I paid for it.

Or was it Jordan's way of telling me she had nothing to do with Godfrey's death?

Short of asking her point-blank, I didn't see any way to answer those questions for now.

Diesel warbled at me, bringing me out of my wool-gathering. "Time to move on. I know."

I put the book in the car, and Diesel and I walked down the block to the bakery.

Helen Louise Brady, another of my Athena High School classmates, had opened a patisserie and café a few years before I moved back. It quickly thrived, patronized by many of the college faculty and students, and plenty of townspeople as well. Helen Louise's pastries and cakes were sinfully delicious, and I never could resist popping in for something to take home.

Another point in the bakery's favor was that Helen Louise didn't mind having Diesel come in with me. The first few times I took him in some of her regulars raised their eyebrows, but Helen Louise had been known to ban

customers who annoyed her. If she said it was okay for
Diesel to be there, no one was going to argue with her.

Rake-thin and nearly six feet tall, her hair jet black,
Helen Louise beamed with joy when she spotted Diesel.
"Ah, *mon chat très beau*." Helen Louise often lapsed into
French. She had lived in Paris for nearly ten years before
coming back to Athena and to open the patisserie. "Let
me find something for you."

I sometimes marveled that Diesel didn't weigh fifty
pounds, so many people wanted to feed him. I kept an
eye, though, on his little treats, and at home we had play
sessions designed to help him burn off the extra calories.

Helen Louise came around the counter with some
creamy frosting on her fingers and bent to let Diesel lick
it off. He purred, and Helen Louise smiled again.

"Thank you." I smiled back. "I know Diesel thanks
you, too. He's going to have to run an extra lap or two on
the stairs at home, but I'm sure it's worth it."

"I should hope so." Helen Louise laughed. She went
behind the counter to a sink and washed her hands. As
she dried them, she asked, "And what can I get for you
today, Charlie?"

She made a wicked chocolate gateau, and I pointed to
one in the glass case. "That will do quite nicely. And I'll
have to run up and down the stairs a few times myself."
I grinned.

"*Quel dommage.* But every mouthful a little heaven on
the tongue." Helen Louise expertly boxed my selection
and rang it up at the register.

"*Oui, certainement.*" I knew some French too, and
Helen Louise laughed.

"Come again soon," she said. "You too, Charlie."

I grinned as I led Diesel to the door. Helen Louise was charming, and her personality was one ingredient in her success.

I put the gateau carefully on the backseat of the car, while Diesel sprang into the front. My two most important errands of the morning accomplished, I thought Diesel and I might drop by the public library for a few minutes. It was only a few blocks away, on the route home.

I was about to back out of the parking space when my cell phone rang. I shifted back to park and pulled the phone out of my shirt pocket. Glancing at the number on the display, I frowned. Someone from the college was calling, but I didn't recognize the number.

"Hello, this is Charlie Harris."

"Hey, Charlie, it's Rick. How you doing?" Rick Tackett was operations manager for the college library.

"Doing fine, and you?"

"Pretty busy," Rick said. "Got a big delivery for you, and I wondered if you wanted it up in your office maybe? Or somewhere else?"

"How big?" I asked, puzzled. I wasn't expecting anything.

"Fifty-four boxes," Rick said. "Pretty heavy. Maybe somebody's papers or something."

Papers?

For a moment I couldn't remember any recent agreement to take someone's papers for the archive.

Then it hit me.

Could these be Godfrey Priest's papers?

SIXTEEN

||||||||||||||||||||||||||||||||||||||||||||

Who else could the papers have belonged to? Godfrey had estimated he had fifty or sixty boxes of papers and books to give to the college archive.

But when had he shipped them?

"Charlie, you still there?"

Rick's voice brought me back to the conversation. "Yeah, I'm still here. Just a bit stunned, that's all."

Rick chuckled into my ear. "Yeah, it's a huge shipment. And pretty heavy, too. Probably cost a coupla thousand bucks, I bet."

"If they belonged to whom I think they did, he had plenty of money." Yeah, the papers were Godfrey's. He must have called someone and had them shipped right after our conversation yesterday.

"Must be nice." Rick laughed again. "Anyway, they're here on the loading dock. Oh, and there's a letter, too."

There was silence for a moment. When Rick spoke again his tone was somber. "Return address says it's from Godfrey Priest. I heard he died last night."

"Yes, he did." What should I do with Godfrey's boxes? The sheriff's department would probably impound them if they knew about them, though I couldn't imagine what use they would be to Kanesha Berry. Technically they were now the property of Athena College, although I didn't think Godfrey had signed anything to that effect yet.

Maybe there was something in his letter that stated his intentions.

"I'd better come over there. I'll meet you on the loading dock in a few minutes."

"Sure," Rick said. "I'll be here."

I ended the call and stuck the phone back in my pocket. Diesel butted my elbow with his head.

"No, I didn't forget about you," I told him. "But we've got to take a detour. Sit."

Diesel sat in the passenger seat. I'd been meaning to get him one of those pet car seats, but since I mostly just drive around town, and pretty slowly at that, I kept putting it off.

About six minutes later I pulled into the loading dock of Hawksworth Library. Built in the 1920s and added to several times over the past eight decades, it was named for an illustrious president of the college who had served right after the Civil War. Altogether it occupied half a block of the street on the north side of the antebellum mansion that housed the archive and some administrative offices.

Rick Tackett, a friendly, stocky fireplug of a man about

ten years my senior, stood on the loading dock beside a pallet of boxes.

I rolled the front windows down a little before shutting off the car. "You stay in the car, boy. I won't be long."

Diesel yawned at me and curled up on the seat. Sometimes, like now, he was remarkably obedient. Other times he was as headstrong as a Brahma bull. I never knew how he'd react to a command.

Or a suggestion, from a feline point of view.

I climbed up onto the loading dock and shook Rick's extended hand.

"Morning, Charlie," he said. He nodded at the neatly stacked and shrink-wrapped boxes. "Here's the letter." He pulled it from his back pocket.

The envelope, made of heavyweight paper, screamed *expensive*, as did the gold-embossed return address bearing Godfrey Priest's name—or rather, "Godfrey Priest Enterprises Inc." I guess being a big bestseller was something like running a business.

"Thanks," I said. "I'll just open this and have a quick look, if you don't mind."

"Sure thing," Rick said. "Here." He handed me a penknife.

I took it and slit open the envelope with the blade and returned the knife to Rick. I extracted the contents, two pages of heavy bond paper.

The top sheet, bearing last Wednesday's date, was a letter from one Gail Enderby, apparently Godfrey's administrative assistant. Ms. Enderby explained that she had prepared the boxes for shipping per her boss's instructions. Each box, she said, contained an inventory of its contents, and box number one—I glanced over at

the pallet, and the boxes I could see did bear numbers—
contained a master inventory.

With the amount of time all this would have taken to
organize, Godfrey had evidently been planning this do-
nation for several months.

The second sheet was a letter from Godfrey himself,
dated the day before his assistant's note. He proclaimed
his intent to donate his papers to the Athena College archive. He didn't mention giving any money along with
the papers to cover the costs of processing and housing
the collection, but at least this letter ought to give the college clear ownership.

"Good news?" Rick asked when I looked up from the
letters.

"Yes. Now I feel like I can answer your question about
what to do with these boxes."

"Great. Where do you want them? Over in your
building?"

I eyed the pallet, trying to estimate how much space
I had in one of the storage rooms allotted to the archive.
"Could you have the boxes numbered one through ten put
in the office? I think the rest of them will fit in the archive
storage room."

"No problem." Rick glanced at his watch. "My guys'll
be having lunch soon. How about they get 'em up there
by two? That do?"

"That's fine." I was itching to get into box number one
and take a gander at Ms. Enderby's master inventory, but
that could wait. "Thanks. I really appreciate it."

Rick smiled, and I climbed down from the loading
dock and rejoined Diesel in the car.

We sat there for a moment as I stared at the boxes

above us. How bizarre this was. And yet, how typical of the man.

Godfrey, with his irrepressible ego, was so sure the college would want his papers, he had them boxed and ready to go. What would he have done yesterday, I wondered, if someone had told him the college wasn't interested?

He would have found a home for them somewhere, but in reality, Athena College, like most private schools these days, couldn't afford to turn down a gift from a prominent alumnus like Godfrey. Athena would accept anything in the hope that more money would follow.

Diesel rubbed against my arm and chirped loudly, interrupting my train of thought.

"Let's go home for lunch," I said, scratching his head. "Then we're going to come back this afternoon and take a look at those boxes."

I drove us home and, once we were in the kitchen and I'd taken off his harness, Diesel headed straight for his litter box in the utility room. I went to the refrigerator, feeling a bit peckish. After the big breakfast I'd had, I didn't want much for lunch.

Azalea had anticipated that, for I discovered a bowl of salad with mixed greens, chopped egg, and cheese sitting on the top shelf. Add some of Azalea's homemade thousand island dressing to that, and it would be just fine.

I prepared my salad and filled a glass from the pitcher of fresh tea on the counter and took them to the table. Diesel came back and settled on the floor near my chair. The house was quiet, and I figured Azalea had probably gone to the grocery store, one of her usual Wednesday activities.

About fifteen minutes later, finished with lunch, I put

my dirty dishes in the sink. Upstairs, I brushed my teeth while Diesel lolled on my freshly made bed. When I first moved back I had made it myself on the days Azalea was due, vaguely embarrassed to have her doing it instead. She quickly informed me that if she wanted me to do her job she'd let me know, and after that I left the bed-making to her. She did it even better than I did anyway.

I glanced at the clock—a few minutes before twelve-thirty. There was no sense rushing back to the archive, because the boxes wouldn't be delivered for at least another hour or so. Spotting Godfrey's latest book on the bedside table, I decided I might as well read a bit of it to pass the time.

I picked up my reading glasses and the book and settled into a comfortable armchair near the window. Diesel appeared to be sound asleep, for which I was grateful. Sometimes he insisted on sitting in my lap while I read, and that could get uncomfortable because of his weight.

Godfrey's book was titled *Moon of the Hunter.* I skipped reading the jacket blurb because sometimes it gave away too much of the plot. I turned past the title page and started reading his acknowledgments. I always found them interesting. Occasionally an author gushed, thanking everyone he knew. Others made poignant remarks about loved ones. Sometimes they were just plain funny.

Godfrey was pompous. He thanked his various agents—in New York, Hollywood, and London—along with members of his staff in California, including Gail Enderby, for ensuring that his life ran smoothly. He mentioned a couple of technical experts he had consulted, and that was it.

The last time I'd read one of his books was probably six or seven years ago, and as I read the first page, I remembered why I stopped. The graphic violence in the opening paragraphs was shocking in its intensity, but somehow compelling. I didn't like the fact that I found it compelling and wanted to read further. But I ignored that and kept turning the pages. Godfrey knew how to pace a story.

A hundred pages later I remembered to check my watch. It was now almost quarter to two. By the time I reached the archive, the boxes of Godfrey's books and papers should be waiting for me. I stuck a bookmark in the book and laid it aside, albeit a bit reluctantly. *Moon of the Hunter* was the story of a serial killer who lured young women to his isolated cabin in the mountains of east Tennessee and the determined sister of one of his victims who was intent on tracking him down and killing him.

I could easily have sat in the chair and finished the book in another couple of hours, but my curiosity over Godfrey's boxes won out. I got up from the chair, stretched, and approached the bed.

"Come on, boy, let's go."

Diesel yawned and rolled over on his back. I reached down and rubbed his stomach. He purred loudly in appreciation.

"I'm not going to stand here and do this for the next two hours." I gave him a final rub and withdrew my hand. "Come on."

A few minutes before two, I unlocked the door to the archive storeroom. Rick's assistants had delivered the boxes, and there was little open space left in the room now. I did a quick count while Diesel sniffed around the boxes. There were forty-four of them, all numbered. Boxes one through ten should be in the office.

I pulled Diesel away from his perusal and headed down the hall to the archive. Inside, the lights on, I dropped Diesel's leash, and he began inspecting the boxes stacked on the floor in three piles in front of my desk. Diesel hopped on top of the first pile of three, and then I realized there were eleven boxes, not ten. The other two piles had four boxes each.

Then I noticed that ten of the boxes were numbered, one through ten, but the eleventh box didn't have a number.

That was interesting. It had to be part of the shipment, because Rick didn't mention any other delivery for the archive today.

I moved forward to pull the eleventh box from the bottom of the center stack but my cell phone rang. I pulled the phone out of my pocket and glanced at the number display. It was the sheriff's department. I answered and identified myself.

"Good afternoon, Mr. Harris." Kanesha Berry's voice was cool and professional. "I'd like to talk to you right away. Can you come down to the sheriff's department please?"

Dang. I really wanted to delve into the boxes, especially the oddly unnumbered one. But I didn't think putting the deputy off would be a good move. I might as well get it over with.

"Okay, I'll be there in a few minutes." I ended the call, stuck my phone in my pocket, and got Diesel down from atop the boxes.

"Come on, boy. Off to jail we go."

SEVENTEEN

I parked a few spaces down from the front door of the Athena County Sheriff's Department. If I had ever been inside the building, I didn't remember it. The building dated from before the Second World War, but there was a new jail behind it, built about five years ago.

"This will be a new experience for both of us," I told Diesel as we approached the door. Diesel's nose twitched in anticipation. He was always curious about strange places.

Inside, the chilled air and fluorescent lighting reminded me of a hospital. Diesel strained against his leash several paces ahead of me. He had spotted the reception desk and a uniformed man sitting behind it. He wanted to go say hello.

"Good afternoon," I said as I approached. "I'm Charles Harris. I'm here to see Deputy Berry. She's expecting me."

The officer behind the desk was too busy staring at Diesel to acknowledge me at first. I cleared my throat a couple of times, and he finally looked up at me.

"Sorry, sir, what did you say?" Before I could respond, he continued. "What kind of cat is that?"

"He's a Maine coon. They get to be pretty big." I smiled at his reaction to my cat. I repeated my name and the purpose for my visit.

"Sure," the deputy said. "She's got someone with her right now. Why don't y'all have a seat over there, and soon as she's done, I'll take you back to her."

"Okay," I said, disconcerted. I led Diesel to the chairs the deputy indicated and sat down. Diesel climbed onto the chair next to me and looked around.

If Kanesha wanted to see me right away, why was I being made to wait? Was this some little power trip on her part? Or had someone turned up to talk to her before I arrived?

I kept checking my watch as I waited. Five minutes passed. Then ten. Fifteen.

Finally, twenty-one minutes after I sat down, I looked up to see Julia Wardlaw coming out of door behind the reception area.

The deputy let her through the security gate, and she came straight to me. I stood to greet her.

"Hello, Charlie." Dark circles under her eyes told me she'd had little sleep since last night. She reached down to stroke Diesel's head.

"Are you okay? You look exhausted." Not the most gallant thing to say, but it was the truth.

"I am," Julia said. "I was up most of the night at the hospital with Ezra. They moved him to a room yesterday, and he's not doing very well at the moment."

"I'm so sorry." Such inadequate words.

"Thank you." Julia gave me a weak smile. "I'm going home for a bit now to try to get some sleep."

"Good idea," I said. "Did Kanesha call you in? She did me."

Julia nodded. "She had more questions. And I told her about going to the hotel to see Godfrey yesterday. She wasn't happy, but it's done."

"Did you tell her about seeing Jordan Thompson there?"

"I did."

"I'm sorry," I said. "I shouldn't hold you up. You need some rest."

Julia gave me a quick peck on the cheek and another tired smile. "I'll talk to you later. I want to come by to see Justin."

"Of course," I said. "Anytime."

As she turned to leave, the deputy on duty called me. I approached the desk, Diesel in tow.

"Come on back. I'll show you the way." The deputy let us through the security gate before escorting us part of the way down a corridor. "Deputy Berry's in the last room on the left, sir."

I thanked him, and Diesel and I moved on toward the room he indicated.

I paused at the open door and knocked. Kanesha Berry looked up from a computer and frowned when she spotted Diesel with me. She stood. "Come in, Mr. Harris. Please have a seat." She indicated a chair in front of her desk.

The office, about ten by ten, held two desks, bookshelves, a few chairs, and stacks of paper. Kanesha's desk appeared orderly, in contrast to the haphazard piles on her office mate's desk.

I pulled another chair next to mine for Diesel, and the cat and I sat. On the way over from the library I speculated why Kanesha had waited so long to question me when she'd had several opportunities already. This morning, of course, she had been effectively routed by her mother, because I doubted she had come to my house simply to tell me to avoid the news media.

"What can I do for you, Deputy?" I squirmed a bit in the hard chair, probably chosen for its discomfort factor. Beside me Diesel sat up and watched Kanesha, his head almost level with my own.

Kanesha seemed not to be able to take her eyes off the cat for a moment. Then she shook her head and focused on me.

"When we questioned you at the hotel, why didn't you tell us Justin Wardlaw was with you?"

I had to choose my words with care, because I didn't want to give her the impression I suspected Justin of killing Godfrey. "Justin had a pretty rough time of it yesterday. I don't know how much he might have told you about the events of the day, but I was concerned. I thought he needed a little time to get himself together before talking to anyone."

"That was very thoughtful of you." Kanesha's jaws clenched for a moment. "You were obstructing an investigation. You do realize that?"

She was definitely pissed.

"Yes, I suppose so," I said. "But I did what I did for the boy's sake. If you have to charge me with something, go right ahead."

"Believe me, I'm very tempted." She paused. "I'm not happy about it, but I've got to live with it. You, Justin, and Mrs. Wardlaw had time enough to collude on your stories by the time Bates and I got to your house last night. I'm not happy about that either, but if I find out one of you lied to me about anything—*any thing*—I will come down hard on you."

"Understood." She was angry already, so I might as well ask for an answer to something that had puzzled me since last night. "Why didn't we do this last night?"

"Because I chose not to."

In other words, I thought, *you goofed and won't admit it*. The murder rate in Athena County was very low, and Kanesha probably had little real experience investigating homicides. The last murder here—that I knew about— occurred seven or eight years ago when an outraged husband killed the man who'd been sleeping with his wife. Since he did it in plain sight of several people, there wasn't much to investigate.

Kanesha picked up a pen from the desk and put a notepad in front of her. She scribbled something. "Take me through your day yesterday, starting with Godfrey Priest's arrival in your office."

Suppressing a sigh, I complied with her request. Diesel curled up and went to sleep, and I talked for what seemed like half an hour.

Kanesha interrupted me only twice before I reached the point when I decided to go to the hotel to check on Godfrey and Justin.

"Why were you so concerned about a man you barely knew anymore? A man you said you didn't really like.

And, according to your statement, one you hadn't seen in nearly thirty years. I'm not sure I understand."

I thought for a moment. "I suppose I was really more concerned about Justin and the fact that he was still gone. He was under a considerable emotional strain yesterday, even before he found Godfrey dead. Plus, Godfrey probably never missed any opportunity for people to pay lots of attention to him. It just seemed odd somehow."

"Why are you taking such an interest in Justin? He's not your son." Kanesha leaned back in her chair, her gaze cool, as if she were eying a specimen of some kind.

"No, he's not. But he is in my care, in a way. He boards with me, and naturally I take an interest in the welfare of someone who lives under my roof. He's also the son of an old friend."

"I see" was all she said in response.

I decided to venture a question of my own. "Are you aware of how much Godfrey was disliked by people who knew him?"

A faint smile played on the deputy's lips. "I've picked up on that, yes."

"Then you must realize there were probably people who had far stronger motives to kill him than either Julia or Justin. Or me." Mindful of Azalea's plea to me this morning, I decided I had better share the gossip I had gleaned. I didn't like having to implicate someone possibly innocent of Godfrey's murder, but I had little choice if I was to help Justin.

"Such as?" She put her pen down on the desk and leaned back in her chair.

"Jordan Thompson for one. I spoke to Julia just now,

and she said she told you about seeing Jordan at the hotel yesterday when she was leaving."

"She did," Kanesha said. "But I have no proof as yet that Ms. Thompson saw the victim yesterday."

"Well, I have it," I said, trying not to sound triumphant. "A signed copy of Godfrey Priest's new book. It's dated, too. Yesterday's date."

Kanesha blinked. That interested her. She picked up her pen and jotted something down. "How did you get this signed and dated copy?"

I told her about my visit to the bookstore this morning, including the gossip from Patty Simpson about Jordan's affair with Godfrey. Kanesha scribbled more notes as I talked.

"Since Jordan saw Godfrey *after* Julia did, it seems to me she's a better suspect. And one with a pretty strong motive, perhaps."

"Possibly." Kanesha laid the pen down again. "I'll check it out, of course, but that doesn't mean anyone else is off the hook now."

"Of course," I said, refusing to be nettled by her dismissive tone.

"Any other little tidbits you want to share?" Kanesha's lip curled. "Especially since you seem to be so up on the latest dirt."

She wasn't making this easy.

With a quick mental apology to my boss I told her what I knew about Peter Vanderkeller's intense dislike of Godfrey and the cause of it.

Once again she took a few notes, but this didn't appear to impress her any more than the information about Jordan Thompson.

"I think that's all, Mr. Harris. If I have further questions, I'll be in touch."

That was a bit abrupt, I thought. "Good day, then." I stood, and Diesel jumped to the floor. Kanesha turned to her computer and started typing.

Azalea would be appalled at her daughter's lack of manners, I thought. Kanesha could have at least thanked me for coming in after her peremptory summons.

Diesel and I left her office and headed back up the corridor to the reception area. We paused at the desk for the deputy to open the security gate. I could tell Diesel wanted to explore around the desk and visit with the deputy, but I couldn't wait to get away from here.

"Come on, boy," I said, tugging lightly at the leash. "Time to go back to work."

"Bye, kitty," the deputy said. Diesel rewarded him with a few trills as we moved toward the door.

Outside I blinked a few times, adjusting to the afternoon sunshine. Kanesha's manner still rankled, but I supposed I shouldn't have expected anything different. At least I had given her two new potential suspects to consider.

Back in the car, I drove to the college library and parked in the lot behind it. Diesel and I entered the house through the back door, near the staff lounge. I was thirsty, and I figured Diesel might be also. I led him into the lounge, unoccupied at the moment. I found an oversized mug in the cupboard and filled it from the cooler. I drank it down quickly and then refilled it and set it on the floor. Diesel lapped at the water. When he was finished I would wash out the mug in the sink.

"Hello, boys. What are you two doing here this afternoon?"

I looked up to see Melba Gilley in the doorway of the lounge. She advanced with a smile, a mug in her hand.

"There's something I want to check on upstairs," I said.

After she exchanged further greetings with Diesel, Melba filled her mug with coffee and took a sip. She made a face. "This has been sitting here awhile. But it'll have to do." She sipped again. "You talking about all those boxes? What the heck are they anyway?"

"They're full of Godfrey's papers," I said. "He had them shipped last week."

"Without even waiting to see if we'd take them." Melba laughed. "Typical." She shook her head. "I never dreamed when I called you last night that he was dead. Bizarre."

"Yes, it is." Diesel was finished drinking. I took the mug to the sink and turned on the hot water. Raising my voice over the sound of the water, I continued. "The whole thing is really bizarre. Godfrey probably ticked off a lot of people, but who hated him enough to kill him?"

"The Lord only knows." Melba moved closer to the sink. "Maybe one of his ex-wives sneaked into town and did it."

I squirted a little dish soap in the mug and scrubbed it with a brush. I gave it quick rinse and set it upside down on the draining board.

As I dried my hands on a towel, I said, "That's possible, I guess, but why would one of them have waited until now to do it? I think it's somebody right here in Athena."

"You're probably right." Melba poured the remains of her coffee out and set the mug in the sink. "You think you'll find anything interesting in Godfrey's papers?"

"I might. I'm sure they'll be interesting," I said.

"Maybe there's a clue to his murder."

Before I replied, we both heard a floorboard squeak out in the hall.

Melba and I exchanged glances.

I waited a moment to see if whoever was in the hallway entered the room. No one did.

I took a step toward the door. "Who's there?"

There was no answer.

EIGHTEEN

|||||||||||||||||||||||||||||||||||||||||||||||||||

The floorboard creaked again, and then we heard the
sound of footsteps in rapid retreat.

I strode over to the door, about six feet away, but whoever was listening to our conversation had disappeared. I
walked down the hall and around by the stairs, but I still
didn't see anyone. Nor did I hear anything other than the
muted sound of street traffic.

Melba and Diesel had followed me out of the staff
lounge.

"That was peculiar." Melba frowned. "And kind of
creepy."

"It was definitely odd."

"I'm going back to my office and keep an eye on the
door." Melba stepped past me, smiling uneasily. "Don't
turn your back on anyone."

I picked up Diesel's leash. "Don't worry. I won't."

I waited until Melba disappeared into the director's office suite. "Come on, boy. Let's go upstairs."

Before I unlocked the door of the archive office, I checked inside the storeroom. Nothing seemed to have been disturbed. I shut the door and examined the lock. It looked sturdy enough, like the one on the office door.

The eleven boxes in the office hadn't been touched, as far as I could tell. Diesel started sniffing around them again, and I had to push him gently away in order to uncover the unnumbered box. When I pulled it free, I restacked the three cartons that had been on top of it before picking it up and setting it on my desk.

Diesel hopped on top of the middle tier of boxes and watched while I cut open the box. After I pulled out the wads of paper used for packing material, I found several smaller boxes and trays of computer disks and even a couple of thumb drives. The disks probably contained the texts of Godfrey's books and perhaps some of his correspondence.

I wondered why the box hadn't been numbered. Perhaps this box hadn't been intended for inclusion in Godfrey's archive.

The master inventory in box number one ought to answer that question. I moved around my desk to check. The box I wanted was underneath the one Diesel was sitting on. I moved him aside to the sound of annoyed chirping.

I extracted box one and set in on the floor. I retrieved my scissors from the desk and cut open the box. Right on top, under more packing material, lay a small report folder labeled "Inventory."

Back at my desk, folder in hand, I sat down and began

skimming through it while Diesel played with the discarded packing material on the floor.

Calling these few sheets of paper a master inventory was a gross overstatement. Each box was listed, but there was little detail of the contents. Godfrey's assistant had merely listed categories, like fan letters, business letters, reviews, awards, newspaper clippings, contracts, review copies, books in English, books in other languages, convention programs, and speeches. Nowhere in the inventory did the words *disk* or *diskette* appear.

It seemed fairly clear to me the box of disks had been shipped by mistake. Otherwise it would have been numbered and included on the inventory. The number of boxes in the inventory matched the quantity of numbered boxes received.

What should I do with it? Send it back to Ms. Enderby in California?

I found the two letters on my desk and scanned the one from Gail Enderby. There was a phone number included. I might as well call her and ask.

I used my cell phone, rather than the office phone, because I could never remember the long distance dialing code I was supposed to enter to authorize a call.

The call went to voice mail after five rings. A perky, young-sounding voice informed me that Gail Enderby was on vacation, and her stated return date was a couple of weeks away. She gave no alternate contact information. I wondered if she had seen the news yet about her boss's death. I left a message, asking her to call.

That was that. The disks were in my custody for now. I replaced the packing material and re-taped the box. Instead of putting the box back with the others, I put it behind some shelves a few feet away from my desk. Perhaps the mysterious eavesdropper had spooked me, but the disks might be valuable. As long as I was the only one who knew they were here, I might as well keep it that way.

I picked up box one and placed it on my desk. Consulting the inventory list, I saw that this box contained fan mail. Curious, I pulled out one of the folders, dated twenty years ago, and began leafing through it.

The first couple of letters were full of praise for Godfrey.

"*Trapped* kept me up until three in the morning," one fan wrote.

Another one said, "I had to get up and check all the locks in the house when I finished *Midnight Killer.*"

On most of the letters I examined there were notes that indicated when Godfrey responded, though copies of Godfrey's answering letters were not in the folder.

The most interesting letter of those I read was one that took Godfrey to task for abandoning the gentler, more traditional mysteries he wrote at the beginning of his career in favor of "bloodthirsty, needlessly violent trash." Godfrey's note on this one was a terse "no response."

I laid the folder aside and was about to pick up another one when my office phone rang.

"Good, you're still here," Melba said when I answered. "Peter wants to see you right away. I told him about the boxes."

"I'll be right down." Sighing, I hung up. I wasn't in the mood for a talk with Peter, but then I realized it was a good opportunity to do a bit of sleuthing.

I picked up the letters that came with the boxes and called to Diesel. "Come on, boy. Let's go."

I paused long enough to lock the office door behind me before following Diesel down the stairs. I found him in Melba's office on top of her desk.

"It's okay," Melba said, flashing me a guilty look. "I let him get up there."

"I guess there's no point in arguing. You'll keep an eye on him while I talk to Peter?"

"Of course." Melba rubbed the cat's head. "You go right on in."

I knocked on Peter's door and then opened it.

"Ah, Charles," he said, rising from his chair. "Do come in."

I took a seat, and Peter resumed his.

"Melba tells me that you have received a shipment of the late Mr. Priest's archival material." Peter tented his fingers together and regarded me owlishly.

"Yes, the boxes arrived today." I leaned forward and handed him the two letters. "It's all very well organized, so he must have been planning this for some time."

Peter read through the letters quickly. He laid them on his desk. "No doubt. Given the colossal ego that man possessed, he would have assumed the college would accept his papers without demur." He sniffed.

"I agree," I said. "But he certainly had no idea he was going to die so soon, and in such a brutal fashion."

"One cannot pretend to feel sorrow for such an unmitigated bastard, despite the distasteful manner of his death. The drivel he wrote will sell even better now, though he won't be able to reap the benefits." Peter smiled with grim satisfaction.

I never suspected our library director possessed such

a deep streak of vindictiveness. He really had hated Godfrey.

"His sales will jump, for a while at least," I said. "You're probably right about that. But I wonder who *will* benefit." Oddly enough, this was the first time I had stopped to think about the matter. Who would inherit Godfrey's wealth? Justin?

"One can only hope he made suitable provision in his will to enable the college to house and process his collection of papers. Otherwise they will have to remain as they are." Peter lifted his chin in a determined manner as he regarded me. "I trust we are in agreement on that point."

"Certainly," I said. I had more than enough to do as a part-time employee. I would far rather catalog rare books than process Godfrey's papers, despite my curiosity.

"Excellent." Peter beamed at me.

"Barring some provision in Godfrey's will, do you think that letter is sufficient for the college's ownership of the collection?"

"I should think so," Peter said. He picked up the letter and read it again. "He states his intentions perfectly clearly, though it is a great pity he did not mention any pecuniary bequest to accompany it."

"All this is going to generate a lot of publicity for the college and for the town," I said.

"Sadly, I fear you are correct." Peter frowned, his distaste evident. "Why the man had to come here to get himself murdered, I simply do not understand."

Peter colored faintly, perhaps having realized the fatuousness of that remark. I decided to ignore it.

"The whole thing is very odd," I said. "There are a lot

of things I'm curious about. For one thing, that call God-frey made to say he was too ill to attend the dinner in his honor last night. It seems a little too pat."

Peter didn't respond. He just stared at me.

"I wonder if it was Godfrey who really called?"

"Why shouldn't it be?" Peter said, his fingers tapping on his desk.

I shrugged. "Just a thought. When Melba called me, she said Godfrey had called the president's office to in-form him. Then I guess someone from his office must have called you."

Peter's fingers ceased their rhythmless tattoo on his desk. "Actually, that is not quite accurate."

"Why not?"

"Melba, I'm afraid, somehow misunderstood." Peter paused for moment. "She quite often does because she fails to listen properly, and I have spoken to her severely on the subject several times."

I waited, and after a moment he continued.

"You see, I was the one who spoke to Godfrey and who in turn informed the president's office, at his request."

NINETEEN

||||||||||||||||||||||||||||||||||||||||||||||||||

That was definitely odd. Why would Godfrey call someone in the library, rather than the president's office?

"When I spoke to him," Peter continued, "he complained of a rather nasty stomach virus. He regretted the
inconvenience—or used words to that effect—and asked
me to pass along the word. As I did." His fingers resumed
their tattoo upon the desk.

"Out of curiosity," I said in a diffident tone, "do you
remember what time that was?"

"Around five-thirty, I suppose," Peter said after a moment's thought.

"Has anyone from the sheriff's department spoken
with you yet?"

"Whatever for?" Peter paled slightly. "One would not
wish to be involved in something so sordid as a murder
investigation."

"No, one wouldn't," I said, a wry twist to my voice. "But unfortunately one already is." I was beginning to lose patience with the man. He was being overly fastidious, in my opinion. "You might have been the last person—barring the killer, of course—to speak to Godfrey. The deputy in charge of the investigation needs to know that."

"I see." Peter reached for a glass of water on the credenza behind his desk and took a long swallow. He set the glass down with a hand that trembled. "Then one must do one's duty."

He was still pale, obviously unsettled, but apparently willing to follow through. I dictated the number of the sheriff's department and told him to ask for Deputy Berry. He laid the pen aside and said he would call.

"Very well," I said. "Shall I leave these letters with you?" I pointed to his desk as I stood.

"Yes, for now. I shall have Melba make copies of them for you. One imagines that the college's legal counsel will want to keep the originals."

"Of course. Well, if that's all, I'll get back to work," I said.

Peter nodded, and I turned for the door.

"Oh dear, I almost forgot."

I turned back. "Yes, Peter?"

He made a moue of distaste. "I received a call from the president's office, shortly before you came, informing me that there is to be a memorial service for Godfrey this Saturday afternoon at two in the college chapel. I suppose I shall have to attend, though one could easily think of far more pleasant things to do on a Saturday." He sighed.

"It would be the proper thing to do," I said. "I'll have to attend, too."

Peter didn't reply. I don't think he heard me, because he had turned to look out the window behind his desk.

I left his office, shutting the door gently behind me. He was an odd duck, no two ways about it.

Diesel still sat on Melba's desk, watching her as she worked at her computer. The keys clicked at a rapid pace, and the cat appeared mesmerized by Melba's flying fingers.

"Sorry to interrupt," I said. "Come on, Diesel, back upstairs."

Melba ceased typing and turned to smile at me. "See you later, then, boys." She gave the cat an affectionate scratch on his head. Diesel purred his thanks.

"Come on now," I said, and Diesel leaped gracefully to the floor. He followed me to the stairs and dashed up them as soon as I placed my foot on the first step.

Back in the office, Diesel began to play with the loose packing material, batting it around and then leaping on top of it. I watched him for a moment. He was still very kittenish, despite his size.

As I sat down at my desk, I noticed the message light blinking on the phone. I listened to a message from circulation at Hawksworth Library next door informing me that a book I'd requested was available.

I checked my watch—it was nearly five o'clock now. Time to head home. I could delve more into Godfrey's papers tomorrow. Before we left, though, I repacked the open box on my desk, taking away Diesel's toy. "You can play with it again tomorrow."

He turned and sat with his back to me until I headed for the door. I attached the leash to his harness, locked the door behind us, and set off down the stairs and out the back door. I wanted to pick up the book, but first I had to put Diesel in the car. Hawksworth was one of the few places I couldn't take him. A couple of staff members had complained that his presence was too disruptive, because invariably students clustered around him, wanting to pet him. They made too much noise, according to the complainants.

So, into the car Diesel went. The day was cool, and I cracked the front windows enough to allow air to circulate—but not enough for a large and enterprising cat to squeeze through.

"I'll be back in five minutes," I told him, but I could tell he wasn't happy at being left behind. He never was.

Inside the library, I went straight to the circulation desk. While I waited for the student worker to find my book, a recent study of the late antiquity and the early Middle Ages, I listened idly to a conversation at the nearby reference desk. Willie Clark was on duty and being his usual charming self while helping a female student.

"No, we haven't received that issue yet. Can't you read the screen? Do you see any mention of volume thirty-three, issue ten?"

I watched as Willie tapped the computer screen in front of him while the student, red-faced, mumbled something.

"Then you'd better go back and check your citation again. You probably wrote it down wrong." The disgust in his voice was obvious.

Head down, the student scurried away. She was probably a freshman. Older female students learned to avoid the reference desk when Willie sat behind it. He could be gruff with male students as well, but his voice had a particular edge to it whenever he talked to a woman.

Not surprising, then, that he had never married. He wasn't gay either, as far as I knew. Too crabby, in my experience, for a partner of either sex to put up with long enough to establish a relationship.

Willie caught me looking at him, my expression no doubt critical. He scowled at me and turned away.

Book in hand, I left the library and went back to my car. Diesel complained nonstop to me on the short drive home, and I scratched his head a couple of times in apology for having abandoned him in the car.

The moment I opened the kitchen door appetizing smells tickled my nostrils. Diesel sniffed appreciatively too, though he was bound to be disappointed. I tried not to feed him from the table, though he often sat nearby and stared hard, as if hoping to bend me to his will.

I glanced at the clock after I released Diesel from his harness. It was a little after five, and Azalea had left for the day. There was a pot of green beans on the stove, and when I peeked in the still-warm oven I found a chicken, mushroom, and brown rice casserole. There was a tossed salad in the fridge as well and, as usual, Azalea had prepared enough food for at least four people.

I checked Diesel's bowls, and Azalea had taken care of them already. She might fuss at him sometimes, but she wasn't about to let anyone in the house go hungry. Diesel examined them before loping off to the utility room.

The doorbell rang. I hoped it wasn't Kanesha Berry, dropping by with more questions.

Julia Wardlaw stood on my doorstep, looking wan and tired.

"I apologize for dropping by like this without calling first," she said as I stepped aside for her to enter. "But I wanted to see Justin before I went home."

"You're always welcome here, Julia," I said. "You have an open invitation to visit whenever you like." I shut the door and examined her with concern.

"Thank you," she said.

"How are you? And how is Ezra?"

"I'm tired, but Ezra's doing better, thank the Lord. They're keeping him one more night, and he should be able to come home tomorrow."

"That's good," I said. "Why don't you come on in the kitchen and sit down. Let me get you something to drink, and I'll go get Justin for you, if he's here. I just got home myself, and I haven't seen him yet."

"I'd appreciate that," Julia said as she followed me. "Right now I don't feel up to climbing those stairs, I have to say."

Diesel came to greet our visitor, and Julia petted and talked to him while I poured her a glass of the sweet tea Azalea had made.

As I climbed the stairs I thought, not for the first time, about having an intercom system installed. But then I reflected that I could always use the exercise.

Puffing slightly by the time I reached Justin's door, I knocked.

"Come in."

I opened the door and took a step inside. Justin sat at his desk, working at his computer. He tapped the keys a moment longer before he turned to greet me. "Hello, sir."

"Hello," I said. "Your mother is downstairs. She'd like to talk to you."

"Thank you," he said. "I'll be right down. I need to do one more thing to this"—he indicated the computer with a quick nod—"but that won't take two minutes."

"Fine," I said. "I'll tell her." I backed out and shut the door. Justin seemed a bit more animated today. All day yesterday he had appeared depressed, occasionally almost catatonic in his lack of response. A good night's rest had helped, I supposed, along with a little distance from the events of yesterday.

Julia had finished her tea by the time I got back to the kitchen, and I offered her more after I relayed Justin's message. She declined.

"You're welcome to visit with Justin in here," I said, "but you might be more comfortable in the living room."

"This is fine," Julia said. "As long as you don't mind. This is such a lovely, comforting room."

I glanced around it with affection. Yes, it was comforting. When Aunt Dottie was alive, it was usually the center of the house, the room where she spent so much of her time. I liked to think her warmth and generosity lingered here.

"It is that," I said. "Why don't you stay and have dinner with me, you and Justin both? Azalea left more than enough for the three of us, and I can guarantee it will be delicious. That woman is a wonderful cook."

Julia smiled. "I really shouldn't impose on you after all you've done already. But I can't face the thought of going home to cook for myself. Thank you. I'd love to have dinner with you."

"Hi, Mama." Justin came clattering into the kitchen. Yes, he was definitely more animated tonight. He bent to kiss his mother on the cheek. She touched his head as he did so, and he didn't move for a moment.

"If you'll excuse me, I'll just run upstairs for a few minutes," I said. "Then if you're both ready to eat, we'll have dinner."

Julia smiled her thanks, and as I headed for the stairs I heard her relaying my invitation to her son.

I dawdled in my bedroom, wanting to give Julia and Justin enough time to talk. I wondered whether Julia was going to tell her son about Ezra's health problems. She ought to do it soon. Postponing it wouldn't be doing Justin any favors in the long run.

Diesel did not appear, and I figured he was downstairs with Justin. He was really fond of the boy, and Justin certainly seemed attached to the cat. Diesel always seemed to have the ability to sense when someone needed comfort, and right now Justin did. If Diesel could help Justin through the difficult times ahead, I was delighted and very thankful that such a special four-legged friend had come into my life.

Almost half an hour passed by the time I went back downstairs. Julia and Justin were quiet when I entered the kitchen. It looked as though Justin had been crying, but now he appeared calm. Diesel jumped down from the boy's lap and came to greet me.

"I told Justin about his father," Julia said simply.

I nodded. "I can't tell you both how sorry I am." I reached down to rub the cat's head.

"Thank you," mother and son said in unison.

Julia stood. "If you'll excuse me a moment, I'd like to freshen up a bit. Justin, why don't you help Charlie set the table?"

"Yes, Mama," Justin said. He got up from the table and went to the cabinet. Diesel padded after him.

I started to point Julia toward the downstairs bathroom, but she waved me away with a smile. "No need for directions."

Justin brought three plates out and set them on the table, Diesel matching him step for step. "Thank you for inviting my mother to dinner."

"You're both very welcome," I said. "If you'll finish setting the table, I'll get the food there."

Justin nodded and worked in silence for a moment. As I was putting on oven mitts, he spoke again.

"Um, sir, I guess there's something I need to tell you." He stood, utensils in hand, his head slightly down. He appeared embarrassed. Diesel rubbed himself against the boy's legs, but Justin didn't seem to notice.

"What's that?" I asked as I reached into the oven for the casserole dish. I thought it might be easier for him to talk if I wasn't looking at him.

"It's about what I told you yesterday," Justin said. "About my dad—Ezra—hitting me."

I set the casserole dish on top of the stove, realizing I needed to put a trivet on the table first.

"Go on," I said, my voice neutral.

"I guess I kind of lied about it," Justin said. His face colored. "Yesterday was the only time he ever hit me like that."

"Why did you lie about it, then?"

Justin shrugged. "He was being so weird about the whole thing, about Godfrey Priest being my dad, too. He kind of freaked out, maybe, and I guess I wanted to get back at him by making him sound bad."

"I can understand that," I said. "What he did yesterday is inexcusable. He never should have struck you like that."

"No, sir." Justin began to lay the utensils at each place.

"I can't blame you for being angry with him. No one could. But I'm glad to know that yesterday was the only time something like that happened."

"Yes, sir." Justin smiled briefly. "And he promised me at the hospital that he'd never ever hit me again, no matter what." His face crumpled. "And now he's going to die, too." Diesel rubbed against his legs again.

Julia came back in time to hear that last sentence, and she gathered her son into her arms. Diesel moved away from them but sat nearby, watching. Justin wept for a moment, and Julia regarded me with a question in her eyes.

"Justin told me he lied to me about Ezra beating him," I said, my voice soft.

"Good," Julia said. "I told him he had to."

Justin pulled away from his mother. "I'm sorry, Mama."

"I know, sweetie." Julia patted his cheek. "Why don't you go wash your face and blow your nose?"

Justin nodded and headed for the bathroom in the hall. Diesel went with him.

"He really is a good boy most of the time," Julia said when Justin was out of earshot.

"I know," I said with a smile. "Diesel wouldn't be so fond of him if he weren't."

Julia laughed. "That cat is such a little character."

I politely refused Julia's offer of help, and by the time Justin returned to the kitchen everything was ready.

We all sat, Julia to one side and Justin across from me. I asked Justin to say grace.

He bent his head over his plate. "Bless this food, oh Lord, to the nourishment of our bodies. We thank you for our many gifts, and we pray that you will watch over us and over the loved ones who are not with us. Amen."

Julia and I echoed his *amen*. I held my hand out for Julia's plate and filled it with casserole and green beans while Julia filled her bowl with salad.

For a few minutes we were busy preparing our plates and bowls of salad, passing things back and forth. Diesel sat near my chair, watching every movement of my hands with great interest. When no tidbits were forthcoming, he moved to the other end of the table to try his luck with Justin.

By unspoken agreement, it seemed, we spoke of things other than the events of the day before. Julia asked Justin about his classes, and he expressed enthusiasm for his freshman English and history courses. He was not so fond of the science and math classes, however.

I talked a bit about my work cataloging rare books, and Julia listened to each of us in turn. Occasionally she prompted with a question, but for the most part she appeared content to let the males at the table carry the burden of conversation. I turned a blind eye to the occasional morsel of chicken or green bean that Justin so casually slipped from his plate.

An hour passed pleasantly, and I realized how much I missed having dinner with other people. I wished Sean and Laura, my children, weren't so far away. But most of all, of course, I wished Jackie and Aunt Dottie could sit at the table with us, too.

Even Azalea's chocolate turtle cheesecake couldn't tempt Julia to stay for dessert. She looked much better now than when she had first arrived, but she was still tired and ready to go home for some rest.

I waved away any offers to help clear the table and set to work while Justin saw his mother out.

He stepped into the kitchen long enough to thank me again, and Diesel followed him upstairs when he said he had to get back to studying.

I took my time in the kitchen, doing my best to keep my mind off Godfrey's death and Ezra's terminal illness. It all seemed too much somehow, and I needed a mental break.

Finished at last, I turned off the lights downstairs and headed up to my bedroom.

After brushing my teeth and changing into my pajamas, I climbed into bed. Diesel was absent, no doubt still with Justin. He would appear eventually to claim his share—and more—of my bed.

I reached for Godfrey's book and got comfortable. I read twenty pages or so before putting the book aside. The heroine wasn't a particularly likable person, and I remembered that was another aspect of Godfrey's books that had always bothered me. There was a strain of misogyny in the books that made me uncomfortable. For all the women Godfrey had apparently married and romanced, he didn't seem to like women very much.

Still not ready to turn off the light and go to sleep, I retrieved my library book. Reading nonfiction would be a good way to cleanse my palate, I decided.

At some point I must have nodded off, book on my

chest, because when Diesel jumped on the bed, I came to with a jerk. The book slid off me, and I yawned. While Diesel made himself comfortable, I put the book on the nightstand, turned off the light, and settled down to sleep.

TWENTY

‖‖

The next morning, as I unlocked the door to the archive office a little after eight, I thought about Godfrey Priest. Only two days ago he walked in here, very much the Godfrey I knew in my youth, self-involved and full of life, and less than twelve hours later he was dead. I never liked him, but he didn't deserve to be murdered.

Diesel couldn't wait to investigate those intriguing boxes, and he sniffed around them while I got comfortable in my chair and turned on the computer.

I heard a small sound, as if something had fallen onto the floor, and looked up. Diesel, from the top of one tier of boxes, chirped at me and began grooming himself. What had he knocked over?

On the floor in front of the boxes I found the folder containing the inventory of Godfrey's papers. As I bent down to pick it up, I frowned. What was it doing on top of the boxes? I was sure I had left it on my desk yesterday.

If it had been on my desk, Diesel couldn't have knocked it off onto the floor in front of the boxes, I reasoned. He was a clever feline, but even he could not have picked it up off my desk and then dropped it onto the floor.

The more I thought about it, the more convinced I was that the inventory had been on my desk when I left the office yesterday.

That meant someone had been in here meddling last night or early this morning.

I went back to my chair and placed the inventory on the desk. I examined it, and it was intact, no pages missing.

Who could it have been?

Had the intruder tampered with the boxes? That was an unpleasant thought. If the intruder had taken anything, I would never know, because the inventory wasn't detailed enough.

I got up and examined the boxes. They appeared to be intact. I went down the hall to check the boxes in the storeroom. They also seemed to be undisturbed. I also checked the locks on both doors, and from what I could see, no one had forced them.

Back at my desk, I considered the problem. As far as I knew there were only three sets of keys to the office and the storeroom. I had one set, Melba had one, and the operations staff had the third.

I couldn't imagine Melba or any operations staff member coming in here after I was gone to poke around. I should check with Melba, though, to make sure she still had her set of keys.

And what about the extra box?

I was relieved to find it where I had left it, untouched as far as I could tell. It was a good thing I put it out of the way, I thought. I went back to my desk.

How many people even knew that Godfrey's papers had arrived here? Rick Tackett or some of his staff could have mentioned it to someone, but I couldn't see that it would be that exciting a bit of conversation. Peter knew, naturally, and so did Melba.

Then I remembered the odd incident yesterday, when someone had eavesdropped on my conversation with Melba—a conversation about Godfrey's papers.

Was that who had done it?

If so, that put a different spin on the incident.

Someone was interested in Godfrey's papers but didn't want anyone else to know.

Why?

Was it a deranged fan seeking mementoes of a dead idol?

Or was it simply someone sly and secretive who liked to poke around in things?

Even if it turned out to be someone harmless, I didn't want anyone entering the archive without supervision.

"Come on, Diesel. Let's go see Melba." Time to check on the status of her keys.

I locked the office door behind us. In the past I hadn't done it while I was in the building, but perhaps I needed to change that.

Melba was on the phone when Diesel and I walked into her office. She smiled and held up a finger, by which I understood the call was almost done.

"Sure thing, hon," Melba said. "I'll let Peter know." She hung up the phone. "Geneva Watterson. Sick again, poor thing."

Geneva was one of the reference librarians, and she seemed to have a lot of health problems. I had pinch-hit for her a couple of times when the reference department was short-staffed. I made commiserating noises, but at the moment I had other things on my mind.

"What's up with you two?" Melba smiled as Diesel hopped up on her desk.

I shook my head at the cat, but he ignored me. I sat down in the chair by Melba's desk. "I think someone was poking around in the archive without my permission."

"What?" Melba's eyes nearly bugged out of her head. "That's outrageous. Did they make a mess?"

I explained my reasoning, and Melba nodded. "I know how you like things a certain way, and if you say you left that inventory on your desk, then that's where you left it."

"Thanks," I said with a grin. "Whoever it was got in with a key. There's no sign of forced entry. I have my keys. Where is your set?"

"Right here in this drawer," Melba said promptly. She pulled the drawer open. "I keep them in this tray."

I leaned forward to look, and Melba hissed in annoyance. "If that don't beat all. Someone got in my desk and took those keys."

"Do you lock your desk at night?"

"I sure do." Melba's tone dared me to argue with her.

"What about during the day, if you leave your desk for a few minutes? Or for lunch, say?"

"When I go to lunch, I lock it," Melba said. "But if I'm just going to run to the bathroom or to the lounge for coffee, I don't usually take the time."

"What about the keys to get into your office after hours? Could someone do that?" I was trying to think of all the possibilities.

Melba nodded. "All the department heads have a key to this office, in case of emergency. So one of them could have got into my office last night, I guess."

"That's one possibility," I said. "But it's also possible the intruder saw you were away from your desk, found the keys, and took them. The other question is, who would know you had the keys and where they were?"

Melba thought about that for a moment. "People are always dropping by to chat," she said slowly. "This drawer gets opened a lot, because it's where I keep aspirin and antacids and stuff like that. People come by all the time asking for things because they know I keep them on hand."

"Then anyone could have seen the keys in the drawer," I said. "But how would they know what they're for?"

"Because I had a tag attached to them that said 'Archive,'" Melba said, sighing. "Labeled on both sides, of course."

"You *always* lock your desk at night?" I wanted to be sure.

"Yes, of course I do."

"And the lock hasn't been tampered with?"

"No, it hasn't, or I would have noticed this morning." Melba was getting a bit testy with this drawn-out interrogation.

"Sorry, just trying to get the facts straight." I smiled, and she relaxed. "Various people have access to this office after hours, but your desk is kept locked. That rules out someone coming in after hours to get the keys."

"Sounds reasonable to me," Melba said.

Diesel, apparently annoyed by the lack of attention, reached out and prodded Melba's arm with his paw. She smiled as she rubbed his head.

"Therefore the intruder must have swiped the keys while you were away from your desk late yesterday afternoon."

"The boxes weren't in there until around two, and at that point very few people even knew they were there." I frowned. "Either the intruder saw the boxes being moved over here from the loading dock at Hawksworth and asked Rick and his guys about them, or else it was probably the eavesdropper. Remember?"

Melba shivered. "That was creepy."

"There could be some other explanation, but that's all I can think of at the moment."

"You need to tell Peter about this," Melba said.

"I know. I think we also need to get the locks changed right away. You think he'll go for that?" With Peter, one never knew.

"I don't see why not," Melba said. "He's due at a meeting at nine-thirty, but he should have time to talk to you now. He got here a few minutes before you and Diesel." She buzzed his office.

When Peter answered, Melba told him I needed to talk to him about something urgent. She listened for a moment. "Go on in," she said, hanging up the phone. "I'll keep an eye on Diesel."

"Thanks," I said. I got up, a bit reluctantly. I did not relish repeating all this to Peter, because he could be amazingly obsessive sometimes about the tiniest details. I might be in for an extended inquisition.

I opened the door and stepped into Peter's office. "Good morning, Peter," I said.

Peter looked up from his desk. "Good morning, Charles. I am most pleased to see you. There is something I feel I should discuss with you. I value your judgment, and I know you will offer sage advice."

He seemed to have forgotten that I wanted to talk to him, but I knew there was no point in trying to divert his attention.

Suppressing a sigh, I sat down. "Tell me about it, and I'll do my best."

Peter stared at me, as if suddenly mute. As I watched him, beginning to grow concerned, his face reddened. Was he having some kind of attack?

"Peter, what's the matter? Do you need a doctor?" I rose from my chair, ready to yell for Melba.

He waved a hand, indicating that I should sit down. "There is no need," he said, his voice low. "I am simply embarrassed by what I have to tell you in order to solicit your counsel."

"There's no need to feel embarrassed," I said. "I won't betray your confidence, I assure you."

"Thank you," Peter said. "I know you are a man of honor." He sighed. "And that is the crux of the matter. I fear that I have acted in a dishonorable manner."

"How so?" I did my best to maintain a patient tone, but Peter could be maddeningly slow getting to the point.

"I refer to the matter of the phone call which we discussed yesterday," Peter said.

"You mean the call from Godfrey? About his feeling too ill to attend the dinner in his honor?"

"Yes, that is correct." Peter drew a deep breath. "I lied to you, Charles. There was no phone call."

TWENTY-ONE

||||||||||||||||||||||||||||||||||||||||||||||||||||||||||||||||||||||

"No phone call?" I stared at Peter in disbelief. "Were you playing some kind of joke on Godfrey?"

"Would that were all it was," Peter said, his face reflecting his pompous tone. "The message from Godfrey Priest was real enough. The method of delivery was quite different, I regret to say."

Peter's conversational style was giving me a headache. I yearned to grab him and shake him a few times, maybe knock loose some of the extra words so he would get to the point sooner.

"Then tell me how and when you talked to Godfrey." That came out far calmer than I expected.

Peter grimaced. "I yielded to a base impulse. I have just cause to despise the man, though perhaps you are unaware of said cause." He paused for a moment.

I didn't want to tell him I already knew about his wife,

in case he asked me for the source of my information. Melba wouldn't thank me for snitching on her.

When I failed to respond, Peter continued. "Before I came to Athena College to assume the position as director of the library, I lived for many years in California. In Los Angeles, to be exact. I was also married then, and my former wife had personal ambitions centered upon writing for the cinema."

I decided to speed things up a bit. "And somehow she must have met Godfrey and hoped to use his connections to break into screenwriting."

"Yes, that is more or less what happened," Peter said with a pained look. "Not content, however, simply to approach that detestable man for assistance and befriend him, my former spouse decided the only way to achieve her goal was to marry the man. After divorcing me first, naturally."

"I see. One couldn't blame you for not liking Godfrey," I said, "though your ex-wife certainly bears a lot of the blame."

"Oh, most definitely, the balance of the opprobrium lies with her," Peter said. "But one cannot exculpate Priest. He encouraged her and, after all, he did marry her once our divorce was final." He snickered. "The marriage lasted little more than two years, I believe."

Time to steer the conversation back onto the right track. "We've established your reasons for despising Godfrey," I said. "Now what about your talking to him and getting the message that he was too ill to attend the dinner?"

"Ah yes," Peter said with a frown. "As I have mentioned already, I yielded to impulse and decided to confront the man. Having no wish to make an ass of myself in front of anyone else, I decided that the best place for such an affray was his hotel. There, one assumed, one could be assured of some privacy."

"You went to Farrington House to talk to Godfrey," I said, holding on to my patience because he was actually approaching the point. "What time was that?"

Peter considered for a moment, his head cocked to one side. "Around five-thirty," he said. "Yes, I waited until I was through with my day here, which is generally around five or five-fifteen. Then I proceeded directly to the hotel."

"How did you know where he was staying?"

"I was privy to the arrangements," Peter said. "The president's office consulted me, perhaps because the man was a writer. Had he been an alumnus of the athletic type, they no doubt would have consulted the athletic director."

"And you knew what room he was in?" Things couldn't have been more convenient for Peter, I thought. And surely Peter realized that his having gone to the hotel put him high on the list of suspects.

But with Peter one never knew what tortuous path his thought processes might take.

"Yes, I did," Peter said. "That was indeed fortunate, because had I stopped at the front desk and asked them to ring and announce me, the man might well have refused to see me. Thus I decided the better plan of attack would be to knock on his door and gain admittance before he realized who I was."

I had a sudden vision of Kanesha Berry questioning Peter. How would she handle his inability to get right to the point? She might arrest him out of sheer irritation.

"So you went up to his suite and knocked on the door?"

"Yes, I did." Peter frowned. "But things did not proceed thenceforth in the way I had postulated. Godfrey did not open the door. I was forced to raise my voice slightly and entreat him to let me in. He refused."

"Did he give a reason?" If Godfrey hadn't wanted to talk to anyone, why did he bother answering?

But at least I knew he had been alive at five-thirty if he had talked to Peter.

"He explained that he felt quite ill and that he feared it was some kind of stomach virus. He had no desire to inflict it upon anyone in case it was infectious. He intended to stay in his room until he recovered."

"That was kind of him," I said. But odd, I thought. The bug must have had a quick onset, because he had appeared perfectly fine when I had last seen him at my house.

"Perhaps. I inquired of him whether he had informed the president's office of his illness, and he said he had not. He then asked if I would be so good as to do it for him. Then he excused himself, saying he had to rush back to the bathroom. Seeing no point in remaining there any longer, I went back to my car and used my cell phone to call the president's office. I also called Melba and asked her to inform others on the library staff who were planning to attend, as one presumes she informed you."

"She did," I said. "You need to talk to the deputy in charge of the investigation even more urgently now. This will help narrow down the time of death."

"I suppose so," Peter said, obviously unhappy about the idea. "One has so little desire to embroil oneself in such a sordid happening."

"I quite understand," I said. "But still, one must do one's duty." I stood.

"Thank you for your forbearance, Charles," Peter said. "I appreciate you hearing me out."

"Not a problem," I said. "I'll talk to you later."

I opened the door, ready to leave, when an unsettling thought struck me. Why hadn't it occurred to me sooner? I turned and walked back to the chair and sat down again.

"What is it?" Peter asked.

"During the time when your ex-wife was pursuing Godfrey," I said, "did you ever meet him?"

"Yes, a few times at parties," Peter said. "Though I must say I quite often tried to avoid the man, finding him hideously conceited, with only one subject of conversation—himself."

"How long ago was that?"

"Seven years ago," Peter said. "Why do you ask?"

"When Godfrey spoke to you through the door at the hotel, did you recognize his voice?"

"What a peculiar question," Peter said, clearly taken aback. "One simply assumed that one was talking to him because it was his room." He paused. "I cannot be absolutely certain that it was indeed Godfrey I conversed with, given the circumstances. There is the additional fact that the man claimed to be ill, and I did detect what I thought was a note of strain in his voice."

"But you can't swear that it was actually Godfrey on the other side of the door?"

Justin hadn't said anything about Godfrey's feeling ill, and surely he would have noticed. It wouldn't have been easy for Godfrey to conceal a stomach bug of some kind from his son if he had to rush off to the bathroom periodically.

"No, I cannot," Peter said. "But if it was not Godfrey with whom I spoke, then who was it?"

"It might have been the murderer," I said.

Peter turned so white I thought he was going to faint. I started to get up to attend to him, but he rallied enough to say, "No, thank you, I'm all right. Just a bit of a shock, you know."

"Yes, I know," I said. "It's a shock to me, too. But the more I think about it, the more inclined I am to believe that Godfrey was already dead when you went to the hotel." I kept my eye on him. If he was the murderer, he was putting on quite an act to convince me otherwise. I couldn't see him as a killer unless he were talking someone to death.

The problem was, I couldn't see anyone—at the moment—as a killer, but someone had murdered Godfrey.

"I must say, that is quite an unsettling notion." Peter was slowly regaining some color—not that he had much to begin with, poor man. "To have been that close to the perpetrator of such a vicious act—well, the mind frankly boggles, as I am certain you can understand."

"I can," I said. "Now you have to tell the deputy about what you did. She'll probably draw the same conclusion." Or at least, she should, I amended silently. Kanesha might be a pain in the neck sometimes, but she was bright.

"Yes, I will," Peter said.

"Good. I'll leave you then," I said, and once again I made it to the door. But the memory of why I had come down to see Peter surfaced, and I turned back.

"I forgot something," I said as I walked back toward the desk. "We need to get the locks on the archive office and the storeroom changed right away."

"What?" Peter looked alarmed. "What has happened?"

I explained tersely. Peter shook his head. "I shall certainly speak to Rick Tackett immediately," he said. "This is a serious breach of our security. I wonder whether I should discuss this with the head of the campus police."

"I don't think that's necessary just yet," I said. "Getting the locks changed today, if at all possible, is the most important thing."

"I shall see to it." Peter sighed. "So many phone calls to make." He brightened. "I shall have Melba make the necessary contact with Rick, however."

"That's probably not a bad idea," I said. I knew Melba could probably get results from Rick faster than Peter could. "Good luck with Deputy Berry." I thought a reminder couldn't hurt.

Peter was picking up the phone as I left.

In the outer office Diesel was stretched out on the credenza behind Melba's desk while Melba worked at her computer. She looked up when I shut Peter's door behind me.

"You sure were in there a long time," she said. "It couldn't have taken that long, even with Peter, to talk about what happened."

"It didn't," I said. "There was something else Peter wanted to discuss." I threw up a hand. "And before you ask me, I can't tell you. If Peter chooses to tell you, fine, but don't ask me, please."

Melba pouted for a moment, but she never could stay annoyed or angry with anyone for long. "All right, Charlie. Spoilsport." She grinned at me. "I'll get it out of Peter somehow."

I smiled at her, not doubting for a moment that she could. "Come on, Diesel. Let's go."

Diesel sat up and yawned. Then he stretched for a moment before jumping down. He came up to me and rubbed against my legs.

"We'll see you later." I waved at Melba as I followed my cat out of the office and toward the stairs.

I had plenty to think about when Diesel and I were once again installed in our accustomed places in the archive office. While the cat settled down for a nap, I stared at the computer screen. I should have been checking e-mail, but instead I kept running a list of suspects through my mind:

Julia Wardlaw
Justin Wardlaw
Jordan Thompson
Peter Vanderkeller

Any or all of them could be lying.

For example, Julia could have seen Jordan Thompson *leaving* as she herself arrived, rather than the other way around. Peter could be lying about speaking to someone through the door, or it could have been any one of the others in the room when Peter came to speak to Godfrey. Justin could have killed Godfrey, run out of the room terrified by what he had done, and then sat on the bench in the square until I found him.

Then there was the unknown factor: Mr. X or Ms. X.

Godfrey seemed to have angered enough people in his life that there were probably others in Athena who might have wanted to kill him.

But how to find out who they were, that was the question.

I glanced at the inventory of Godfrey's papers lying on my desk. I knew one place to start.

Sighing, I picked up the inventory and began jotting down the box numbers that contained correspondence. It was going to be a long day.

TWENTY-TWO

||||||||||||||||||||||||||||||||||||||||||||||||||||||||||||||

I worked my way steadily through Godfrey's correspondence, stopping only for lunch and the occasional insistent demand for attention from Diesel. At some point Rick Tackett appeared to change the locks on the office door and the storeroom, but until he came to offer me the new keys and take the old ones away, I hardly noticed him.

He stood in front of my desk for a moment, surveying the boxes. "Lotta stuff here. What are you gonna do with it?"

"Keep it in storage until I have a chance to go through it all and catalog it. But that's going to be a while. I have a lot of other things to see to first."

"Seems like a lotta work for just a bunch of paper," he said.

I shrugged. "Someone may be interested in them at some point, want to do a dissertation perhaps. You never know what kinds of interesting stuff you'll find in a collection like this."

"Is it valuable?"

"Possibly," I said. "Like anything, it depends on how much someone would be willing to pay for it. I doubt the college would want to sell the collection, though."

Rick nodded and turned away. I watched him go, somewhat surprised by the conversation. This was the first time I had heard him express any curiosity about anything archival in nature. In the past when he'd delivered packages to the office he had never asked even one question.

It was probably because of Godfrey's murder, I reasoned. I went back to my work.

Godfrey had accumulated several boxes full of fan mail, not to mention other kinds of correspondence. I scanned each letter as quickly as I could, looking for evidence of some kind of threat to—or ill feeling toward—Godfrey. There were indeed some of the latter but none of the former. If he ever received a threatening letter, Godfrey hadn't kept it, apparently. I also skimmed any notations that Godfrey made on the letters, but I gleaned nothing worthwhile.

By five o'clock I had achieved nothing more than a bad headache and a case of eyestrain. There was still the other correspondence to go through, chiefly business stuff, but that would have to wait. I needed a break, and Diesel was more than ready to go home. I usually spent only half a day in the archive on Thursday anyway.

The walk home helped my headache. Being out in the cool late-afternoon air, plus getting some exercise, made a difference. By the time Diesel and I reached the house I was feeling quite a bit better.

After filling Diesel's food and water bowls and cleaning out the litter box—something I had neglected to do this morning—I contemplated preparing dinner. I found a fresh package of ground beef in the fridge and decided that hamburgers were just the thing. A check of the pantry turned up a large can of baked beans. Add a salad to that, and I'd have a pretty tasty and filling meal for both my boarder and me.

Justin, with Diesel right on his heels, appeared in the kitchen as I was finishing up the burgers. "Good timing," I said. "I'll let you fix your hamburgers for yourself." I pointed with the spatula toward the table. "There's salad there and baked beans in the pot."

"Thank you, sir," Justin said with a shy smile. "I'm really hungry."

"There's plenty." I returned his smile.

Justin never had much dinner-table conversation, and tonight was no exception. I waited until he had dispatched one burger, a large helping of salad, and two helpings of beans before I ventured a question.

"How are you doing?" Still hungry, I reached for the salad bowl, thinking more salad would be better for me than another round of beans.

Justin shrugged. "I'm okay, I guess. It all seems like a really bad dream, you know?"

"I do," I said. "I know it might be difficult to talk about, but I was hoping you wouldn't mind telling me a few things." I had been thinking about the time Justin spent with Godfrey, wondering whether Justin had heard or seen anything that might be a clue to the murder.

"I don't mind," Justin said. He got up from the table to fix himself another burger.

"I'm sure Deputy Berry asked you the same questions I'll probably ask," I said. "The reason I'm doing this, I want you to understand, is because I'm concerned for you and your mother."

"Yes, sir, I know," Justin said. "I know Mama really appreciates it, and I do, too." Finished at the counter, he returned to the table. He smiled at me again, not so shyly this time.

Good, I thought, he's beginning to get some of his old spark back.

"You spent several hours with Godfrey yesterday," I said. "Did anything unusual happen?"

Justin chewed for a moment, and after he swallowed he replied, "Most of the time we just talked. We argued, like I told you, but nothing weird happened."

"Were you in his hotel room most of the time?"

"Yes, sir," Justin said. "He said he didn't want anyone bothering us, so it was better to be somewhere private." He frowned. "That didn't stop people from calling him, though."

"How many phone calls did he get?" These might be slim leads, but they were better than nothing.

"Just two." Justin ate a forkful of beans. "The first one was from his agent, he said. They only talked a few minutes, and he went into the bedroom to do that."

"What about the second call?" I asked.

"Somebody else," Justin said. "He went into the bedroom again, but he wasn't there long."

"Did he say who it was?"

"Not exactly," Justin said. He thought for a moment.

"When he came out of the bedroom he was muttering to himself, so I asked him if everything was okay. He said it was just some guy he knew bugging him about reading a book."

That didn't sound like a clue to anything. "That was all?"

Justin frowned. "Now that I think about it, he didn't say *book*, he said *manuscript*. That's different, I guess." He paused. "I asked him if he read other people's manuscripts and why, and he said he did sometimes because they wanted him to give them some kind of quote to use on the book when it was published. Then he said a lot of times people wanted him to read their stuff because they thought he would help them get it published. But he said this guy was a pest with no talent, and he wasn't going to do it." His face reddened a bit. "Actually the way he said it was a lot ruder, but I'm not going to repeat his actual words."

"I think I can guess the gist of it," I said. Justin was very different from my son, Sean, at that age. Sean had delighted in trying to shock his mother and me with rude language. "So that was it? Just those two phone calls?"

"Yes, sir," Justin said. "Oh, I almost forgot. I did ask him about the guy and how he knew he had no talent if he wasn't going to read the guy's manuscript."

"What did he say to that?" As big a bestseller as Godfrey was, aspiring writers who wanted his help probably approached him all the time. Knowing Godfrey, he probably wasn't that gracious about it, either.

"He said he'd known this guy a long time, but he wouldn't take no for an answer." Justin pushed a couple of beans around on his plate with his fork. "You don't think somebody like that would get mad enough to kill him, do you?"

"I don't know," I said. "It depends on how desperate the man was. And how stable. Someone with mental health problems might respond violently to being thwarted."

"That's pretty freaky," Justin said. He set his fork aside.

"Yes," I said. There was something odd about that second conversation. "Which phone did Godfrey talk on? The hotel phone or his cell phone?"

"His cell phone," Justin said.

"For both calls?"

"Yes, sir."

"Why would Godfrey give his cell phone number to someone he described as a pest?" That was what was bothering me about the second call. "That doesn't make much sense."

"You're right," Justin said. "It doesn't. He talked to me about his writing and stuff, and he said once his books started selling really well, he had people coming out of the woodwork all the time. He had his own security guards at his house in California to keep the crazies away from him." Justin turned a bit pink again, and I figured Godfrey had used a much coarser term than *crazies*.

"I'm not surprised. I've seen it happen before when really big-name authors have signed at the bookstore here in town. I remember one woman who held up the signing line to tell the author in detail about the book she had written. It was sure to be a bestseller, if only she could get someone to read it—according to her. The author politely—and tactfully—declined, but the store staff had to intercede to get the woman out of the line. Even then, she hung around waiting to accost the author again. The staff finally had to eject her. It was embarrassing for everybody."

"Sure sounds like it," Justin said. His mouth twisted in obvious distaste. "But how would they find the person he was talking to?"

"They probably could get a record of his calls and trace the number that way," I said. "Of course, we have no idea where the person was calling from. There's no reason to think he was here in Athena."

"That's true," Justin said.

"You told all of this—everything you told me just now—to Deputy Berry?" I wanted to be sure.

"Yes, sir," Justin said. "I told her, but she didn't say much, just kept asking questions."

"As long as she received the information," I said. "That's the key thing." I stood up, ready to clear the table.

Justin forestalled me. "I'll clean up, Mr. Charlie. Why don't you go relax?"

"Thanks, I think I will." I smiled and looked down at Diesel, who had been napping on the floor near my chair during dinner. "What about you, boy? You want to come up with me or stay here and help Justin?"

Diesel sat up and warbled at me. He stretched a moment before getting to his feet and walking over to Justin's chair. "There's my answer," I said. "See you later, then."

I left the two of them and climbed the stairs to my bedroom. I wanted to change out of my clothes and relax with a book—the history book, not Godfrey's novel. I wasn't in the mood for it right now.

But when I was comfortably in my pajamas, slouched into my chair, book in hand, I found I couldn't concentrate on late antiquity. My mind kept returning to the murder.

Was there someone else who might have a motive for wanting Godfrey dead? The mysterious Mr. or Ms. X?

I needed to know more about Godfrey's past. I needed dirt, if there was any. And I knew the right person to call. Putting my book aside, I retrieved my cell phone and settled in for a long chat.

TWENTY-THREE

IIIIIIIIIIIIIIIIIIIIIIIIIIIIIIIIIIIIIIIIIIIIIIIIIIIIIIIIIIIIIIIIII

The obvious person to call was Melba Gilley. With her healthy interest in the doings of her fellow Athenians and her long-term involvement in a variety of community activities, she was a prime source of information.

Calling her, however, meant that I would have to tell her why I was so involved in Godfrey's murder. If she had somehow heard that I—really, Justin and I—discovered the body, she hadn't let on, and such behavior would be totally out of character.

I found her number in my cell phone's address book and initiated the call. She picked up after two rings.

"Good evening," I said. "It's Charlie. How are you?"

"Hey, Charlie, I'm doing fine. How about you?" She sounded as chipper as ever.

"I'm okay," I said. "Is this a good time? Am I interrupting anything?"

"Only some lame show on TV," she said, laughing. "Sometimes I don't know why I even turn the dang thing on, except it's company. What's on your mind?"

"I need to talk to you about Godfrey," I said. "I need to find out some things, and I figured you were the person to ask."

She gave a hearty chuckle. "You mean you called the biggest gossip you know."

I had to laugh. "Well, if you want to put it like that."

"I'm nosy. I admit it," Melba said. "So what do you want to know? But maybe I should ask *why* first. Godfrey wasn't exactly a buddy of yours."

"No, he wasn't," I said. "And if it weren't for certain circumstances I'd be happy to keep my nose out of it."

"And they would be?"

"First off, you know Justin Wardlaw is boarding with me," I replied. "And I'm sure by now you've heard about his relationship to Godfrey."

"Yes, I have," Melba said. "Can't say I'm surprised. I remember how hard Godfrey was running after Julia back then. And frankly, honey, if I had to pick between Godfrey and Ezra, I'd pick Godfrey. Even knowing he was a class A jerk most of the time."

I started to speak, but Melba went on. "And her already engaged to Ezra. That's what got me. Julia never seemed like the type, but I guess you never can tell, can you? When the baby was born, people started counting up, but it was close enough that no one knew for sure."

Poor Julia, I thought. Having to be the cynosure of all those suspicious people in town, many of them gleefully assuming the worst.

"It was certainly a surprise to me," I said. "I feel a certain amount of responsibility for Justin because he's boarding with me, and I can't help feeling concerned for him and Julia, naturally."

"Of course," Melba said. "They need support right now, because I'm sure the sheriff's department is looking pretty closely at them."

"They are," I said. "But the other reason I'm concerned about this is . . . well, I found the body, basically." I didn't see any point in giving Melba the full details of the situation. This would be more than enough to make her eyes pop.

"You dog," Melba said. "You never said a word to me." She chuckled. "But I won't hold it against you."

"Thanks," I said. "Trust me, I'd rather not have been the one. It wasn't pleasant."

"No, I'm sure it wasn't," Melba said, her tone serious. "It's one thing to read about it in a book, like one of Godfrey's, but it's something else to experience it for real."

"It sure is," I said, doing my best to suppress that ugly image from reappearing in my head. "I guess you can see now why I'm curious about it all."

"Sure," Melba said. "What was it you wanted to ask me?"

"I know Godfrey came back to Athena on a regular basis," I said. "He had quite a track record with women, like the episodes with Julia and Peter Vanderkeller's wife. Are there any other outraged husbands or boyfriends or spurned women in the area?"

Melba was silent for a moment. "The first one that comes to mind is the woman who owns that bookstore on the square. Can't remember her name at the moment."

"Jordan Thompson," I said. "I heard about her. Can you think of anyone else?"

"The other one that comes to mind is Frank Ledbetter." Melba sighed into the phone.

"Frank Ledbetter?" Why did that name sound familiar?

"My ex-husband," Melba said.

"Oh," I said, too stunned for the moment to say anything else.

"I know," Melba said, sounding sheepish. "It's not something I'm proud of, let me tell you. But I had a brief fling with Godfrey about ten years ago, and it cost me my marriage."

"I'm so sorry," I said. "I had no idea." Poor Melba. I knew she was divorced, but that was pretty much the extent of my knowledge.

"Frank and I were going through a bad patch," Melba said. "Old, old story. And here comes Godfrey on a book tour. I went to hear him talk, there were some sparks, and I went out to dinner with him afterward. And you can guess the rest."

I could, but I was curious about one thing. "I do have to ask you one question."

"Shoot," Melba said.

"Did Godfrey hang around town while you had this, er, relationship?"

"I wasn't stupid enough to run off to California with him, thank the Lord," Melba said. "Yeah, Athena was the last stop on his tour, and he was planning to stay here for a couple of months, doing research for a book."

"And when he finished, he went back to California?"

"And I stayed here," Melba said. "By then I'd realized

what a fool I'd made of myself, and poor Frank, too. He filed for divorce right away."

"Another question," I said, "and forgive me for asking it, but I have to. Did either you or Frank hate Godfrey enough to kill him?"

"Ten years ago Frank was ready to skin him alive— and he loved to hunt," Melba said. "But by the time Godfrey came back to town a couple years later, Frank was remarried."

"And you?" I prompted her gently.

"I hated him, too," Melba said. "But I hated myself more, let me tell you. I learned my lesson from that." She laughed, a little wildly, I thought. "I got back at Godfrey in my own way, though."

"How so?" I was almost afraid to ask, uncertain of what I would hear.

"I took every one of his books I owned and sat down in front of the fireplace. I ripped out every page, one by one, and burned them. It felt pretty good, though of course I don't normally hold with burning books."

"That's a good thing," I said, trying to ease the tension a little. "Especially since you work in a library."

She laughed, and I felt relieved. I couldn't completely cross her off the suspect list, but it sounded to me like she had worked through her feelings.

I wondered if things might be awkward between us at work after her confession, and I hoped they wouldn't be. I liked Melba. Her sunny, upbeat disposition made her fun to be around, and I would hate for her to feel embarrassed with me.

"I appreciate you telling me all this," I said.

"No big deal," Melba said, though her tone belied the

words. "I figured somebody was bound to bring it up sooner or later, and I'd rather you heard it from me."

It was time to move on. "Can you think of anybody else?" I didn't want to say it, but Godfrey, I was sure, probably found a different, but willing, woman whenever he popped back into town for a visit.

"Besides Julia, the bookstore lady, and me?" Melba snorted. "The notches that man must have had on his bed. Well, there is one more that I know of. Janette Turnipseed."

"That's an odd name," I said. "I don't recall anybody by that name."

"No reason you should," Melba said. "She was a professor at Athena, a post-doc in the English department. She was here about six years ago. Godfrey spent three months here one fall in that writer-in-residence program they have, and apparently they had quite an affair."

"She left after her post-doc?" I said.

"Before it was finished," Melba replied. "Poor woman. She left at the end of the fall semester. I think I heard she went to some school out in Nebraska or Oklahoma."

"Why did women keep falling for him? Surely they knew about his past?" I realized my questions could be insulting, but Melba seemed not to take them that way.

"He could be incredibly charming when he wanted to," Melba said. "He'd focus those eyes on you, and suddenly you felt like the most desirable woman in the world." She laughed. "Listen to me. I sound like a teenager. But he made me feel that way."

"I'll have to take your word for it," I said wryly. "I've been reading his new book, and I have to say, the way he writes about women makes him seem like a misogynist."

"That's the weird thing," Melba said. "I got that from his books, too, but in person he wasn't like that. I think he truly liked women, and that was his problem. He liked them so much he couldn't limit himself to one, or even one at a time."

"Then I wonder why he wrote about them with such disdain?"

"Only his shrink knows for sure," Melba said.

Diesel appeared in the doorway and ambled over to my chair. He leaped into my lap, and I tried not to wince from the impact. I grunted into the phone anyway.

"Are you okay?" Melba asked.

"I'm fine," I said. "Just a bit winded from being the landing spot for a large cat."

Melba laughed. "I can see it now. He's pretty big for a lap kitty."

"Try to tell *him* that," I said as I shifted in the chair to redistribute some of Diesel's weight. "Okay, now I can breathe again."

Diesel chirped at me, and I rubbed his head with my free hand. He would be happy to sit like this for an hour or two—or until my hand cramped and my legs went to sleep, that is.

He laid his head against my chest, and when he did that, I forgave him everything. He was such a loving companion, and if it hadn't been for him, I don't know what I would have done the past couple of years.

"Thanks for all the information," I said. "So far, though, I don't think any of these people—especially you—sounds like a good suspect, though. Can you think of anyone else? I believe Godfrey's parents have passed away, but did he have any other family?"

"Some distant cousins, I think," Melba said. "On his father's side. But they live in south Alabama. I don't think Godfrey's parents had much contact with them, though."

I was about to ask another question when Melba continued.

"The only other one I can think of is his half brother," she said.

"Half brother?" That was news to me. I didn't remember ever hearing that Godfrey had any siblings.

"Yeah, he's about ten years older. Godfrey's mother was married to someone else before she married Mr. Priest."

"I never knew that," I said. "And I sure didn't know about a half brother."

"You know him. You just don't know you know him," Melba said, an impish tone in her voice.

"Okay, I give. Who is it?" I said. I really had no idea.

"Rick Tackett, the operations manager."

TWENTY-FOUR

|||||||||||||||||||||||||||||||||||||||||||||||||||||||||||||||||||||||||||||||||||||

"So Rick is Godfrey's half brother," I said.

Was that why he was so interested in the value of Godfrey's papers?

"Yeah, I guess a lot of people probably don't know that. I don't think they ever had much to do with each other," Melba said. "What I heard was that the boys' mama left her first husband, Mr. Tackett, and Rick for Godfrey's daddy. This was back in the fifties, and I reckon it was a real scandal for a while."

"She left both her first husband *and* her son?" I said. "That's really sad for the son."

"I know," Melba said. "I've always felt a bit sorry for Rick on account of it. His daddy wouldn't let him have anything to do with his mama. But apparently Godfrey took after *his* daddy in a lot of ways."

"So old man Priest was a ladies' man, too?"

"From what my mama told me, he was," Melba said. "But they stayed married, even if he did run around on her. She got paid back for running out on her son like that."

"They sound like such lovely people," I said, my tone sour. I had no respect for men who behaved like that. Or for women who ran off and left their children for some man. I didn't know all the details, so I could be misjudging Rick and Godfrey's mama, but still.

"Mrs. Tackett, as she was then, was the organist at her church, and her sister was the preacher's wife. *That* sure caused some talk."

"I guess Peyton Place had nothing on Athena," I said.

"Not then, or now," Melba said. "People don't change that much. They're always gonna get themselves into all kinds of messes."

"I guess so," I said. "But what I have to wonder is, could one of those messes be related to Godfrey's death? What about Rick, for example?"

"Like I said, I don't think he and Godfrey ever had much to do with each other. I never heard that they did, anyway. Rick, though, has had a pretty hard life."

"I don't really know anything about him," I said, knowing that Melba would fill in the details.

"For one thing, he was in Vietnam, right at the tail end of the war, and the Lord only knows how that affected him," Melba said, the pity obvious in her voice. "Old Mr. Tackett was a hard man, they say. He was a farmer, and you know that's not an easy life. Rick worked on the farm until he was old enough to enlist in the army."

"Couldn't wait to get away, probably," I said. "That's what it sounds like."

"Probably," Melba said. "Rick's been married a couple of times too, and has three kids, I think." She paused for a moment. "Yeah, three. Two boys and a girl. He had another daughter, though, but she died when she was only nine or ten."

"That's awful," I said. I couldn't imagine anything worse than the death of one's child.

"She had some kind of cancer," Melba said. "They took her to St. Jude in Memphis, and I reckon they did everything they could for her. But they couldn't save her."

"Poor Rick," I said.

"Yeah, he's had a hard row to hoe all his life," Melba said. "And there's his half brother, rich as all get out from his books, and Rick struggling to raise his family and get them through school."

"Godfrey probably never did a thing to help them," I said. I couldn't imagine Godfrey being that charitable. Of course, Rick might not have wanted anything from his brother.

"Not that I ever heard," Melba said. "Those kids are smart, though, and one of them's really talented. I heard her sing in the church choir. She has a beautiful voice, and the last I heard she was off to one of those high-toned music schools back east. I think she wants to be an opera singer."

That wouldn't be cheap, I thought. Godfrey's money could make all the difference, if he were inclined to help.

I chatted a few minutes longer with Melba, but she had no further skeletons to reveal. I finally ended the call and put my phone aside.

Diesel was sound asleep in my lap, and my legs were

beginning to ache a bit from his weight. I woke him gently and shifted him off my lap to the floor. He blinked up at me, yawned, and hopped on the bed where he went back to sleep.

I got up and stretched my legs before going into the bathroom for a drink of water. My throat was dry after the long conversation with Melba.

After I brushed my teeth I climbed into bed beside Diesel, thankful that for once he had left me plenty of room, so I didn't have to move him.

I lay there in the dark for a while, thinking about all Melba had told me. Godfrey had caused a lot of heartache—as had his mother and father, apparently. But out of all those sad little stories, was there one relevant to Godfrey's death?

The one that seemed like the only real possibility was that Godfrey had a half brother. I could see where Rick might resent his brother, especially since Godfrey had become rich and famous while he had to struggle just to get by.

Even if Rick resented Godfrey, though, was that a strong enough motive for murder? From what Melba told me, it didn't sound likely to me that Godfrey would have put Rick and his family in his will. There was probably no monetary gain, then, from Godfrey's death.

Or could it have been the product of sheer envy, turned deadly by years of disappointment and resentment?

Troubled by these questions, I had a hard time going to sleep. Eventually I drifted off, Diesel by my side.

When the alarm sounded the next morning, I felt groggy and inclined to stay in bed. My sleep hadn't been restful, and I knew I'd be logy all day. Diesel poked his nose close to mine and warbled at me. When I didn't move, he put a paw on my arm and warbled again.

I opened my eyes and glared at him. "Oh, all right. I'll get up. I'm sure you'll faint from hunger if I don't get up and feed you right this minute."

Diesel walked across me and jumped down onto the floor, ignoring my grunt of pain as he stepped on my stomach. That put me in my place, so I got up.

Downstairs I put the coffee on, filled up Diesel's bowls, and cleaned the litter box. While the cat munched happily on his food, I retrieved the paper from the front lawn and sat down to read it. *That coffeepot better hurry up*, I thought. I needed the caffeine to kick-start my brain into gear.

Godfrey's death was still front-page news, though I was pleased to see the article mentioned no names of suspects. I'd have to thank Kanesha Berry later for keeping my name, as well as those of Julia and Justin, out of the paper. I realized then that the local reporter had not been pestering me any further either, so I owed Kanesha for that, too.

Azalea came bustling in while I was finishing my second cup of coffee.

"Good morning," she said, and I returned her greeting.

"How's Kanesha doing?" I asked.

"Sore as a long-tailed cat in a roomful of rocking chairs," Azalea said. "She better get this thing figured out soon, else I don't know what I'm going to do with her."

"She's under a lot of pressure," I said. "I can understand why she might be feeling stressed out."

"That's why I been hoping *somebody* might find out something to help her with," Azalea said with a pointed look at me.

"I'm doing my best," I said. "I've been digging, but so far I haven't come up with anything solid. Godfrey managed to make a lot of people angry with him over the years, and it seems like his parents did, too."

Azalea sniffed. "With that trashy mama of his, and that hound dog of a daddy, it ain't no wonder."

"Did you know them?" From the disdain in her voice, I thought Azalea must have had personal experience of the Priests.

"I sure did," Azalea said with a pained expression. "Worked for that woman six weeks or so when I was sixteen. You ain't never heard so much yellin' and cussin' in your life as the two of them, and that poor child having to hear it all. No wonder he turned out like his daddy."

"Sounds pretty awful," I said.

"It was," Azalea replied. "Wasn't no amount of money worth working for them folks, let me tell you. I got me another job fast as I could. That's when I come to work for Miss Dottie." Her face softened with a smile. "She was a true lady, and I loved every minute of working for her."

I knew that Aunt Dottie had treasured Azalea, but I didn't dare say so. This was about as sentimental as I had ever seen Azalea, and I didn't want to offend her by some well-meant but unwelcome comment.

Instead I said, "Yes, she was one of a kind."

Azalea turned back to the stove. "I'm going to be scrambling some eggs and frying up some bacon."

"Sounds good to me," I said. "I think I'll head upstairs for my shower. I'll be back down in about fifteen minutes."

Azalea nodded, and I left her in the kitchen. Diesel followed me up, but he kept on going when I stopped on the second floor. He would make sure Justin was up in time for breakfast.

I was almost finished eating by the time Justin appeared. He ate quickly, explaining that he needed to get to the library before class to meet a friend for a study date. The way he bolted his food down, I doubt he tasted much of it, but I remembered the hasty meals of my own student days and forbore commenting.

Diesel and I spend three Fridays a month at the public library where I volunteer. I fill in as needed, helping with reference, doing a bit of cataloging, and running one of the reading groups for retirees. Today, however, was not one of those Fridays, so I decided to go instead to the archive and poke around some more in Godfrey's papers.

By the time Diesel and I reached the campus, the building was open. I debated seeking Rick out and talking to him about Godfrey, but what pretext could I use? Nothing that wouldn't make me sound like a tabloid journalist on the hunt, I realized. I decided to wait and see if a good opportunity presented itself. Perhaps Rick would attend the memorial service tomorrow.

We made it upstairs without Melba spotting us. I would just as soon she didn't know—at least for a while—that Diesel and I were here today. I wanted to focus on Godfrey's papers, and Melba would only be a distraction.

I shut the door behind us and turned on the lights. The boxes of Godfrey's papers appeared undisturbed, and I hoped that the change of locks would keep them that way.

Diesel made himself comfortable in the window. I eyed the inventory as I sat down at my desk. Where to start?

I didn't want to read more letters this morning, so I decided against starting on Godfrey's business correspondence. While I sat there, I remembered the box of computer disks. I might as well see what was on them and start making an inventory of their contents.

I retrieved the box and set it on my desk. I pulled out one of the containers of disks from inside and opened it. They were the large floppy disks that hadn't been used for years. Under normal circumstances these disks would cause a problem, since few people these days had computers that could accommodate them.

The archive, however, was prepared for just such a contingency. I had a computer that could handle them, and it was loaded with various word-processing programs. I ought to be able to read the contents of the disks with one of them.

This computer was on a desk in a corner, behind a range of bookshelves. I took all the disks with me and turned on the computer. While I waited for it to boot up, I examined some of the disks. They were labeled, and I recognized the words as the titles of some of Godfrey's early books. There were also dates on them, so I could put them in chronological order.

When the computer was ready, I inserted the earliest disk of the group and executed a DOS command to see the directory of its contents. Judging from the file extensions, I didn't think I'd have any trouble opening them.

I scanned the directory. There were only twelve files, and they all had numerical names. Chapters one through twelve no doubt.

I opened the file named "one" and scanned through it. I recognized the text of what I thought was Godfrey's first thriller, *Count the Cost*. The change in style from his early, more traditional mysteries, was clear. I closed the file and removed the disk. I didn't see much point in reading through the text of the books, because I wasn't interested in analyzing Godfrey's prose.

There were three disks labeled "Cost." I inserted the third one in the drive and executed the directory command. There were more files names with numbers, but there was one file called "letter." I opened it and began to read.

The letter was addressed simply to "G." I presumed that meant Godfrey. The writer stared by thanking G for taking time to read the manuscript and expressed the hope that G would like it enough to help get it published. The letter referred to the title *Count the Cost*.

By the time I finished the letter—unsigned, unfortunately—I was convinced Godfrey had not written a book that bore his name.

TWENTY-FIVE

Stunned by the contents of the letter, I stared blankly at the computer screen, trying to get my mind back into working gear.

If this letter wasn't some kind of joke, then the implications were clear. Godfrey had stolen the work of another writer and published it as his own.

But how had he been able to get away with such a thing? Surely the writer, Mr. or Ms. X, would have figured it out. Godfrey even used the same title referenced in the letter.

I read through the letter again, more slowly this time, searching for any possible clues to the identity of the writer.

Here's the manuscript I told you about when you were here a few months ago. Thanks for taking the time to read it. I hope you'll like it enough to want to help me get it published. It's different from your books—a lot darker and harder-edged—but you said you liked thrillers when you talked to the group. I call it Count the Cost, *but that might not be the best title. Any suggestions you have about that would be appreciated, too. I know a catchy title seems to be important, but you know more about the business than I do. At least for now, that is. I'm hoping to know a lot more about it one of these days. Thanks again. I'm looking forward to hearing what you have to say.*

There were no real clues to the letter writer's identity, not even a hint of the gender. Two things might be helpful: "when you were here a few months ago" and "when you talked to the group." There was no date in the text of the letter, but then I got the bright idea of looking at the date stamp in the directory of files on the disk.

Before I did that, however, I printed a copy of the letter. Once that was done, I called up the directory and looked at the date: August 3, nineteen years ago. The last time the file had been altered was nineteen years ago.

Nineteen years ago. I thought for a moment.

Justin was eighteen.

Godfrey would have been in Athena roughly nineteen years ago.

Could this mean the letter writer lived in Athena?

He or she must. There had to be a local connection to Godfrey's murder. Otherwise, why was he killed here and not somewhere else?

Slow down, I told myself. *You're jumping to conclusions pretty fast.*

I did a screen print of the directory and clipped it to the letter.

Before I examined any of the other disks, I wanted to check something. This computer was not connected to the Internet, so I went back to my desk. Diesel appeared sound asleep in the window when I glanced at him. I connected to the library's online catalog and searched for Godfrey's name. I wanted to check the publication dates for his books. The library should have all of them in the collection because he was a local writer.

No doubt Godfrey had a website that provided the information, and I would check that later. But I preferred the information from the catalog—it was probably more accurate than the website.

I performed the operations necessary to create a brief citation list of all of Godfrey's titles and printed it out. The citation included publisher and date of publication.

When the printer finished, I examined the sheets. I had sorted the citations in ascending publication order, so I could trace Godfrey's books as they were published, from the first one to the most recent.

His first five books were published within four years, and then there was a four-year gap before his sixth novel, *Count the Cost*. It was published seventeen years ago, and that meant a two-year gap, roughly, between the date stamp on the disk and the actual publication of the book.

Godfrey's first five books were different in style and tone from the later books. Light, amusing, fluffy, they featured a bickering duo of amateur detectives who fought their attraction to each other as they stumbled over dead bodies. *Count the Cost* signaled an almost radical change, and if I had thought about it at all, I probably assumed Godfrey did it for commercial reasons. He wasn't a bestseller before, as far as I was aware, but *Count the Cost* made the bestseller list. He had been a fixture there ever since.

In that letter was the reason for the abrupt shift in Godfrey's work.

It wasn't his, plain and simple.

But was that the only one? What about the other fifteen books published in the years since *Count the Cost*?

Diesel stood up from his perch, stretching and yawning. I reached over to rub his head. He rewarded me with a couple of happy chirps. He jumped down and accompanied me as I took the list of Godfrey's books back to the other computer. The book published the year after *Count the Cost* was entitled *Abide with Me*. I checked the box of disks, and there were three labeled "Abide."

I inserted the first one into the drive and looked at the list of files. Only numbers. I checked the second and third disks as well. Same thing. No letter this time. Diesel rubbed against my legs a few times before he wandered off to prowl around the office. He was not usually destructive so I let him have free run in the room.

I checked the next book on the list: *Dead Men's Plans*. There were four disks for this one. This time I put the disk numbered four in and checked the contents.

Bingo. Another letter, again addressed simply to G. No signature. That was frustrating.

The arrangement seems to be working out pretty well, though I thought you were at least going to mention me in the acknowledgments. I don't mind you getting

*all the attention from the media—I hate that kind of
thing. But why couldn't you at least include my name
somewhere? I expected a bit more gratitude, frankly.
The money's good—I'm not complaining about that,
but if it weren't for me, your name wouldn't be on the
bestseller list, you know. I'm glad it's time for a new
contract. I'm going to want some changes, but I'll let
you know what they are after I've had a chance to
think more about them.*

The letter went on to describe, only in the briefest
terms, the idea for the next book and asked for feedback
on it.

This was pretty clear evidence that Godfrey was putting his name on another writer's work. It also sounded
like X was getting a bit restive over the lack of attention.

Why had Godfrey kept these disks? If he'd had any
sense, he would have destroyed them years ago. They
clearly weren't intended to be part of his archive, since
the box was not included on the inventory. Knowing the
man's arrogance, however, I figured he never thought it
possible that anyone would find out about his deception.

Some overzealous person must have seen the box and
simply included it with the rest. Godfrey would no doubt
have had a fit if he had known.

But what a stroke of luck. I silently thanked whoever
had stuck the box of disks in with everything else.

This was something Kanesha Berry needed to know
about, and I planned to tell her.

First, though, I wanted to dig further and see if there
were other letters. Had Godfrey continued to put his
name to X's work?

I realized I should also check the acknowledgments in all of the books to see if there were any clues in them.

Did his agent know? I wondered. I would have to start keeping note of the questions that occurred to me.

Back to checking the disks. I went through them chronologically. There was no letter included on the disks for the next book on the list. I went on to the fifth book.

Pay dirt. My eyes widened as I read this letter.

You bastard, I should have known better than to trust you. You haven't changed, still intent on screwing anybody to get what you want. I thought a contract would protect me, but you saw to that, didn't you? I can't believe how naive and stupid I was. I should have talked to a lawyer, but you said it wasn't worth the money. Did your agent really review the contract like you said? Frankly, I don't believe it. I have a good mind to call her and have a little talk with her. But I can't afford to pay back the money, you bastard, and you know that. I'm stuck, but this doesn't mean I won't try to find some way out.

What kind of contract had X signed? I wondered. Godfrey had only too obviously taken advantage of X's naivete and lack of experience, but this sounded bad, even for Godfrey.

There was a mention of contracts in the inventory, but I suspected that there wouldn't be a copy of the contract with X. Even Godfrey wouldn't be arrogant enough—or stupid enough—to include something that potentially damaging with the rest of his papers.

That contract, however, could be the key to everything.

Had X finally become so enraged over the unfairness and decided that Godfrey had to die? If only I could find it— or figure out some way of discovering who X was.

The answer might be in the box of disks. All it would take was time.

Stopping long enough only to walk home for a quick lunch, I spent most of the day at the computer, going through every disk in the box.

I found a few more letters, some of them filled with X's anger over Godfrey's behavior, others with a tone of resignation. Occasionally X mentioned the increasing profits the books brought. X apparently had no complaints there.

That was another point to consider. Godfrey had made millions from these books. Even I had read some of the articles in magazines about his lifestyle. X must have made some pretty significant money as well.

Was there someone in Athena living beyond his or her apparent means? Had X resisted the temptation to spend conspicuously? That would be something Kanesha could check better than I—once one of us could put a name to X, that is.

After all the time spent with the disks, I had no solid clue to the identity of X. X had obviously known Godfrey a long time, but there were plenty of people in Athena and elsewhere who had.

There was the mention of a group—probably a writers' group—but there were such groups all over the place.

I believed there was a local connection, though. It was at least a place to start. I could talk to one of the librarians who had been at the public library for nearly thirty years. If there was a writers' group in the area, she would know about it.

I finished printing copies of the letters on the disks and arranged them chronologically. I made sure the disks were organized in their containers as well.

Time to quit stalling, I told myself. I couldn't put it off any longer, though I wasn't looking forward to the inevitable explosion.

I went back to my desk, noticing Diesel once again asleep on the windowsill. I picked up the phone and called the sheriff's department.

TWENTY-SIX

|||||||||||||||||||||||||||||||||||||||||||||||||||||||||||||||||||||

When Kanesha Berry walked into my office, I could see the thunderclouds forming. "What is so urgent? I don't have time for some amateur interfering in this investigation, Mr. Harris."

"I understand that, Deputy," I said. "If I didn't think this was significant, I wouldn't have called you away from what you were doing."

She did not appear mollified by my placatory tone. I gestured to the chair by my desk. "Please, have a seat, and let me tell you what I've found."

Behind me on the windowsill, Diesel stirred. He always reacted to a harsh tone of voice, and Kanesha had disturbed him.

The deputy took the proffered seat, but her glare did not diminish.

Before I sat down I handed her a folder of the letters I had printed out for her.

"What's this?" She accepted the folder but didn't open it.

"It could be evidence of a strong motive for Godfrey Priest's murder," I said. "Let me tell you about what I found, and I think you'll agree this is serious."

Kanesha nodded before glancing pointedly at her watch.

"When Godfrey showed up in my office three days ago, he told me he wanted to donate his papers to the college archive," I said. "What I didn't know at the time was that he had already made arrangements to ship his papers here. They arrived the day after his death."

"And you waited two days to tell me about this?" The intensity of Kanesha's glare sharpened.

"Yes, I did," I said. "Godfrey's papers basically belong to the college now. In a letter that came with the papers Godfrey pretty much assigns ownership to the college."

"That may be," Kanesha said. "But that doesn't mean you can suppress information that could be relevant to this case. I have a good mind to charge you with interfering with an official investigation."

"I'm not suppressing it, and I'm not trying to interfere," I said. "There was simply a delay in telling you about them. I realize that's not an excuse, but as the person who will have to process the collection at some point, I wanted a chance to see what it contained. A lot of the content won't be of any use to your investigation whatsoever."

"It's kind of you to make that judgment for me," Kanesha said, the sarcasm dripping from her words. "And how do I know you haven't already destroyed anything in these papers that might link you to the crime? Or link someone else, like Julia or Justin Wardlaw?"

"You don't," I said with what I hoped was a disarming smile. "And if you want to charge me with anything, go right ahead. But first, at least let me tell you what I did find. I think it might be the key to Godfrey's murder."

"Go ahead," Kanesha said. "I'll listen." *But not for long*, her expression told me.

I picked up the inventory of the papers and handed it to her. "This is the inventory that came with all the boxes. It's very general, which is unfortunate. But the interesting thing is that there is an extra box."

"What do you mean?" Kanesha was scanning the inventory.

"All the boxes were numbered except one. And the numbers match the inventory. The unnumbered box contains computer disks."

"You think that box wasn't meant to be included?" Kanesha handed the inventory back to me.

"Judging by what I found on some of the disks, no, I don't think Godfrey wanted anyone else to see them. I don't know why he kept them, other than his unbelievable arrogance. He probably figured no one would ever see them and he would be safe."

"Safe from what?" Kanesha glanced at her watch again.

"From the letters I found on some of the disks." I pointed to the folder I gave her earlier. "They're all there in chronological order. Take a look at them, and I think you'll see very quickly."

She still thought I was wasting her time. I could see

it in her face. She was also angry that I hadn't let her know about the boxes sooner. But after clenching and unclenching her jaw for a moment, she opened the folder and began to read.

I watched. She read quickly, and after the second letter she glanced up at me with a frown. I maintained a bland expression, and she went back to the letters. I believe I had finally piqued her curiosity.

Eight minutes later—I timed her—she was done. She closed the folder and looked at me, her expression thoughtful.

"He basically paid someone else to write the books for him," she said. "And whoever he paid wasn't happy over the terms of the contract."

"Exactly," I said. "I think X—that's what I've been calling the unknown writer—might finally have become so incensed over Godfrey's treatment that he—or she—killed him."

"Uh-huh," she said. She handed the folder back to me. "If X was so unhappy about the contract, why didn't he or she hire a lawyer and take Mr. Priest to court?"

"Not knowing what the contract stipulated," I said, "I don't have a solid answer for that. But reading between the lines, I figure that the contract between Godfrey and X must have bound X to complete secrecy, otherwise the deal was off."

"That's a possibility, I suppose," Kanesha said. "But what's at stake here? Mr. Priest's reputation, of course, but what about money? How much could he make from the books?"

"While I was waiting for you to arrive, I did some research on the Internet," I said. "I found an article published a little over a year ago that ranked the top-selling American writers by their projected annual incomes. Godfrey was in the top ten. According to the article, his annual earnings were in the neighborhood of twenty million dollars."

Kanesha wasn't expecting that. Her eyes popped wide open. "That's significant money," she said. "How could he make so much?"

"For one thing, the books are published in something like thirty languages, and they apparently sell really well all over Europe, and in Japan, too. Then there are the movie adaptations. If Godfrey had a cut of the profits, that could add up to a lot of money, too. Several of the films based on the books have been big hits, both domestically and in foreign countries."

"Twenty million dollars a year." Kanesha shook her head as if she still couldn't take it in.

"X had to know the books were generating huge income," I said. "And what if his cut was small compared to what Godfrey was raking in? Add to that the fact that he's not getting any credit for his work, and he might have become more and more frustrated every year."

"It's possible," Kanesha said. "I grant you that. And it makes as much sense as anything else I've been able to discover. But how the heck am I going to figure out who X is? I don't even know where X lives."

"I think X lives in Athena," I said. I explained my reasoning, and Kanesha picked up the folder again and glanced through the letters.

"It makes sense," she said when she finished. "Now all I have to do is track down some writers' group that X belonged to." She rolled her eyes. "Talk about looking for needles in haystacks."

"I can help with that," I said. "There's a librarian at the public library who's been there for about thirty years. If anyone would know about local writers' groups, she would. Her name is Teresa Farmer."

"I know her," Kanesha said. "She does the summer reading program for kids."

"That's her," I said. I tapped the inventory list on my desk. "We can also look in the boxes that contain contracts. There might be some information there. And you can always talk to Godfrey's agent. She's supposed to be here for the memorial service tomorrow."

Kanesha nodded a couple of times. "I already have an appointment with her. She gets into Memphis late tonight and is driving down tomorrow morning."

"Good," I said.

"Why are you doing all this?" Kanesha regarded me, her eyes narrowed.

"You mean poking my nose into your investigation?" I said, trying not to sound too flippant.

Kanesha nodded.

"Natural instincts, I suppose." I shrugged. "Librarians are trained to help find answers, and the identity of Godfrey's killer is an important question. Plus I find myself involved because of Justin and Julia Wardlaw. I can't believe that either of them killed Godfrey, and I want to do what I can for their sakes."

I wanted to add—but knew I didn't dare—*And because your mother asked me to, and I couldn't figure out a way to say no.*

"If anything you've done compromises my investigation in any way, you are going to be in a lot of trouble. Are you clear on that?"

I resisted the urge to salute. Kanesha sounded like a drill sergeant dealing with a bunch of raw recruits fresh out of the cotton patch. I hadn't expected her to turn suddenly effusive with gratitude, but I guess I shouldn't have been surprised she was taking a dim view of my "interference."

"Yes, I am," I said. "But let me ask you this: If I had called you the minute these boxes of papers arrived, what would you have done? Would you have rushed over and impounded them, or whatever the term is, for your investigation? And would you have gone through those disks the way I did? Do you even have a computer that can handle old floppy disks?"

"Whoa." She held up a hand. I had gotten a bit carried away. "You might have saved me some time on these disks, but I still can't be sure that you haven't destroyed other evidence. Frankly, how can I even be sure that you didn't create this stuff about X yourself as a smoke screen?"

Aghast, I stared at her. Never would I have thought she'd react this way. I didn't know what to say.

"By not letting me know the minute these papers arrived, you basically tainted the evidence—if any of this could be called evidence. If I could have been assured that the contents of these boxes were untouched once they arrived here, I'd feel a lot more comfortable with all this. But you took it on yourself to investigate, and now I'm left with a difficult situation."

"I'm sorry," I finally managed to say. I had never thought about any of this, and I realized I had goofed big time. "I really don't know what to say other than I'm sorry."

"Where are the disks?"

They were still in the box back by the other computer. I retrieved them without a word and handed the box to Kanesha. She looked inside.

"I see what you mean about old disks," she said.

If that was some kind of olive branch, I'd accept it.

"I'll take them," she said. "If you can make out a receipt, I'll sign it. But these need to go with me."

"I'll do that," I said. "But what about the rest of Godfrey's papers?" I realized suddenly that I should tell her about the unauthorized person who had been in my office Wednesday night. She was going to be even happier with me.

"Where are the rest of the boxes?" she asked.

"In a storeroom down the hall," I said.

"Is it secure?"

"It is now," I said. "I have something else I need to tell you."

"Go ahead." She had one of those pained *What now?* looks on her face.

As briefly as I could, I related the facts about the unauthorized visitor.

"And you still didn't call me." She examined me like I was an exotic insect that she found distasteful.

"No," I said. "But I made sure the locks were changed that day. There are only three sets of keys. I have one, of course. Melba Gilley, the library director's assistant, has a set, and Rick Tackett, the head of operations for the library, has the other set."

Kanesha continued to regard me like a specimen.

"By the way," I said, feeling more uneasy by the second, "did you know that Godfrey had a half brother? It's Rick Tackett. Do you know him?"

"I don't know him," Kanesha said. "But I knew of the relationship. You might find this hard to believe, but I did make an effort to find out as much as I could about the victim and his family right off the bat."

"Sorry," I said, abashed.

She simply stared at me, and I tried not to squirm. Feeling like a delinquent ten-year-old was a new experience for me.

"For now we will move these boxes into the storeroom with the others, and I will seal the room until I can send someone here to pick them up and bring them down to the sheriff's department."

"Okay," I said. "Sounds like a good idea to me." I wasn't going to argue. If the college for some reason had a problem with this, I would deal with it later.

I had an inspiration. I found some of the cotton gloves I used to handle rare books and offered her a pair. She accepted them with a nod, and then we moved the boxes from my office down to the storeroom.

Diesel, very curious about where we were going with the boxes, followed us back and forth until we completed the move.

"Since we're here," I said, waving a hand to indicate the storeroom, "why don't you have a quick look at some of the contracts? That would answer one question pretty quickly."

"Meaning you want to know, so you want me to do it right now and tell you before these boxes are removed." Kanesha didn't smile, but I could have sworn she was the tiniest bit amused. That was a surprise.

"Well, yes," I said.

"Go get the inventory and the box of disks, and I'll stay here," Kanesha said. "I'll have a look at the contracts."

I nodded and went back to my office to retrieve the inventory. Diesel remained with Kanesha. He was prowling around the boxes as I left the room. I thought Kanesha might object. She ignored him, however.

I came back with the box of disks and the inventory. "The contracts are in box twelve," I said. "I looked already." I set the box down on the floor.

We both turned to hunt for box twelve. Kanesha spotted it first, at the bottom of a stack of four. I helped her move the three on top, and she pulled box twelve out of the way.

"It's pretty light," she said, frowning up at me.

She squatted down and removed the lid.

It was empty.

TWENTY-SEVEN

If I could have crawled into that empty box and pulled the lid over me, I would have. Kanesha's expression was implacable enough to stop a charging rhino in its tracks.

She stood after replacing the lid on the box. She walked out into the hall, and I fancied I could see the anger in every step she took. She turned and waited for Diesel and me to join her in the hall.

"Please lock the door," she said.

When I had done so she held out her hand for the keys. "I'm sorry," I said as I complied.

She didn't respond. Instead she walked down the hall to my office, unlocked the door, and stood pointedly by the door. Diesel followed me as I went down the hall and into the office.

"I'll be back in a few minutes," she said. "I'll return your keys then." She headed for the stairs.

I went to my desk and sat down. I had really screwed things up, and Kanesha had every right to be furious with me. I had let myself get too caught up in the situation and hadn't thought things through clearly enough. I wasn't one of the Hardy Boys, happily assisting my famous detective father.

As a basically law-abiding citizen, however, I had interpreted what I saw as my civic duty to assist the deputy in her inquiry a little too broadly. I did think I had helped her in some ways. How long would it have taken her to find the letters on those disks, for example? But did that outweigh my blunder in allowing someone to steal a whole boxful—if not more—of Godfrey's papers?

To distract myself from spinning mental wheels to no effect, I turned to my computer to check my e-mail. Diesel, seeming to sense my inner turmoil, kept rubbing against my legs and purring. I scratched his head and, as always, that made me feel better. Seeing his pleasure from the attention was an effective calming agent.

After a couple of minutes of scratching, Diesel pulled his head away and climbed into his window seat. Still purring he settled down for a siesta while I tried to focus on work.

As I read through my e-mail, I heard Kanesha return, but I didn't look up from my task. Some minutes later I was aware that she entered my office, and I swiveled in my chair to face her.

"Here are your keys," she said as she placed them on my desk. "I've put an official seal on the room, but I'll be sending someone here within the hour to remove those boxes to the sheriff's department. If you will have a receipt ready, I'd appreciate it."

I glanced at her face. Her expression had lost some of the rigidity it had earlier, and I relaxed a bit myself. Maybe she wasn't going to bless me out after all.

"I'll be glad to do that," I said.

"Fine." She glared at me a moment. "I realize that you had good intentions, Mr. Harris, and generally we appreciate cooperation from the public. But you stepped too far over the line. You realize that, don't you?"

"Yes, I do," I said. "I can't tell you how much I regret not notifying you right away about Godfrey's papers. I can only hope this won't cause serious problems for your investigation."

She listened, but when I finished, she simply nodded and walked out.

After that I tried to focus on my e-mail, but it was no use. I was still too unsettled by what had transpired between Kanesha and me. I glanced at my watch. It was almost four-thirty. *Might as well get out of here.*

"Come on, boy, time to go," I told Diesel as I shut down my computer.

Yawning, he sat up and stretched. He stood patiently, as always, for me to put him in his harness, and a few minutes later we were ready to go. The afternoon was cool but sunny when we left the building. During the brief walk home, I thought about what I might do this evening.

A quiet night at home would be just the thing. That's what I told myself, but a little niggling voice kept insisting that there was something else I could do.

Teresa Farmer, the librarian I mentioned to Kanesha Berry, was usually at the public library until six on Friday evenings. I had time to go over there and have a quiet chat with her and find out what she might know about local writers' groups.

This would mean treading on Kanesha's toes again, but I knew I could trust Teresa's discretion. If I told her why I was asking, she would not talk about it to anyone until the deputy asked for her assistance.

When you want something, you can generally come up with the reasoning to justify it, I have discovered over the years. Even when you know you shouldn't.

At home all was quiet. I let Diesel have time to use the litter box and eat something before heading to the public library in the car. I contemplated leaving him home, but if I walked through the front door of the library without him, I would have to look at any number of disappointed faces. Diesel was very popular there.

I pulled into the parking lot at the library a few minutes after five. Diesel walked ahead of me, pulling a bit on the leash, eager to go inside. He enjoyed the public library because of the attention he always received.

The first few minutes inside we spent accepting greetings from some of the children who were there, not to mention the adults on the library staff. Teresa was not at the reference desk, and I was afraid for a moment that she wasn't at work today.

But a few minutes later she appeared from the office area behind the reference desk, alerted no doubt by the increase in noise. A petite dynamo a few years my senior, Teresa smiled broadly when she discovered the reason for the noise.

As soon as I could I extracted Diesel from his cadre of young admirers and led him behind the reference desk where Teresa waited. She had three cats of her own, and she was as fond of Diesel as anyone here.

"Charlie, what are you doing here? This is an unexpected pleasure," Teresa said. "And Diesel, how are you?" She squatted in front of the cat in order to give him some attention, rubbing his head affectionately.

Diesel purred and warbled while I explained.

"I came to see you," I said. "I need your help with something."

Teresa stood. "Sure, come on back to my office."

Diesel and I followed her. Teresa was the head of reference for the library as well as the assistant director. She also supervised the library's few volunteers, and I had worked closely with her for almost three years now.

She sat down behind her desk and motioned for me to take a seat across from her. I did so and unhooked Diesel's leash from his harness. He padded around the desk and climbed up into Teresa's lap. When he sat up his head was actually a bit higher than hers, and I had to smile at the sight.

"What can I do for you, Charlie?" Teresa said as she rubbed Diesel under the chin.

"It has to do with Godfrey Priest," I said.

Startled, Teresa looked at me. "That's odd," she said. "How so?"

"I had a call just a few minutes ago from Detective Berry," she said. "She's coming in tomorrow morning to talk to me about something to do with Godfrey. She didn't say what, exactly, just that she needed some information and someone had suggested me to her. Was that you?"

Kanesha had acted more quickly than I expected. At least she had accepted my suggestion, I thought.

"Yes, it was," I said. "I'm being really naughty in coming to talk to you before she does, but I'm letting my curiosity get the better of me, I'm afraid."

Teresa laughed. "I promise not to rat on you. What is it you and Deputy Berry want to know?"

"Information on local writers' groups," I said. "If there are any, I figured you'd be bound to know."

"Thanks," Teresa said. "We do try to keep track of any community activities to be prepared for the inevitable questions."

"I know," I said, grinning. "I'll never forget the time I got a call from a woman—this was in Houston—who was looking for information on an organization for cats." I had to laugh, just thinking about it.

"What's so funny about that?" Teresa asked.

"She had heard about a group that knitted socks for cats, she said, and she wanted to join them," I said. I chuckled again.

Teresa joined in my laughter. "I can't imagine one of my cats allowing me to put socks on her or him. They'd have a fit."

"I thought it was pretty funny," I said. "But of course I couldn't tell her that. So I found her the name of a contact person for a local cat fanciers' group. I never heard whether she found what she was looking for."

"At least you gave her something," Teresa said, still smiling. "Now, about writers' groups. Yes, I can think of several. There's one group that's been meeting here at the library for about twenty years. They're all poets, though, and somehow I don't think that's what you're looking for. Not if it has something to do with Godfrey Priest."

"Right," I said. "I want to know if there was a group

he was ever a part of, or maybe whether he spoke to local groups when he came back to Athena."

"And you can't tell me exactly why you want this information?"

"No, I can't," I said with regret. "You don't mind, I hope."

"I can live with it," Teresa said wryly. "Okay. Godfrey Priest and writers' groups." She frowned as she thought. By now Diesel had settled down in her lap, his head against her chest as he purred in deep contentment. Teresa stroked his head gently.

I kept quiet while she dredged through her memory banks. She had amazing recall—one reason she was such a terrific reference librarian. If there were something to find, she'd find it.

"It has to be at least twenty years ago now," Teresa said. "Godfrey Priest hasn't spoken at this library in at least that long. He did participate in a fund-raiser we had about seven years ago, spoke at a Friends of the Library dinner, but that was it."

"What about twenty years ago?" I said, prompting her gently when she fell silent again.

"There was a group that met here occasionally back then," Teresa said. "Seven or eight people, I think. They weren't together that long, or at least they didn't ask to use our meeting room for long. They could have continued meeting somewhere else."

"Do you recall who was in the group?" I kept my fingers crossed.

"I can do better than that," Teresa said with a smile. "I can show you a picture of them." She scratched Diesel's head. "But you're going to have to let me up." Diesel sat up, butted his head against her chin, and jumped to the floor at her gentle urging.

"A picture would be great," I said as Diesel came around the desk to sit by my chair.

Teresa got up from her desk. "I'll be back in a minute. What I want is in one of the filing cabinets behind the reference desk."

Diesel and I waited quietly for her return. She was gone less than five minutes.

When she returned she handed me a folder. I examined the label: "Library Annual Reports."

"I put the relevant one on top," Teresa said as she resumed her seat behind the desk.

I extracted it from the folder and laid the rest aside on top of her desk. The report consisted of only a few pages, and it was on page four that I found the photograph Teresa wanted me to see. It was rather small, and the caption only said, "Writers' Group Meets with Local Novelist."

In the center of a group of six people was Godfrey Priest—looking much younger and much less successful than he did when I saw him a few days ago. That was only natural. This picture was taken before he hit it big.

I examined the faces of the others in the group. I recognized two of them right away, and I was stunned as I put the names to the faces.

Julia Wardlaw and Rick Tackett stood on either side of Godfrey, both smiling into the camera.

TWENTY-EIGHT

"You look shocked," Teresa said. "Is anything wrong?"

"I'm just really surprised," I said. "I see two people in this group I never expected to see. Two people I had no idea were interested in writing."

I examined the other faces in the group. Two of them looked vaguely familiar, but I couldn't quite place them. If only the caption to the picture had included their names.

I was about to hand the report back to Teresa to ask whether she knew who they all were when I spotted something odd in the picture. I held it closer and squinted. The resolution wasn't great, but I thought I saw the top of another head peeking out from behind Julia's shoulder, the one next to Godfrey.

"Looks like there's another person here in the background," I said. I held the report across the desk to Teresa. "See what you think. Also, do you know who all the people are?"

Teresa examined the picture for a moment before laying the report aside. She opened one of her desk drawers and rummaged through it. "Ah, here it is," she said. She brandished a magnifying glass. She picked up the report again and examined the picture with the aid of the glass.

"I think you're right," she said after a moment. "That does look like someone's head. It's odd, though. Why wouldn't whoever it was want to be visible in the picture?"

"Beats me," I said. My heartbeat picked up though, because I wondered if the mystery person behind Julia was X. Based on the letters I had read, X shunned the spotlight, and it could be that he or she avoided having photos taken.

Teresa laid the glass aside and looked at the picture again. "I recognize all of them," she said. She named them, and in addition to Julia and Rick, I recognized the names of a couple of professors at Athena, one from the history department and the other from English.

"Would you mind writing those down for me?" I said. "And do all of them still live in the area?"

"One of them passed away a few years go," she said. "I'll put an *X* next to her name. But the others—except Mr. Priest, of course—are still around."

"Thanks," I said. "I really appreciate your help with this. I can't tell you how, or why, but this may be the key to Godfrey's murder."

"That's definitely intriguing," Teresa said. She finished writing and handed a piece of paper across the desk to me. "I'm sure it would help if we knew who the other person was lurking in the background. I've been mulling it over, and I seem to remember that there were a couple of people who met with the group a few times, but the six you see here were the core. They met together for four or five years, I think."

"I know one of the people in the group pretty well," I said. "And I work with another one."

"That's right, Rick Tackett works at the college library," Teresa said. "He's a nice man, pretty quiet. Reads a lot. I hope he's not involved in this."

"I hope so, too," I said. "I agree he's a nice guy. But I think one of the people here may very well be the one Deputy Berry is looking for."

"That's unsettling, to say the least," Teresa said with a frown. "I hope she manages to figure it out soon. If one of them comes in the library before she does, I think I'll be a bit nervous."

"No need to be, I'm sure," I said. "There's no reason for anyone to think you're involved in any way."

"Other than assisting the official inquiry, you mean." Teresa's smile was impish. "And the unofficial one."

"Yes," I said, hoping that my face wasn't turning pink. "I appreciate your help, but I think Diesel and I ought to head home now." I stood, and Teresa came around the desk to shake my hand. "I'll see you next Friday, of course."

"We always look forward to it," Teresa said as she escorted Diesel and me out of the office. "Our volunteers are a huge help, and we definitely appreciate what you do for us." She bent to rub Diesel's head. "And you too, big guy."

Diesel chirped at her, and I smiled as I led him away. We managed to make it out the door after only a few minutes' delay for more attention to Diesel. He loved every second of it, the ham.

Back in the car I examined the list of names for a moment while Diesel settled down on the passenger seat beside me. I might as well start with Julia, I reckoned. Seeing her in the picture had really knocked me for a loop. Her connections to this case were so strong, and though I was sure she had to be innocent of Godfrey's murder, I knew her having been part of the writers' group might make Kanesha Berry focus more intently on her.

Rick Tackett seemed like a stronger possibility in many ways. He was Godfrey's half brother, for one thing, and as the library's custodian, he had easy access to my office and to the archive storeroom. No one would have thought twice about it if he had been spotted upstairs near the storeroom on the evening when someone had obviously entered my office and examined the boxes.

I had to hope that whoever it was hadn't destroyed the contracts. If Kanesha could find those in his—or her, I added, to be completely fair—possession, that would be an important link to the murder.

Surely, however, there were other copies of the contracts. Godfrey's agent had to have copies. I brightened at that thought. The agent would be at Godfrey's memorial service tomorrow. By then she would already have talked with Kanesha, and perhaps I could slip in a few questions without objection.

On the short drive home I pondered the questions I wanted to pose to the agent. How should I start? What

preface to my questions could I use to disarm her enough
to talk to me?

One big question occurred to me right away, and I
knew I would have to be very careful in asking it. Did
the agent know that Godfrey wasn't writing the books
himself?

Then I remembered that Kanesha would probably be
asking her that question, not to mention countless others,
tonight. I would try and see how far I could get.

Julia's car was parked in front of the house, and Diesel
and I found her in the kitchen. We exchanged greetings as
I released Diesel from his harness. He went to greet Julia
before trotting off to his litter box.

"I came to pick up Justin," Julia said. "He's coming
home to have dinner with us, and he'll probably spend
the night."

Justin often spent Friday nights with his parents, and
that meant I had the house to myself one night a week.
At least until the spring semester, I reminded myself. My
other boarder would be back from his semester abroad
then.

"How is Ezra doing?" I asked. "Would you like something to drink while you wait?" I went to the fridge for a
diet drink.

"No, thank you, Justin should be down any minute,"
Julia said. "Ezra is doing okay. Very happy to be home
from the hospital, naturally."

"Good," I said, popping the top on the can and having
a swallow. I came to the table and sat down. "I've come
across something interesting, and I'd like to talk to you
about it, if you have a moment."

Julia frowned. "This isn't a good time, I'm afraid.

I really need to get back to Ezra. Justin needs to get a move on."

"I understand," I said. "But when you do have a moment, it's important."

"Okay," Julia said. "Perhaps when I bring Justin back tomorrow morning. It depends on how Ezra's doing, though."

"Of course," I said. I had to be content with that. Julia obviously wasn't in the mood to talk.

Justin came clattering down the stairs then, his backpack slung over his shoulder and his hair over his eyes. "I'm ready, Mama." He spotted me then and said, "Evening, sir."

"Good evening, Justin. I'll miss your company at dinner tonight," I said, and I realized I meant it. I had grown accustomed to having someone at the table with me—besides Diesel, that is.

"Thank you, sir," Justin said, coloring slightly. He bent to pet Diesel, who had reappeared in the kitchen the moment he heard Justin coming down the stairs.

Julia stood. "We'd better be going. I'll see you tomorrow morning, Charlie."

"I look forward to it," I said.

Julia flashed me a questioning look, but she didn't linger. I hoped she would have time to talk in the morning. For now, however, I would have to curb my impatience.

Diesel followed them to the door, and I heard Justin say good-bye to him before the door shut. The cat came back into the kitchen as I was checking to see what Azalea had left for tonight's dinner.

There was a roast in the oven, along with a baked potato wrapped in foil. A pot of green beans on the stove rounded out the meal. I sighed in contentment. Azalea's roasts were tender and delicious, and I looked forward to my dinner.

On the way upstairs to change clothes, I considered calling Rick Tackett, but I quickly rejected the idea. I could think of no reasonable pretext for calling him out of the blue—for he was probably home by now. Plus I knew such a call could get me into deeper trouble with Kanesha Berry. I discounted my chat with Teresa Farmer and the forthcoming talk with Julia. Concerning the latter, I figured it possible that Kanesha might talk to Julia before I did. She often didn't bring Justin back to my house until lunchtime or after on Saturdays. If Kanesha talked to Teresa early enough tomorrow, she would probably get on to Julia right away.

My son Sean called as I was ready to go downstairs for my dinner. Instead, I sat on the bed and chatted with him for nearly half an hour. That was a long call for Sean. Our conversations usually lasted no more than ten minutes, but tonight I sensed that Sean needed to talk, and I wasn't going to hurry him.

By now he had heard about Godfrey Priest's murder, and I told him of my involvement. Sean, in his second year out of law school, worked for a large firm in Houston that specialized in civil law. He expressed concern for me, and I assured him I was fine.

He kept talking about innocuous things, but all the time he spoke I sensed an undercurrent. Finally, I decided to ask him outright what was wrong.

Sean sighed into the phone. "I don't know, Dad. It's a number of things. The job, for one. It's not really what I thought it would be, and the hours are crazy. I work all the time."

"It's hard, I know. Those big firms work junior lawyers really hard for the first few years." Now that he was talking openly, I could sense a certain amount of relief.

"Yeah, that's part of the problem. It's going to be years before it gets any better, and I'm not sure I'm cut out for this."

That concerned me, because Sean knew he wanted to be a lawyer from the age of twelve when he first read *To Kill a Mockingbird*.

"You wanted to be Atticus Finch," I said.

"I did," Sean said. "I was pretty naive, wasn't I?"

"Idealistic," I said. "There's a difference."

"Well, it's hard to hold on to your ideals when you're working on cases involving millions of dollars and representing big companies who are trying to sidestep the law any way they can."

"What are you going to do about it?" I asked.

Sean didn't answer for a moment. "I'm not sure. I'm still thinking about it. I thought I might spend a couple weeks at Christmas with you, if that's okay. Do you think Laura's coming home then?"

"She hasn't said yet, but I certainly hope she will. And you know, son, you can come and stay as long as you like. There's plenty of room." I didn't dare be too effusive. Sean turned prickly over displays of paternal emotion. He had always been closer to his mother. "Thanks, Dad," he said, the relief obvious in his voice. "I'll let you know when I can get away."

"Good. I'm looking forward to seeing you," I said. I

actually hadn't seen him since his law school graduation over two years ago. He was always too busy to visit me, and whenever I suggested coming to Houston, he put me off.

We chatted a few more minutes, and when I put down the phone I was thoughtful. Sean was in distress, and I wanted to help him. I would have to wait until the holidays, though. I tried not to dwell too much on the possibility that he might leave Houston permanently for Athena. I didn't want to be disappointed. By December he might change his mind about even coming here for the holidays.

Dinner was every bit as delectable as I expected, and when I finished I thought ruefully about that third helping of roast. I felt discomfort in my stomach, and I scolded myself for overeating. I put it down to my concern for Sean. I had always been a stress eater.

I had a restless night as well, partly because I'd over-eaten, but in large part due to worries about my son. When I rose the next morning, bleary-eyed from not getting enough quality sleep, Diesel hopped out of bed, perky as ever. On mornings like this he reminded me of one of my college roommates, who invariably rose from bed chipper and happy. There were times when I could cheerfully have whacked him over the head and stuffed his body in the closet.

Diesel was safe, however. He was much too fast for me.

On Saturday mornings I pottered about the house once I had read the newspaper and eaten my breakfast. Sometimes I worked in the yard, and I knew a couple of the flowerbeds in the backyard needed attention. I was not the world's most enthusiastic gardener, but I knew it would do me good to be out in the clear, cool air, engaged in a useful activity.

Besides, Diesel loved exploring the backyard. The lot was large, and there were plenty of spots for an enterprising feline to delve into in hopes of finding something fun to play with. As I weeded the flowerbeds, Diesel popped into and out of them, batting fallen leaves about and cheering me up to no end.

Near noon I decided to break for lunch. There had been no sign of Julia and Justin, and I hoped they would appear soon. I was eager to talk to Julia about the writers' group.

As I was washing my hands in the kitchen sink, I heard the front door opening. Justin had a key, so I assumed it was he and Julia. Diesel scampered off. He would accompany Justin upstairs, I was sure.

"Good afternoon," Julia said moments later, as she paused in the doorway. "You look like you've been working out in the yard today."

I glanced down and saw the streaks of dirt on my old khakis. "Weeding flowerbeds while Diesel stalked the jungle in search of dangerous leaves."

Julia laughed at that.

"Come in and have a seat," I said. "Would you like something to drink?"

"I'm fine," Julia said as she came to the table. "We finished lunch a short time ago. Justin was anxious to get back. He has a paper due for his English class on Monday."

I filled a glass of water from the tap and sat down at the table. "How are things?"

"Okay," Julia said. "Though we had a visit this morning from Kanesha Berry."

"I see," I said. "I have an idea what you might have talked about."

"How would you know?" Julia asked. "Is she taking you into her confidence?"

"Not exactly," I said wryly. "But I did manage to find out a few things that she didn't know."

"Something to do with a writers' group that I used to belong to." Julia said it flatly. She looked annoyed, whether with me or Kanesha, I wasn't sure.

"Yes," I said.

"Why all the interest in something that happened twenty years ago?" Julia frowned. "I can't see what my belonging to that group for a couple of years has to do with anything." She paused for a moment, a faraway look in her eyes. "Though that *is* when I had my fling with Godfrey, the Lord forgive me, and got pregnant with Justin."

"I can't really say why Kanesha is interested, or why I am either," I said. "But I do think it's important. I never knew you were interested in writing."

Julia shrugged. "I tried my hand at several things back then, trying to figure out what I could do besides being a preacher's wife. I'd always made good grades in English, so I assumed—wrongly, as it turned out—that I had potential as a writer." She laughed suddenly, a bitter sound. "I had visions of becoming the new Phyllis Whitney or Victoria Holt. Not only were books like that not being published anymore—unless you were Phyllis Whitney or Victoria Holt—but I wasn't very good at writing them. Godfrey might have been a jerk in many ways, but at least he convinced me to stop wasting my time."

"You weren't interested in writing thrillers?" She had sounded sincere when talking about her writing, but I needed to be sure she wasn't X and trying to put me off the scent.

"Heavens, no." She laughed again, this time sounding amused. "I almost never read them. I never had a desire to write them, I promise you."

"Good," I said. "What about the other members of the group? Were any of them interested in writing thrillers?"

"Not that I recall," Julia said. She thought for a moment. "Rick Tackett was writing a book about Vietnam. I think it was therapy for him, more than anything else. The other two women in the group were writing romance novels, and one of them was working on a western. The history professor—I think he's actually teaching Justin this semester—was writing this horrendously awful historical novel about an oversexed druid in ancient Britain."

"That's six of you," I said. "Were there others in the group?"

"Occasionally," Julia said. "We had three people join for a brief time, if I remember correctly, but they never lasted."

"Do you remember who they were?" I was thinking of the person lurking behind Julia in the photograph. "Someone who might have been part of the group when Godfrey spoke to you twenty years ago?"

"That's what Kanesha Berry wanted to know," Julia said, her head tilted to one side.

"Oh," I said. "And did you have an answer for her?"

Julia looked at me for a moment. "There was this strange little man who came a few times, but he never showed us any of his writing. Shortly after Godfrey talked to us, he stopped coming."

"Who was he?" I said. I had the feeling Julia was deliberately dragging this out.

"He was one of our classmates in high school," Julia said. She paused for a moment, and I thought I would have to prompt her again. Then she spoke. "It was Willie Clark. He always was an oddball, you know."

TWENTY-NINE

||||||||||||||||||||||||||||||||||||||||||||||||||||||||||||||||||||||||||||||

"Willie." Of course, I thought. Who I had seen the day Godfrey died, scribbling away at something in the staff lounge.

Then I put another piece of the puzzle together. The misogyny of the books. Who had a reputation for it? Willie did. I remembered the conversation I had overheard the other day in Hawksworth Library. Willie didn't like women, while Godfrey did.

Perhaps I was jumping to conclusions, but for me, that clinched it. Willie was the X who wrote the books.

And who had a powerful motive for killing Godfrey.

"Charlie." Julia's voice brought me back to earth. "What is it? Why are you so excited about Willie?"

I tried to restrain myself. I didn't want to give away anything to Julia, not without talking to Kanesha Berry first.

"I can't really say," I told her. "But knowing that Willie was part of your group, even briefly, helps fill in some missing pieces of the puzzle."

Julia scrutinized me for a moment, as if she were trying to read my mind. "It's the oddest thing," she finally said.

"What is?" I asked when she fell silent again.

"About Willie," Julia replied. "Now that I'm thinking about it, I could have sworn I saw him at Farrington House on Tuesday."

"You did?" This was even better—a witness to place him near the scene of the crime.

Julia nodded. "I think it was him. You know how it is, when you're in a hurry and you catch sight of someone in the corner of your eye. I don't think it really registered at the time who he was." She paused and closed her eyes for a moment, as if trying to visualize the scene. "As I was leaving, I was aware of someone in the revolving door, entering the hotel. But I was in a hurry to get to the bank and then back to the hospital, so I didn't think much about it at the time."

"And it was Willie?" This put both Willie and Jordan Thompson in the hotel. I knew Jordan had seen Godfrey. The signed and dated copies of his new book were evidence of that.

"Yes, I'm pretty sure, the more I think about it," Julia said.

If Willie was the killer, he saw Godfrey after Jordan did. According to her, she didn't stay that long with Godfrey. Then in comes Willie with a strong grievance over Godfrey's treatment of him. Perhaps he had wanted more money for his part of the deal, or maybe he simply was tired of the anonymity of his position and wanted recognition.

Whatever the motive, he might have become enraged by Godfrey's attitude and struck Godfrey down on impulse.

Yes, that sounded like a believable scenario.

"When you talked to Kanesha about the writing group," I said, "did you happen to mention that Willie was a member for a while?"

"Yes," Julia said. "She had a picture with her. Actually an annual report from the library. I had forgotten all about that picture. Willie was there that day, I remembered, but he hid behind me. At the time I thought it was peculiar, but you know how he was in high school. Always scurrying from one place to another, trying not to be noticed."

"So the football team wouldn't pick on him, as I recall." Willie's life in high school had to have been pretty miserable. "And Godfrey was one of the worst." How ironic that was, if I was right about Willie being X.

"Yes, he was." Julia sighed. "He really was an out-and-out bastard a lot of the time."

"You need to tell Kanesha that you saw Willie at the hotel that day."

"Of course. As soon as I get the chance." Julia glanced at her watch. "Perhaps I'd better go hurry Justin along."

"Are you going somewhere this afternoon?" I asked.

Julia nodded. "Godfrey's memorial service. I promised Justin I would go with him." She gestured at my clothes. "Doesn't look like you were planning to go."

The moment Julia mentioned it, I realized I had forgotten all about it. I checked my watch. It was 12:32. If I hurried, I could clean up and get dressed and still make it to the service just about on time.

"I can't believe I forgot about it," I said, rising. "If you'll excuse me, I'll run upstairs and get ready. I'll see you and Justin there." *So much for lunch.* But there would be food after the memorial service, I remembered.

"Good. We'll save a spot for you, if we can. I expect a lot of people will turn out, just out of curiosity."

"Probably so," I said. "See you soon." I hurried up the stairs.

I met Justin on the second floor landing. He was wearing a dark suit and looking pale but composed.

"Hello, sir," he said. "Are you coming to the service?" He eyed my clothes with doubt.

"Yes, just running a little late," I said. "I'll see you there. Was Diesel with you?"

"He was," Justin said, pausing on his way down the stairs. "But he disappeared while I was in the shower." He hesitated, as if he was about to add something, but then he turned and continued down.

Diesel was napping on my bed, his head on one of the pillows. He opened one eye when I came in the room, regarded me for a moment, then shut it again. His tail twitched a couple of times while I took off my clothes, but after that he appeared to be sound asleep.

Just as well, I thought. The memorial service was one place I shouldn't really take him. I hoped he would stay asleep while I got ready.

I took a very quick shower, and as I was toweling off, I reconsidered my decision not to take Diesel with me. I remembered Justin's hesitation before he went on down the stairs. This memorial service was bound to be difficult for him, and I guessed he might have been planning to ask me to bring Diesel. Cat and young man seemed to have a special bond, and Justin needed support right now.

Diesel could come with me after all. For Justin's sake.

I dressed quickly into one of my own dark suits. Diesel woke up when I sat on the bed to tie my shoes. "Come on, boy," I said. "Let's go."

Diesel hopped off the bed and was at the door in a flash. He knew those words too well.

I glanced at my watch as I hurried down the stairs, Diesel ahead of me. It was 12:52. I would just about make it.

I had Diesel in his harness in record time, and then we headed out the door. It would be just as fast to walk to the college chapel as to drive and try to find a place to park, I reasoned.

We set off at a brisk pace, and the carillon on campus was chiming one as we approached the chapel, which was down the street from the library buildings.

Campus police were in evidence, as well as members of the sheriff's department and the city police force. I spotted all three uniforms moving among the crowd of reports and photographers on the lawn outside the chapel. I should have realized that Godfrey's memorial service would attract the media. As far as I knew, however, they were still unaware of my role in the case. I really owed Kanesha Berry for that.

Diesel and I weren't the only late arrivals, though I was the only one accompanied by a cat. Diesel's presence occasioned a few frowns, but I didn't care. Justin mattered more than what these people thought.

A couple of reporters tried to get my attention, probably because of Diesel. I knew cameras were busy snapping shots of us as we hurried up the walk toward the front door of the chapel. One reporter with a microphone and a cameraman tried to step around the cordon the police had placed, but a campus officer quickly stepped in and forced her back behind the barrier. Diesel and I scooted into the chapel. I hoped we could avoid them again after the service.

I paused at the entrance to the sanctuary, trying to find Julia and Justin in the crowd. There were very few open seats, and the sanctuary could easily hold three hundred people. I spotted Melba Gilley and Peter Vanderkeller near the front. Willie Clark was here too, in the back row to my left. Jordan Thompson sat nearby, two rows in front of Willie. Standing in the back to my right was Kanesha Berry, dressed in a black skirt and jacket instead of her usual uniform. She saw me and acknowledged me with a brief nod.

I scanned the crowd again and finally picked out Julia and Justin about halfway down on the right in the middle of a pew. There was an empty space next to Justin, and I led Diesel toward it.

I mumbled, "Excuse me," several times as Diesel and I made our way to the middle of the pew. One woman hissed, "Well, I never." A vaguely familiar man with her told her to hush. "That's the cat I told you about," I heard him tell her in an undertone.

I flashed him a quick smile, and then I reached the empty space. I sat, and Diesel moved between Justin's legs and stared up at him.

"Thank you," Justin whispered to me. He bent forward and began to rub Diesel's head. I just hoped the cat wouldn't purr too loudly and annoy the people sitting around us.

Julia glanced down and shook her head, but smiled. She had her arm around her son's shoulders.

The organist began playing. The service had started.

The choir sang two hymns, and the chaplain spoke briefly about Godfrey's accomplishments and lamented a life cut short by violence. The president also spoke and said a few words about Godfrey's generosity to the school over the years. Godfrey had always given money on condition of anonymity, and that surprised me. He always seemed to want to be the center of attention. Knowing this made me think slightly better of him.

The president introduced Godfrey's agent, a petite blonde named Andrea Ferris, who said a few words about the effect of his death on his millions of fans around the world. She herself didn't seem all that grief stricken, however. Perhaps she was simply putting up a brave front. The president stepped back in front of the microphone to invite everyone to move into the chapel meeting room for a reception in the dear departed's memory.

Then it was over. It was mercifully brief, but the whole time I had been aware of the tension coming from mother and son beside me. There had been no mention of Godfrey's recently discovered son during the service, and I imagined that both Julia and Justin were greatly relieved. The last thing they wanted right now was that kind of attention, especially with the media waiting right outside.

I remained seated with mother, son, and cat while the pews around us slowly emptied. Julia was making no move to leave, and I wondered if she planned to go home now and skip the reception.

"Are you leaving now?" I asked when most of the people around us were gone.

"No," Julia said. "We should put in an appearance at the reception. And I want to have a word with Godfrey's agent."

"So do I," I said, smiling briefly. "Shall we?" I stood.

I exited the pew, leading Diesel on his leash, and Justin and Julia followed me through the sanctuary to the meeting room behind.

Not everyone who attended the service stayed for the reception. There were only about a hundred or so people in the room, and I was thankful for that. I tended to be a bit claustrophobic when a large number of people occupied a small space, and this room wasn't really designed to hold as many people as the sanctuary.

Mindful of my lack of lunch today, I followed Julia and Justin as they joined the line of people at the buffet table. From my place in line I could see some of the food. It appeared to be mostly cocktail party–type snacks. Not ideal, but enough. I could easily fill up on cheese and crackers and fruit. There were also deviled eggs, a staple of this kind of gathering—at least in Mississippi. I would have to watch Diesel, though, in case he decided he wanted to investigate the food. When he stood on his hind legs, he was tall enough to reach out and scoop something from the table.

We made it through the line without incident, and along with Julia and Justin I found a place to stand against the wall. While the two of them nibbled at the few things on their plates, I had to restrain myself from gobbling it down. I was hungrier than I realized.

I was chewing my last bit of cheese and cracker when Kanesha Berry approached us.

"Good afternoon." Her voice was low, her demeanor wary.

I returned her greeting, echoed by Julia and Justin. Diesel chirped at her, and she glanced down for a moment. I could almost swear I spotted a brief smile, but when she looked up, her expression was blandly official.

"Julia has something she needs to tell you," I said, eager to the point of rudeness. Now that the solution to the murder was so close, I really wanted to see things happen. Once Willie was arrested—for at this point I had no doubt he, as X, had the best motive for murder, and according to Julia he also had opportunity—we would all rest much easier.

Kanesha turned to Julia with an expectant look.

Julia frowned slightly. "I'm not sure this is the place," she said.

Justin surprised us all by interrupting. "Mr. Charlie, would you mind if I took Diesel for a walk?" He had a slightly desperate look, and I wondered whether the occasion was proving too much for him.

I handed over the leash. "Sure, but why don't you just go into the sanctuary? It should be pretty quiet in there, and I don't think going outside right now is a good idea."

"Yes, sir," Justin said. "Come on, Diesel."

I watched boy and cat make their way through the crowd. Poor kid. So much had happened to him so quickly. No wonder he wanted to find a quiet place.

"You have something to tell me?" Kanesha spoke firmly to Julia.

"I suppose so," Julia replied with a sidelong glance at me. "During a chat with Charlie before the service, I recalled something that happened when I went to the hotel to see Godfrey."

"I see. What was that?" Kanesha shifted her weight from one foot to the other.

"It was talking about the writers' group that brought it back to mind," Julia said. "I remembered that, when I was leaving the hotel that day, I saw someone in the revolving door, entering as I was going out." She paused for a moment. "It was Willie Clark. Charlie seems to think that's significant for some reason."

"How so?" Kanesha could have been discussing today's weather, I thought. She didn't seem particularly interested in Julia's revelation.

I thought I could get her interested, however. I said, "Willie is X."

THIRTY

Kanesha flashed me a warning look, her head moving ever so slightly in Julia's direction.

"X? What does that mean?" Julia frowned at me. "Are you telling me that *Willie* murdered Godfrey?"

I was relieved that she kept her voice down, otherwise the people nearby would have heard it all.

"I really cannot discuss that with you, Mrs. Wardlaw. Do not repeat this conversation to anyone."

Julia nodded. "Certainly I won't."

Kanesha was clearly annoyed with me for speaking in front of Julia. She took my arm and started leading me away. "I need to speak to Mr. Harris alone."

I went without protest. I should have restrained myself and waited until I could speak to her alone, but sometimes I got a bit carried away. I recalled an expression my grandmother used when I did something like this as a child: "His head knows better, but his feet can't stand it."

In other words, despite knowing better, I sometimes put my foot in it.

Kanesha led me back out into the sanctuary. I spotted Justin and Diesel in the choir loft, away from the few people sitting in pews, eating and talking. Kanesha found a spot a good ten feet away from anyone else and pointed to a pew.

I sat.

She sat down beside me, about a foot away on the pew. Her right hand gripped the back of the pew in front of us, and I saw her knuckles tighten. "You cannot blurt out things like that."

"I know," I said, feeling foolish. "I'm sorry. It's just that, now that I know who killed Godfrey, I want this to be over."

Kanesha closed her eyes for a moment, and I wondered whether she was praying for patience. Her grip on the pew didn't loosen.

"You know who killed Godfrey Priest?" Her eyes opened. "I suppose you think Willie Clark did it."

"Yes," I said, eager to atone for my goof. "Once I found out he was part of the writers' group, and knowing what we know about someone else writing Godfrey's books, it all fell into place."

"How so?" Kanesha let go of the pew and folded her arms across her chest.

"The attitude toward women in the books," I said. "Look, have you ever read one of the books?"

"Yes, a few of them," Kanesha said. "I like to read them and find all the mistakes in police procedure." She shook her head. "His books were pretty bad in that respect. But I know what you mean about the women in his books. He didn't like them."

"Well, that wasn't Godfrey. From what everyone says, Godfrey truly liked women. He just couldn't settle down with one. It's Willie who's the big-time misogynist. You should hear him talking to female staff and students sometimes. He can be a real jerk."

"Okay," Kanesha said. "He's a misogynist. I'd need more evidence than that, though. Even if he did write the books. I have to have something that links him to the actual murder."

"According to Julia, he was at the hotel that day. He had to have gone there to talk to Godfrey." I was feeling a bit deflated by her lack of excitement. I thought surely she would see the picture as clearly as I did.

But she was an officer of the law, and I was a librarian. This was her job, not mine.

"I will ask him about it," Kanesha said. "But unless he admits to being there, I'm going to need more than Mrs. Wardlaw's glimpse of him in a revolving door to go on."

"Of course," I said. "You need physical evidence for a stronger case." I had read enough mysteries to know that. "But at least now you have motive and opportunity."

"There are other suspects who have motives and who also had the opportunity," Kanesha said, her logic relentless.

"Okay, you win," I said. Here I thought I had come up with the answer, and she was refusing to accept it.

What if I was wrong? That was an unwelcome thought. There were things Kanesha knew that I didn't—if her investigation had turned up any kind of evidence from the scene of the crime. I didn't even know what the murder weapon was.

"You did help—a little. I found out some things faster because of your interference." Her tone was grudging, but I knew better than to expect outright gratitude.

I nodded.

"But you're done," she said. "Back off now, and leave me to finish this."

I saw the glint in her eye. "You know who did it, don't you?"

Kanesha regarded me for a moment. "I do. I have a few more things to check, however, and I don't want you getting in my way again."

"I won't, I promise," I said.

"Good." Kanesha stood and made her way out of the pew. She disappeared through the door into the meeting room.

I sat there, thinking about our conversation. Kanesha seemed awfully sure she knew who the murderer was. Was that because of what Julia and I had told her about Willie? Or had she known already?

Perhaps that meant Willie wasn't the killer.

Not knowing was going to annoy me to no end. I had a sudden suspicion that was why Kanesha had told me she knew the killer's identity. If so, I supposed it was adequate payback for the annoyance I had caused her.

It was time to head back to the reception. I would have to be careful about what I said, and to whom, though. I had pushed Kanesha far enough.

I stood in the doorway and looked around, searching for Julia. After a moment, I spotted her in the far corner to my right, talking to someone, but I couldn't see who it was. As I moved closer, I could peer through the crowd, and I recognized Godfrey's agent, Andrea Ferris.

At the same time I also spotted one of the campus blowhards, an elderly English professor named Pemberton Galsworthy. Many suspected the name was his own invention because it was so pompous sounding. But in that respect it was apt. He was a self-important windbag who never had an opinion he wasn't willing to share with anyone within hearing distance.

I almost turned away, knowing that I could be stuck there for an hour if I joined the group. Galsworthy never had conversations. He performed soliloquies.

But Julia caught sight of me, and I couldn't ignore the plea in her eyes. I didn't know why she thought I could do anything to stop the deluge of words. We had suffered through Galsworthy's sophomore literature course together, and she knew him as well as I did.

I moved forward and sidled up next to Julia.

Galsworthy noticed me—in itself noteworthy—and interrupted himself to acknowledge my presence. He peered at me. "Harris, isn't it? Librarian, aren't you?"

Without waiting for an answer, he resumed his peroration, peering now at Godfrey's agent. "Contemporary literature has obviously been bastardized to the point of utter banality. Crass commercialism, naturally. Publishing was once the profession of gentlemen—educated, sophisticated, cultured—who chose works for their literary merit and their ability to enlighten and transform. Not because they would sell in the millions and cater to the tastes of the lowest common denominator, so sadly low these days, one fears for the intellectual survival of the species."

He had more to say in that vein, but I tuned him out for a moment, though I faced him with a rapt expression. I had learned to do it in his class, and thankfully it was a skill I hadn't completely forgotten.

I sneaked a glance at Andrea Ferris, dressed smartly in a dark suit and spike heels that made her stand about five-two. She had that glazed look common to anyone in Galsworthy's presence for more than ten seconds.

Julia nudged me, and I looked at her. She frowned and bobbed her head in Galsworthy's direction. I knew what she wanted, but short of clapping my hand over the man's mouth and shoving him into a closet, I didn't know how to shut him up. We could simply have turned and walked away, but generations of Southern grandmothers would spin in their graves if we behaved so rudely. That was the curse of being raised to have good manners and to treat one's elders with respect—no matter how irritating they were.

I tuned back in at the sound of Godfrey's name.

". . . a sad example of a young man with a good mind— a good mind, you understand, not a fine one—but, yes, a young man with a good mind who could have accomplished something more lasting than such ephemera as he chose to create. Then there is his appalling portrayal of females in his work. One has little doubt that a psychiatrist could have helped the poor boy work through his obvious feelings of hatred toward women. Yet I have no doubt that his female readers little suspected his opinion of them."

I exchanged amused glances with Julia. Galsworthy had obviously read some of Godfrey's work, though one wondered why he had allowed his intellect to be sullied by entertainment of such dubious value to mankind.

Galsworthy blathered on, but I could see that Andrea Ferris was about ready to pop. She cut him off suddenly in mid-sentence.

"I'll be delighted to share your observations of contemporary publishing with my colleagues in New York," Andrea said, her tone deceptively sweet. "I have little doubt they will respond immediately by pulping anything that smacks of lowbrow entertainment and instead start printing—in huge quantities, of course—works that cannot fail to *enlighten* and *transform*. This will revolutionize publishing around the world, and your name, professor, will be on everyone's lips."

After his initial shock at being interrupted, Galsworthy appeared delighted to have his opinions received so well. But Andrea's tone altered as she spoke, becoming more waspish by the syllable, until even Galsworthy had to recognize the sarcasm.

"Good day to you, young woman." Galsworthy glared at Andrea, and so upset was he that he failed to include Julia and me in his farewell.

Julia and I both sighed audibly as he stalked off.

"What a pretentious snot," Andrea said. She sniffed. "If I had a dollar for every one of his kind I've met, I could retire." She turned to me and stuck out her hand. "Andrea Ferris, the late Godfrey Priest's agent."

"Charlie Harris," I said. "Archivist here at the college. Like Mrs. Wardlaw, I went to school with Godfrey eons ago."

Andrea nodded, her eyes on Julia. "You're the mother of his son, aren't you?"

Startled, Julia nodded. "I asked Godfrey to keep it to himself for a while, but obviously he didn't."

"Oh, Godfrey told me everything," Andrea said. "He was my biggest client, you know."

Had Godfrey really told her everything, I wondered? Did Andrea know about the ghostwriter?

"I'm not surprised," I said. "Godfrey made millions."

"He sure did." Andrea's smile was smug. "No complaints there." She cocked her head to one side, thinking about something. "But you know, the old windbag did have a point about something."

"What was that?" I said, though I knew what she meant.

"The bit about Godfrey's treatment of women in the books," Andrea replied. "That always bothered me, because Godfrey liked women. No doubt about that. I never could figure out why the tone of the books was so antifemale."

"Did you ever ask him about it?" Julia seemed intrigued by the question, too.

"I did, early on," Andrea said. "I wasn't his agent for his first few books. I took him on on the strength of *Count the Cost*, his first bestseller." She frowned. "I went back and read one of his earlier books, and the tone was very different."

"What was Godfrey's response when you asked him about it?" I said to get her back to the point.

"He just shrugged and said that was the way the book came out. He claimed most thrillers were like that anyway, so why should his be different?"

"And that made sense to you?" Julia didn't sound convinced.

"As much as anything else," Andrea said. "Frankly, he started making so much money for both of us, I didn't really care."

I decided to risk a question. "Did you ever think someone else might have written the books? I mean, because the tone was so different."

Andrea laughed. "Don't be ridiculous. Who else could have written them? Godfrey changed his style, that's all. He wanted to break out and make serious money, and he did."

She seemed sincere, and I thought Godfrey had kept his ghostwriter a secret from her, too. She was in for a rude shock, though.

Julia regarded me, obviously curious. She knew that I wouldn't have asked such a question without a reason.

Before either of us could respond to Andrea's last remark, she spoke again. "He made it after all." She waved at someone.

Julia and I turned our heads to look. "Who is it?" I asked.

"The tall man in the suit there, talking to the deputy. You know who I mean, don't you?"

"Yes," Julia and I said in unison.

About twenty feet away Kanesha Berry was deep in conversation with a distinguished-looking man about sixty years old.

"Who is he?" Julia asked.

"Miles Burton," Andrea replied. "Godfrey's attorney." She grinned at Julia. "And if Godfrey managed to get his will changed like he was planning to, your son is going to be really rich, Mrs. Wardlaw."

THIRTY-ONE
||||||||||||||||||||||||||||||||||||||||||||||||||||||||||||||||||

After her announcement, Andrea excused herself, saying she wanted to talk to Miles Burton.

"That was hardly discreet," I said as she walked away.

"No," Julia said. "But I already knew that. Godfrey told me he changed his will to include Justin and acknowledge him as his son." She smiled with what appeared to me to be grim satisfaction. "And he died before he could change it again."

"Why would he want to change it again?"

For a moment Julia looked uneasy. "Well, Justin did quarrel with him, and you know how nasty Godfrey could be when he didn't get his way."

That didn't make much sense to me. One disagreement on the day Godfrey met his son for the first time didn't mean he would disinherit Justin. Godfrey was too excited about having a son, I figured, to do something vindictive after one meeting.

I didn't express my doubts to Julia, though. She was watching Andrea Ferris speak with Kanesha Berry and Miles Burton. Her face betrayed her avid interest. I wondered why she didn't simply go up to them and introduce herself to the lawyer.

Kanesha saved her the trouble. She beckoned for Julia to join them, and I decided I was included in the invitation. Julia needed support, especially since Ezra wasn't here with her.

Kanesha frowned at me as she introduced Julia to Miles Burton.

"I regret that we are meeting under such tragic circumstances," Burton said, his voice a mellow baritone. "Where is your son? Did he attend the service?"

"Yes, he did," Julia said. "He's here somewhere."

"He was in the sanctuary, up in the choir loft the last time I saw him." I introduced myself. "Would you like to speak to him?"

"Yes, I would," Burton said with a grave smile. "I have matters to discuss with him and with Mrs. Wardlaw."

"I'll go find him," I said, and Burton nodded his thanks.

As I left them, Julia was asking Burton how long he had been Godfrey's attorney. I didn't hear the answer.

Out in the sanctuary, I turned to look up into the choir loft. Justin and Diesel weren't there. I scanned the sanctuary, but there was no sign of them. Perhaps Justin had gone to the restroom.

I went down the hall on the side of the chapel opposite the meeting room and checked inside the men's room. All was quiet, and I didn't see any legs, human or feline, in any of the stalls. Had Justin and Diesel gone home?

How had they made it past the media outside? I had visions of Justin being pinned to the front steps of the chapel while reporters bombarded him with questions. But I realized that, unless they knew who Justin was, they probably would have asked him only general questions. Like why did he have a cat with him?

On a hunch, I went further down the hall to the back of the chapel. There was another short hallway running across the rear of the building, which led to a back door. I opened the door and peeked outside. There were no reporters out here.

I stepped outside on the stoop and looked around. No sign of boy and cat here, but I realized that Justin and Diesel could easily have slipped away without attracting attention. They could have taken a roundabout way to the house without having to cross paths with the media.

I made my way back into the meeting room to report to Miles Burton and the others. As I approached them, Andrea Ferris was speaking.

". . . shame that after the new book is out next fall, there won't be any more. Thank goodness Godfrey finished it before he came here." She tittered. "It's the best thing he's done yet, and I predict it will outsell his last two."

"How tragic," Julia said. She turned to look at me.

I answered the unspoken question. "No sign of Justin, nor of Diesel. I think they slipped out the back and went home."

"Diesel? Who is that?" Miles Burton frowned.

"My cat," I said. "Justin is very attached to him, and I

brought him along to the service to help comfort the boy. This has all been a severe shock to him."

"Naturally," Burton said, though he eyed me doubtfully. "I would like to speak with the young man sometime today, if possible. My plane leaves Memphis very early tomorrow morning. I have a case coming to trial on Tuesday in LA."

"I can bring him to your hotel," Julia said.

"Or you can come back to my house now." I made the offer with a smile. "There will probably be reporters at the hotel, and if we go out the back way to my house, you can avoid all that."

"Excellent idea," Burton said. He turned to Julia. "If that is okay with you, Mrs. Wardlaw." He looked in Kanesha's direction. "And you too, Deputy."

"It's fine," Julia said.

"Okay with me," Kanesha said. "I'm in no hurry to make a statement to the media, and I need to hear what Mr. Burton has to say."

"In that case," Burton said, pulling a small notebook from the jacket of suit. He opened it and flipped through a few pages. "If Mr. Harris wouldn't mind, I'd like to request that a few others be present as well. I might as well address all beneficiaries of Godfrey's will at one time."

"It's fine with me," I said. "You're welcome to use my living room."

Kanesha frowned. Would this interfere with her plans for arresting the murderer? To me it looked like she was figuring something out, and after a moment the frown relaxed.

"I think that's okay," Kanesha said. "Who else do you need to speak to?"

Burton consulted his list. "Richard Tackett and William Clark. And a representative of the college, if possible."

Beside me, Julia tensed. What was bothering her? I was surprised at hearing Willie's name, and no doubt she was, too. But perhaps it was the mention of Godfrey's half brother that concerned her. After all, she had dated Rick for a while before Godfrey and she had the fling that produced Justin. And she knew perfectly well, unlike me until recently, that the men were half brothers.

"I work for the college," I said. "And I'm the archivist. Godfrey spoke with me earlier in the week about donating his papers to us. I saw the president leave a few minutes ago."

"You should be sufficient as a representative for the moment," Burton said. "Official notice will come later, and that can be addressed to the president and board of trustees."

I scanned the crowd in the meeting room. I caught sight of Rick and pointed him out to the lawyer. Burton strode off to speak to him.

"Do you see Willie anywhere?" I asked Julia. "I'll go around the room. He's short enough that we might not be able to see him in a crowd."

"I'll help you look." Julia started off in one direction and I in the other to make a circuit of the room. Andrea Ferris chattered at Kanesha.

I found Willie behind a clump of people, hectoring a history professor about his students and their lack of library skills. I had heard this song many times before.

When I interrupted Willie, the history professor shot me a grateful look and disappeared quickly.

"What do *you* want?" Willie was gracious as ever.

"Godfrey Priest's lawyer is here, and he wants to speak with you."

Willie looked taken aback at first, but then a smile spread on his homely face. "Maybe there will be justice at last." He started forward.

"What do you mean by that?" I asked, although I was certain I knew the answer.

"You'll find out soon enough," Willie said. "Where is this lawyer?"

"Over here," I said. Burton had rejoined the three women, and Rick Tackett was with him.

"This is William Clark," I said when we reached them.

Willie stuck out his hand. "I sure am pleased to meet you."

"And I you." Burton shook the hand. "You are all acquainted already with Mr. Tackett, of course. Why don't we proceed now to Mr. Harris's house?"

"Just follow me," I said. I offered my arm to Julia, and she clasped it with a trembling hand. I shot her a sideways glance and was surprised to see her pale. Was she excited or nervous? I couldn't tell. Perhaps it had something to do with Rick Tackett. I had seen him watching her intently when Willie and I joined the group.

I led the group on a slightly circuitous route to my house, but even with the detour we arrived in less than ten minutes. I unlocked the front door and ushered everyone into the living room.

Miles Burton set his document case on the coffee table as the others found seats. I offered refreshments, but everyone declined.

"I'll go check on Justin," I said. "I'm sure he's upstairs with Diesel."

He'd better be, I thought as I climbed the stairs. I couldn't imagine where else he could be right now.

Sure enough, he and Diesel were in his room. Justin was lying on his back in his bed, still wearing his suit. Diesel was stretched out beside him, purring as the boy rubbed his head.

"How are you doing?" I asked.

"Okay."

He didn't look okay. He looked miserable, and no wonder. I wished he could have been spared all this. The months—and perhaps years—ahead were going to be hard for him. To have his biological father snatched away from him so cruelly just after they'd met for the first time—it was truly tragic.

"Godfrey's lawyer is here, along with your mother and a few other people," I said. "The lawyer needs to speak to all of us about Godfrey's will."

"I don't care about his will," Justin said. "Can't everyone just leave me alone?" He turned his face into the pillow, away from me.

I sat on the edge of the bed. "Son, I'm sorry you have to go through all this. But you need to come downstairs and hear the lawyer out. Godfrey obviously remembered you in his will, and for his sake, you need to listen."

Justin lay there, unresponsive for a moment. I waited, and then he sat up. He had been crying.

"Go wash your face," I said gently. "Then we'll go downstairs."

Justin nodded and got out of bed. Diesel stretched and came over to me on the bed. I scratched behind his ears. I suspected he was going to be spending a lot of time with Justin in the near future. I hoped Diesel could provide the comfort the boy would need.

Justin came back, and we set off down the stairs, Diesel running ahead of us.

All heads turned when the three of us entered the living room. Miles Burton came forward, hand extended. He introduced himself and shook Justin's hand. I could see the sympathy he felt for the boy.

Burton led Justin to a seat on the sofa next to Julia and near his own chair. Diesel climbed into Justin's lap. Andrea Ferris, who occupied the other spot on the sofa, stared at Diesel in fascination. Rick Tackett and Willie Clark had pulled chairs close in a semicircle.

Kanesha stood a few feet away, arms crossed. I found another chair and offered it to her, but she shook her head. I took it instead, sitting a little behind Rick Tackett. I had a clear view of Julia and Justin and the lawyer from this vantage point.

Miles Burton held a thick document in his hands. "I regret deeply the occasion that has brought all of us together. Godfrey Priest was my client for many years, and I wish he could have been with all of us for many more." He glanced down at the papers he held. "But it is now my duty to share with his beneficiaries the terms of his will. Godfrey changed his will recently because of the knowledge that he had a son.

"He was thrilled with the knowledge, and I also deeply regret that he had such a short time with this young man. I know how excited Godfrey was to meet him for the first time." He smiled at Justin, who ducked his head. Diesel rubbed his head against the boy's cheek.

"I will spare you all the unnecessary details of a testament such as this. You must realize that, in the case of such a large estate, there are many details that have to be considered. Those, however, are of little concern to you at the moment.

"There are a number of relatively small bequests to which I will return in a few minutes. The important point is that Godfrey stipulated that these small requests should be paid first, and the remainder of the estate would be divided as follows:

"'To my biological son, known as Justin Henry Wardlaw, I leave two-thirds of my estate;

"'To my half brother, Richard Horace Tackett Jr., I leave the remaining third of my estate.'"

Burton paused, as if to gauge the impact of his words. In front of me, I could see Rick Tackett's shoulders relax and his head go down. I thought I could hear him muttering a prayer of thanks.

Julia's eyes glittered with triumph, and her smile was wide. Justin stared at the lawyer, as if he found it difficult to understand what the man had said.

"What are we talking about, in real terms?" Julia surprised me by the obvious note of greed in her voice.

Miles Burton eyed her with what I presumed to be slight distaste. "A conservative estimate of your son's share, Mrs. Wardlaw, would be something in the range of seventy million dollars."

Justin's mouth dropped open, and even Julia appeared thunderstruck. She had obviously never realized how rich Godfrey was.

Burton turned to Rick Tackett. "And that means Mr. Tackett's share would approach thirty-five million."

"I can't believe it," Rick said. "After all these years of ignoring me, why now?" He kept shaking his head.

"Godfrey made no explanation," Burton said.

"It was his way of saying he was sorry, probably," Andrea Ferris said. "He was like that. He always thought money could excuse anything."

"What about me?" Willie Clark startled everyone. "What did he say about me?"

Burton frowned as he consulted Godfrey's will.

"To my high school friend, William Ebenezer Clark, I leave the sum of one million dollars and my grateful thanks for his friendship over the years."

I waited for the eruption, and it came almost immediately.

"That's all? That's all he had to say?" Willie was screaming. He leaped out of his chair and tried to snatch the will from Burton.

Kanesha stepped forward and put herself between Willie and the lawyer. "Sit down, Mr. Clark. Now."

Willie backed away, but he was still furious. His face was so red, he looked like he was going to have a stroke any moment now.

"That cheating bastard, I can't believe he did this to me. Even dead he's screwing me."

"What are you talking about?" Andrea Ferris glared at Willie. "I don't think a million bucks is anything to feel bad about."

"You stupid cow," Willie said. "I wrote the freaking books, not Godfrey."

THIRTY-TWO

||||||||||||||||||||||||||||||||||||||||||||||||||||||||||||||||||||||||||

There was dead silence for a moment. Andrea Ferris jumped up from the sofa, the outrage plain in her face.

"You are totally nuts, you little creep." For a moment I thought she was going to crawl over the coffee table to get to Willie. "I was Godfrey's agent, and I know damn well he wrote those books."

"Shows how much you know, you ignorant bitch," Willie said, not in the least cowed by Andrea's response. "I have proof that I wrote the books. Godfrey always said you knew, but I guess he didn't trust you enough to tell you the truth."

"What kind of proof?" Andrea sounded a little less certain now. "You're damn well going to have to prove it."

"Well, for one thing," Willie said in a smug tone, "I can give you a copy of the manuscript for the book that's coming out next September. How do you think I'd have a copy of it if I didn't write it?"

"Godfrey could have asked you to read it for some reason," Andrea said. "It's set here in Mississippi again, and he could have asked you to do some fact-checking for him."

During this exchange I had been trying to get Kanesha's attention, but she steadfastly ignored me. She was intent on the argument between Willie and Andrea.

Willie laughed. "You can argue all you like, woman. It's not going to change anything. I wrote those books, and I have proof. I have a contract with Godfrey."

"You can produce this contract?" Miles Burton frowned. "This is a serious allegation, you understand. I'm not certain what the ramifications will be, because Godfrey assigned his copyrights to his son."

Willie howled in rage and made a move toward the lawyer. Kanesha, who was still standing between Willie and Burton, held a hand up in front of Willie's face. "Calm down. Now. Or I will have you taken out of here. You understand?"

Faced with Kanesha's commanding tone and stance, Willie backed down. He resumed his seat, and I could feel the tension in the room drop a little.

"I can and will produce the contract," Willie said. "We will discuss it later, you can be damn sure."

Kanesha stepped to one side of the lawyer, but her gaze remained fixed on Willie.

For a moment there was silence, and in that brief interval I heard a car pull up in front of my house. I got up and went to the window. The curtains were open, but I had to pull aside the sheers in order to see clearly.

There were two sheriff's department cars in front of my house. I glanced toward Kanesha, and she was watching me. She inclined her head a fraction, and I went back to my chair, thinking hard. She was going to arrest someone in my house. My heart started beating faster. I wasn't sure I liked the idea.

Burton resumed announcing the contents of Godfrey's will. "There is a bequest of five million dollars to Athena College, and of that amount two hundred and fifty-thousand dollars is to be used for the processing and preservation of the papers he is donating to the school." Burton glanced at me.

"I'm sure our president and trustees will be delighted," I said. Godfrey had obviously made his plans for the archive before he ever consulted me. He came to me simply to talk about Justin, and I could understand that.

"There are bequests to a few charities," Burton said. "And that is it."

"How soon will my son actually be able to receive his bequest?" Julia leaned forward on the sofa, watching Burton like a proverbial hawk.

"The will must go through probate, naturally. There is also the investigation into Godfrey's death," Burton said. "Until that is concluded, nothing much can happen. And now there is an additional issue to consider, the true authorship of the novels that bear my client's name. I really cannot say how that will affect the disposition of Godfrey's estate."

"What does the investigation have to do with it?" Rick Tackett asked. "I'm not sure I understand."

"In Mississippi," Kanesha said, "murderers are not allowed to profit from their crimes. If one of the beneficiaries in the will is found guilty of Mr. Priest's murder, he or she will not inherit."

"Is this true?" Julia looked right at Miles Burton.

"I'm sure Deputy Berry knows this particular statute better than I," Burton said. "Since the crime occurred here, that law would obviously be in effect."

Julia now directed her gaze at Willie Clark. I had been watching her in fascination, seeing a side of her that I hadn't expected to see. She was far more avaricious than I would have guessed, judging by her behavior these last few minutes.

Julia pointed across the coffee table to Willie. "I think you have a pretty darn good motive. Plus, I know you were in the hotel that afternoon."

"Me? You're nuts, Julia." Willie's voice came out in a squeak.

"I saw you," Julia said. "In the revolving door as I was leaving." She sat back and crossed her arms across her chest. Her smile was grim.

Willie laughed, startling us all. "Yes, I was there. I went to see Godfrey to talk about the new book. Not the one that's coming out next year, the one after that."

"And you got into a fight and bashed him over the head." Julia nodded. "I can see it now."

I looked to Kanesha to intervene, but she didn't. She simply stood there and watched.

"Well, I saw you too, Julia." Willie did not appear in the least perturbed by Julia's accusation. "But you've got it backward. I was in the revolving door with you, but I was the one leaving, not you. I saw Godfrey around two-thirty, after waiting for him almost twenty minutes. He was upset about something when I finally did get in to see him, and he said we'd have to talk later. By then I couldn't really hang around any longer either. I was due back on the reference desk at three. One of my staff called in sick that morning, and I had to take his stint at the desk."

"The reference desk?" Julia had paled.

"Yep," Willie said. "At three, and in full view of plenty of people for two hours, because I manned the desk until five. Then I had a meeting with the chair of the history department, and I was with him until nearly six."

It appeared that Willie had a pretty good alibi for Godfrey's murder. Based on what Julia had told me, it was nearly three when she left Godfrey. That statement lent credence to Willie's assertion.

But if she had lied about when she saw Willie, had she lied about anything else?

Kanesha broke the tense silence that had fallen. "I have to ask you, Mrs. Wardlaw, if you would like to revise what you told me earlier. Is Mr. Clark correct? Did you see him as you were *entering* the hotel?"

"Perhaps I got it wrong, and I did see Willie as I was entering," Julia said. "But he could have come back later and killed Godfrey."

"I most certainly did not," Willie said. "After I finished the meeting with the head of the history department, I walked over to the patisserie for something to eat, and then I went to the bookstore for a poetry reading. I didn't have time to go to the hotel and kill anybody."

All eyes appeared to be on Julia now. Except for Justin's. He had his head against Diesel, hugging the cat closely to him.

"Mrs. Wardlaw, refresh my memory. What was it you

did after you left the hotel and your interview with Mr. Priest?" Kanesha took a step closer to the sofa.

Julia watched Kanesha, the unease evident in her face. "I went to the bank to deposit a check Godfrey had given me. Then I went to the hospital. I got there in time for the shift change, a little after three."

"Were you given a receipt for your deposit, Mrs. Wardlaw?"

What was going on here? From Kanesha's demeanor I began to wonder if she had decided Julia was the murderer. My stomach began to knot up in distress.

"Yes, I suppose so," Julia said, shrugging. "Don't they always give you one?"

"They're supposed to," Kanesha said. "And generally those receipts record the time of the deposit. Were you aware of that, Mrs. Wardlaw?"

The relentless use of *Mrs. Wardlaw* was like a nail being slowly hammered into a coffin.

Julia stared at the deputy but didn't respond. It was clear that she had never given a second thought to the time stamp on her bank receipt.

"I believe also that the bank is open until six P.M. during the week," Kanesha said. "I can of course check with the bank, and I will, to determine at what time you made your deposit, Mrs. Wardlaw. I have already spoken with hospital personnel in order to verify your whereabouts."

Kanesha paused, but there was only the sound of hard breathing. Julia was afraid, and the fear was almost palpable in the room.

"Do you have anything you wish to say about the time you made your bank deposit, Mrs. Wardlaw? It's only a matter of time before I know the truth."

Julia took a deep breath. "It was a few minutes before six."

Justin raised his head and looked at his mother. "Mama, what's going on? Why did you lie about the stupid bank deposit?"

"I guess I was just mixed up," Julia said, but even Justin didn't believe her. The pain in his eyes as he looked at his mother was heartrending.

"Mr. Priest wanted to take Justin back to California, didn't he? You were afraid you might lose your son, weren't you? And you weren't going to let that happen."

"No, that's not right. Godfrey wasn't going to do that. I talked to him and he promised he wouldn't, at least not until Justin finished college." Julia sounded desperate, but at this point I didn't think anyone believed her.

"Can I ask a question?" Rick Tackett spoke, his voice low and hesitant.

"Yes, Mr. Tackett, what is it?" Kanesha appeared surprised at the interruption, but she nodded encouragement when Rick failed to speak right away.

"Justin, when is your birthday?" Rick watched Justin, his hands on his knees. I saw that his knuckles were white.

"August fourth," Justin said after clearing his throat. Then he added the year.

"Thank you," Rick said. "He wasn't premature, was he, Julia?"

Tears welled in Julia's eyes. "No, he wasn't." We could barely hear her.

Rick nodded. He took a deep breath as he looked straight at Justin.

"He's not Godfrey's son," he said. "He's mine."

THIRTY-THREE

I wasn't the only one in the room who was stunned. I sneaked a quick look at Kanesha's face, and I could have laughed at her expression. The English have a term for it: *gobsmacked*. Translated roughly, it means *utterly astounded*.

That's exactly how Kanesha looked.

Rick spoke again. "Son, I'm truly sorry you had to find out this way."

"Mama, is it true?" Justin put a trembling hand on Julia's arm.

Julia didn't answer.

"It has to be," Rick said, his voice steady. "I suspected it for a long time, and I just let it go, I guess. Julia had dumped me for Godfrey. And then she went and married Ezra. She made it clear she didn't want me, even though I'd asked her to marry me." He paused. "I didn't realize until today that she was claiming Godfrey was the boy's father. I couldn't let the lie go on any further."

"How can you be sure?" Kanesha asked.

Rick shrugged. "The last time I saw Julia back then"— and we all understood that *saw* was a euphemism—"was in early December. Godfrey didn't blow into town until mid-January."

We could all do the math. If Rick was right, Godfrey couldn't have been Justin's father.

"Did Mr. Priest know about your relationship with Mr. Tackett?" Kanesha went back on the attack.

"No," Julia said. "He was only here for about two weeks that time, and I made sure he didn't hear about it. He never knew."

I had to speak up, though it hurt me to do so. "He found out about it on Tuesday," I said. "I told him. It just came up in the conversation. My family and I were here for Christmas that year, and we saw Julia and Rick together. I told Godfrey that, and he seemed surprised by it."

"She told Godfrey the boy was a preemie." Andrea Ferris got off the sofa and came to stand near me. "When Godfrey first told me about it, he said he was thankful the boy hadn't had any significant health problems despite being two months premature."

"Mr. Priest confronted you that afternoon, Mrs. Wardlaw. He had figured out that he might not be Justin's father. I imagine he was very angry with you." Kanesha glared at Julia.

Julia was sobbing now. All she could do was nod.

Rick got up from his chair and extended a hand across the coffee table to Justin. "Son, I think you should come with me." He glanced at Kanesha, and she nodded.

Justin, obviously torn, still clutching Diesel, looked

first at Rick and then at his mother. Julia said, "Go. Please." She wouldn't look at her son.

Justin hesitated, then kissed her cheek. He gently pushed Diesel aside and got up from the couch. He moved from behind the coffee table, and Rick put an arm around the boy's shoulders. We all watched as he led Justin from the room. Diesel came to sit by my chair.

"Mr. Harris, would you go to the door and wave at the cars parked outside? They'll know what it means." Kanesha moved closer to Julia, and I got up from my chair to do what the deputy asked.

As I headed for the front door, Andrea, Willie, and Miles Burton all moved to the other side of the room.

I opened the door and waved. A moment later three deputies stepped out of the cars and headed up the walk. I moved aside to let them in. I kept an eye out for Diesel in case he decided to wander outside.

I saw him scampering up the stairs when I closed the door behind the deputies. I was tempted to follow him, because I didn't think I could bear to see Julia being arrested. I was appalled by what she had done, but I also hated the thought of her being so alone now.

I went back into the living room and sat down on the couch with her. Kanesha had begun the process of arresting her for murder.

On Monday morning when I was about to leave for the college library, Justin walked into the kitchen. With Julia in custody, he had gone home to Ezra Saturday afternoon. I went with him, to try to explain to a very bewildered man what had happened.

Ezra's illness was taking its toll and Justin stayed with him until the evening, when Rick Tackett arrived. The boy was too dazed to make any decisions for himself, and I encouraged him to go with Rick. He was going to need a father, and Rick had the quiet strength, I thought, to help his son.

All Julia had wanted to do was help her son, too, but she had gone about it the wrong way. Godfrey had treated her badly, driving her to choose Ezra instead of going back to Rick. I had no doubt now she bitterly regretted that choice. She seemed determined, however, to make Godfrey pay for what he had done, and even though Godfrey realized Justin wasn't his son, he must have felt guilty enough to give her money anyway. He probably thought he could simply buy her off, but by then Julia was, I suspected, so irrational that she simply acted without any consideration for the consequences. Otherwise she wouldn't have forgotten Justin's cell phone or have let something so simple as the time stamp on her deposit receipt trip her up.

The tragedy of it all was stunning, and I felt such pity for Julia. I could do something for her, though, by continuing to look after her son however I could.

"How are you?" I examined Justin with concern. He looked like he had slept very little the past two nights.

Justin shrugged. "I don't really know. It's all too freaky."

Diesel rubbed against his legs, and Justin squatted down to hug the cat.

"Yes, it is," I said. "I want you to know, though, if I can do anything to help you, I will."

"Thank you," Justin said, looking up at me. Besides

the fatigue, I thought I could see the beginnings of a new maturity in his face. He stood.

"Actually, there is one thing you can do for me, if you will." Justin watched me calmly. "I'd like to stay here with you for now."

"Of course you can," I said. I had to speak around a lump in my throat. "Diesel would miss you terribly, you know."

Justin gave me the ghost of a smile. "I'd miss him, too. Rick wants me to move in with him and my brothers and sisters." He shook his head. "That sounds so weird. I have brothers and sisters now. Half, that is, but still."

"I'm glad. It's good to have family." I paused. "But it can be a bit confusing to try to get to know them all at once. Maybe you need a little time to get used to the idea."

"Yes, sir," Justin said. "Thank you, Mr. Charlie, and you too, Diesel."

He stood there for a moment, and my heart ached for him. But Diesel and I would do our best to help him.

"I think I'll go up to my room and take a nap," Justin said.

"Sounds like a good idea." I smiled at him. "And I'll bet you can talk Diesel into coming with you."

"Come on, boy," Justin said, waggling his fingers at the cat. "Let's go upstairs."

I sat down at the table, forgetting about work for the moment, as boy and cat left the kitchen. I heard Justin clumping up the stairs, and I realized what a reassuring sound that was.

In the years since my wife died, I had done my best to isolate myself from all but the necessary daily contacts with other people. With my son and daughter off living their own lives, I had only Diesel for any kind of emotional companionship.

That had been enough for a while. But the shock of the events of the past week had broken through that shell I had almost unknowingly put up around me.

For a moment I fancied I could see both Jackie and Aunt Dottie sitting at the table with me. "It's time," Jackie would say, and Aunt Dottie would nod in agreement.

I smiled as the images I conjured up faded away, leaving only the glow of happy memories.

Yes, it was time.

I gathered my things and headed for work.

THE *NEW YORK TIMES* BESTSELLING
BOOKTOWN MYSTERIES FROM

LORNA BARRETT

CONTINUES WITH

BOOKPLATE SPECIAL

Bookstore owner Tricia Miles has put up—and
put up with—her uninvited college roommate
for weeks. In return, Pammy has stolen one
hundred dollars. But the day she's kicked out,
Pammy's found dead in a Dumpster, leaving
loads of questions unanswered.

Penguin Group (USA) Online

What will you be reading tomorrow?

Patricia Cornwell, Nora Roberts, Catherine Coulter,
Ken Follett, John Sandford, Clive Cussler,
Tom Clancy, Laurell K. Hamilton, Charlaine Harris,
J. R. Ward, W.E.B. Griffin, William Gibson,
Robin Cook, Brian Jacques, Stephen King,
Dean Koontz, Eric Jerome Dickey, Terry McMillan,
Sue Monk Kidd, Amy Tan, Jayne Ann Krentz,
Daniel Silva, Kate Jacobs...

You'll find them all at
penguin.com

*Read excerpts and newsletters,
find tour schedules and reading group guides,
and enter contests.*

Subscribe to Penguin Group (USA) newsletters
and get an exclusive inside look
at exciting new titles and the authors you love
long before everyone else does.

PENGUIN GROUP (USA)
penguin.com